ALSO BY SOPHIE LARK

Minx

Brutal Birthright

Brutal Prince

Stolen Heir

Savage Lover

Bloody Heart

Broken Vow

Heavy Crown

Sinners Duet

There Are No Saints

There Is No Devil

Grimstone

Grimstone

Monarch

Kingmakers

Kingmakers: Year One

Kingmakers: Year Two

Kingmakers: Year Three

Kingmakers: Year Four

Kingmakers: Graduation

MONARCH

SOPHIE LARK

Bloom books

Published by Bloom Books, an imprint of Sourcebooks
P.O. Box 4410, Naperville, Illinois 60567–4410
(630) 961-3900
sourcebooks.com

Cataloging-in-Publication data is on file with the Library of Congress.

Printed and bound in the United States of America.
LSC 10 9 8 7 6 5 4 3 2 1

For my grandma Anna, who came to
Canada from Ukraine as a bride

For Fergie, with her stories and secrets

For my daughter Paige, and all the
ways she communicates

Sophie Lavz

CONTENT WARNING

The Grimstone series is a dark, contemporary romance in a Gothic setting. Triggers for *Monarch* may include violence, attempted murder, murder, nonconsensual drug use, kidnapping, torture, coercion, child with neurodiversity, child neglect and endangerment (not by a main character), ableism (not by a main character), attempted sexual assault (not by a main character), and cheating (not against a main character).

SOUNDTRACK

1. "Got it Bad"—LEISURE
2. "Too Sweet"—Hozier
3. "Wet Dream"—Wet Leg
4. "Oxytocin"—Billie Eilish
5. "Deceptacon"—Le Tigre
6. "Charmed"—Etella, Red-inho
7. "A Girl Like You"—Edwyn Collins
8. "Babydoll"—Dominic Fike
9. "Devil in Paradise"—Cruel Youth
10. "Kill of the Night"—Gin Wigmore
11. "Paint The Town Red"—Doja Cat
12. "bellyache"—Billie Eilish
13. "Wildfires"—SAULT
14. "Howlin' for You"—The Black Keys
15. "bad idea!"—girl in red
16. "I hope that you think of me"—Pity Party (Girls Club), Lucys
17. "Spooky"—Dusty Springfield
18. "Never Felt So Alone"—Labrinth
19. "i am not who i was"—Chance Pena
20. "Coming Home"—Leon Bridges

 Spotify Apple Music

WELCOME TO

1

2   3

14

16

15

Town Square

GRIMSTONE

9

8

7

6

5

4

MAIN STREET

13

10 11 12

17

Echo Park

CHAPTER I
ELENA ZELENSKA

I HOPE I RECOGNIZE MY FIANCÉ. FACES HAVE NEVER STAYED STILL in my mind, and I've only seen him once in person.

I scan the forest of figures in the airport baggage claim, looking for someone with untidy brown hair and a big, bright American smile.

Unfortunately, now that I'm in America, that describes a lot of people.

He sent me three photographs, but they all looked slightly different. I pored over them with my cousin, on her phone with the cracked screen. In the first, his hair was longer, almost touching the collar of his shirt, the backdrop dark, like a studio portrait.

"From school?" I said confusedly.

Mina, eighteen months older and wiser, said, "It's his author portrait. You know, for the back of his books."

In the second, he wore outdoor clothes, jaw unshaven, pine trees all around.

"Hiking," Mina explained.

She's been on the Sunflower Brides site for two years now. She knows everything about American men. Brits and Canadians, too. She doesn't trust the Australians.

"I'm not living on the upside-down part of the world, not for anything."

When I said *we* were upside down to them, she shivered in horror. "*Exactly.*"

In the last photograph, my fiancé stood with his hands on the shoulders of a small girl with hair as pale as a dandelion puff.

That time, I supplied the answer: "His daughter."

The trouble was, I couldn't decide which of those images—serious academic, rugged outdoorsman, or hesitant father—most represented the man I'd met at the wife swap. Then, he'd seemed shy and nervous and sweet.

And so I couldn't fix any image of his face in my mind, and now I don't know what to look for.

I wish I would have had my camera on me that day. Mina said it was too big and clunky to bring along. *"You hide behind that thing."*

So I left it at home in our tiny, shared room and then regretted it bitterly when I couldn't snap a picture of him.

The airport seems crowded because it's small, smaller even than the one in Lviv. I don't think anybody else who rode the transatlantic jumbo jet into the Portland airport switched to the rickety little Grimstone puddle jumper with me. My fellow travelers all seem to be coming home, ready for the brisk weather in their boots and scarves, plaid shirts, and heavy jackets.

Americans don't dress up to travel; I'm realizing that now. Most wear jeans or sweatpants, and at least one girl seems to have rolled straight out of bed in her pajamas. I'm the only one in my best dress and heels, sticking out like Minnie Mouse at a hayride.

An older man catches my eye, but not the one I'm looking for. Faces blur like smeared thumbprints. My heart jitters.

If I knew he was going to bring Ivy, his daughter, I wouldn't worry. Pale and wispy as a winter's moon, I couldn't miss her in a crowd. But he already told me he's coming alone.

I'm glad it won't be both things at once: meeting her and the reunion. Either one on its own is a lot.

None of this felt real until I stepped off the plane. Then I breathed air that smelled nothing like I'd encountered before: sweeter, thinner, damper, with threads of smoke and pine. No hint of diesel or that fried scent from home.

The dreamlike, floating feeling that propelled me all the way from Lviv popped like a bubble and I realized, *Oh my god, I actually did it. I flew nine thousand kilometers to marry a man I've met once.*

And now I'm standing here freaking the fuck out.

So it's a good thing the kid won't be here to witness it. As long as I can calm down, paste a smile on my face, and remember *what the hell my future husband looks like,* everything will be fine.

I catch the eye of a tallish man in a tweed jacket with hair almost long enough to touch his collar. His hair is a bit lighter than I remember, and his face is clean-shaven, but when he smiles at me, I'm pretty certain...

"Lorne," I say, stepping forward.

He smiles, displaying a set of impossibly perfect teeth, and I become sure. Just in time to tilt up my lips to receive his kiss.

His mouth is soft, extremely soft, no prickles around the edges like he had in Lviv. Then and now, he tastes minty and fresh. I hope I do, too, after a quick rinse in the airport bathroom. I should have brought a toothbrush in my purse.

"God, you look incredible!" He holds the outsides of my arms, leaning back to look at me.

The couple passing by turns their heads because he said it pretty loudly.

I'm embarrassed even though I spent a lot of time getting ready, hoping to elicit exactly this sort of reaction. It's just that a Ukrainian man would never say it like that for everyone to hear. He probably wouldn't say it at all; he'd just give me a certain kind of smirk.

But we're not in Ukraine anymore. That was the whole entire point.

So I look downward and smile and say, "Thank you," even though Lorne slides his hands down my arms, grabs my wrists, and pulls my hands outward like a butterfly, which is even more embarrassing.

"I can't believe you're here!"

"Me, too." This seems like a good time to step forward for a hug to stop everything else that's happening.

I slide my arms around his waist. He's warm and firm. When I press my palms against his back, I can feel that he works out.

I'm hugging him. I'm hugging my *fiancé*.

I turn my face against the side of his neck where the hair curls a little and breathe in his smell, pleasant and clean. Soap, pine, and pencil shavings. It's a nice smell. I could love this person.

The fact that I don't yet is okay. Love takes time; everyone says so. And I'm patient.

Lorne has everything a girl needs to fall in love. Mina was madly jealous when I told her all about him—fit, fortyish, attractive, well-read, well-spoken, successful enough to wear a Breitling.

"And you just met him in the café? Not even inside the swap?" she squawked.

At the very first event I attended. Even I had to admit, it wasn't fair.

But Mina's too generous a soul to be overly envious. "About time you got lucky, Sprout" was all she said.

Mina calls me Sprout, and I call her Bean. I've always been tall, and she likes jellybeans. We were six when we came up with it, and we thought it was genius.

As further evidence of my undeserved good fortune, Lorne isn't short, which means I won't have to scrunch in photos. Even in Mina's stilettos, we stand eye-to-eye.

It seems perfect to me.

But Lorne steps back, squinting slightly. "You're taller than I remember. What kind of shoes are you wearing?"

I twist my foot to show him.

"You won't be able to wear those here. Not in winter."

His dismissive tone makes my face hot. I only wore these heels again because he complimented them last time. But then, I was sitting down.

It doesn't matter; he said I look pretty. No, better than pretty—incredible.

So I smile back at him, even though he isn't smiling right at this moment. "That's okay. I have other shoes."

Only one pair, actually. But that's fine; they're sneakers.

The rigidness in Lorne's face melts away like it was never there at all. "Why don't I just take you shopping? You want to fit in."

I *do* want to fit in, desperately. But I'm not stupid enough to think it will be that easy.

I'm noticing all kinds of things I did wrong already. Like, I'm wearing *way* too much makeup compared to the other women in the baggage claim. It's less than Mina wears to her waitressing job and a fraction of the full-face paint job she spackled on for the wife swap, but I don't see a single other person wearing lipstick, blush, shadow, and liner at two o'clock on a Tuesday.

Also, my suitcase looks tacky tumbling down the conveyor belt: dirty purple nylon with a strip of duct tape sealing the pocket that lost its zipper.

Lorne doesn't seem to notice. He hauls it off the belt for me, waiting for more.

"That's all I have."

He looks at me in surprise. "You only brought one suitcase?"

I shrug, not entirely sure how to respond. It's a big suitcase, and it wasn't that hard to fit all my clothes inside. I'd have liked to bring more books, but then it would have been too heavy.

To my relief, Lorne just laughs. "That's what I love about you, Elena—you're so practical. If an American woman were moving halfway around the world, she'd need ten of these."

I nod, smiling. Really I'm thinking that an American woman would never trade places with me precisely *because* of her ten suitcases of luxuries. She's already got everything she needs right here.

And soon...so will I.

I've been drooling over the American life since I was six years old and I found my aunt's old stash of Sweet Valley High books. I learned English purely to devour the adventures of those outrageously blessed California twins who swam in their own backyard pool in a land of perpetual summer and drove a cherry-red convertible to school.

Lorne can try to scare me about Oregon winters all he likes—there's no way it gets as bad as Lviv, where cold fronts roll down from Siberia. If you take a glass of water outside, it freezes solid in your hand in minutes. Summer is the rainy season.

So I'm not worried about the weather.

It's the man leading me by the hand who concerns me.

We exchanged forty-two emails and spoke on the phone seventeen times. But I only saw his face during that one conversation, across a café table at the Ambassador Hotel.

Mina dragged me along to what Sunflower Brides calls a "romance tour" and the locals call a "wife swap." Mina attends all the time, not hunting for an actual husband but for more of a raunchy pen pal who will send her money for laptops and purses.

I had never been to a wife swap before. Never even considered it. But I had to get out of Lviv quickly and could only think of one way to make that happen.

I met the foreign men and gave up after an hour. No matter how Mina dolled me up, I'm shit at flirting. I'd never had a local boyfriend even once in my life, so I don't know how I thought I was going to charm some exotic doctor.

Also...most of them were strange. Not awful, exactly, but you could tell there was a reason they had to board a plane for a date. One guy was just pouring sweat, shirt soaked through. I could imagine that being slightly alarming on a normal sort of date. Instead, he was sharing a small sofa with four voluptuous twenty-year-olds.

That's the other thing I learned: there's no way I could compete with the girls who'd already attended dozens or even hundreds of wife swaps. One day of work with Mina could never match their level of investment.

I'm twenty-seven, not twenty. A twenty-seven-year-old virgin. Over the hill in the Lviv dating market, and apparently on romance tours.

I felt relieved but then depressed. Without a quickie marriage, I hadn't solved my problem. So I bought a pastry at the café on the ground floor of the hotel and sat down to stew.

I hadn't noticed the man already taking a seat at the one and only open table—or he hadn't noticed me. After a moment of confusion, he gave me a nervous look, sweet and awkward, saying, "We could both sit. I won't bother you; I was planning to read anyway."

I didn't realize he was from the wife swap, silly as that might seem. A lot of tourists go to that café. He seemed so different from everyone upstairs.

He'd left the romance tour for the exact same reason as me, out of disgust.

"At them or yourself?" I said.

He laughed. "Both, absolutely. The whole human race, actually—what are we doing?"

He was so easy, so funny. I hardly noticed how we started talking or how we continued on. He never did open that book.

It seemed we had everything in common. I mean, he's an author and my favorite thing in the universe is books…everything else was just frosting on the cake.

It was almost too romantic, too perfect, the hours flying away unnoticed. When it was all over, I had to give my head a shake. I thought, *He's already married. Or he was lying the whole time, making things up to impress you…*

But Mina looked him up online, and everything he said was true. His books, the award he won, even his daughter, all there in black and white on his Wikipedia page. *The man has his own Wikipedia!*

Author Lorne Ronson lives in the American West with his daughter, Ivy Ronson, 9 (Mother, Linda Lovelace, d.).

Neither the Wikipedia page, nor Lorne himself, had explained how he came to have a daughter with a woman who was now dead and apparently hadn't shared his last name.

Through all our emails and phone calls, the closest I got was asking after Ivy's mother. Lorne sighed and said, "She's not in the picture." Since I already knew she was dead from my snooping, it felt tacky to press for more information, and possibly cruel, though my curiosity was killing me.

Lorne told me all about Ivy. *"The good and the bad,"* as he put it. I hope he did the same for himself. I hope *I* did.

I really tried to be honest. About everything. *Almost everything.* I mean, would it be so crazy if this could actually work out?

When Lorne smiles at me, it doesn't seem so nuts.

I want it to work out. I want to build a life here. That's what he wants, too, right?

Still, I can't shake the feeling that I'm holding the hand of a stranger.

We cross the parking lot, Lorne lugging my suitcase easily, though the lot is unpaved and my suitcase is janky.

Grimstone is remote; Lorne warned me of this. But he promised the house he's building will be really nice. *"Luxurious, even."*

I don't want to be materialistic. Or a hypocrite—I flew in with single suitcase. But Lorne told me he does pretty well for himself, and we're coming up to the first test. Does this guy exaggerate?

I scan the bumpers of the cars, trying to guess which is his. I'm hoping it's at least a Toyota. *Please, just not that truck held together with twine...*

Lorne stops behind a shiny BMW.

Something in my brain relaxes like a rubber band. *Okay. So he's not a total liar.*

If anything, he undersold it. This car is really nice. The trunk whooshes up before we touch anything, like it saw us coming. When I slip inside, the leather smells brand-new. Does his kid even ride in here?

I sink into the cloudlike front seat. Lorne slides in beside me, donning a pair of sunglasses that also look pretty expensive. I start to get a weird feeling. How much do authors make?

It's disorienting. If he were a teacher, I could have looked his salary up online. *How much does a teacher make in Oregon, USA?*

I told him what I earned at the bookshop.

"I know it's pitiful," I said when his laugh came snorting over the phone. "I'm there for the discount. If my uncle made me pay full rent, I'd have to get some other job."

That would have broken my heart. I *loved* working at the bookshop. Besides Mina, it was the best thing in my life.

I worked there for almost eight years, from the time I was a teenager. The discount let me build the best little library in Lviv.

But that was all coming to an end, one way or another.

I sold my beloved library for cash before I left because I knew I couldn't bring it, and god, it hurt more than I expected.

If I think about it now, I might bawl, and then Lorne will think I'm one of the girls with a secret child back home. I'm a shithead for even thinking it, but that's how it feels in my heart. That library *was* my child. I protected it, nurtured it, grew it for years.

That was the price of coming here, paid with my dearest treasure. If life were a fairy tale, that sacrifice alone would guarantee my success.

But I don't think I'm in a fairy tale.

I'm hoping for a nice, boring memoir. I'll write it when I'm a hundred. Maybe Lorne can help me.

I smile at him.

"What?" he says, smiling back.

"You're a good driver. Careful."

"Precious cargo," he says, and he puts his hand on my knee.

His palm fills the whole bare space below my skirt. His skin is warm and dry. His thumb presses in just a little.

My heart rate shoots up like a strongman dinged it with a hammer at a circus. Lorne is behaving so easy and natural, while my head fills up with sirens.

I'm realizing that this man conceived a child with somebody named Linda, while I've never put a toe on third base.

Lorne knows I'm inexperienced; I've told him. But there's no way he remembers what it was like the first time someone slid their hand up your bare thigh.

Now *I'm* that dude from the wife swap who couldn't stop sweating. If Lorne puts his hand all the way up my skirt, will I feel sweaty down there?

I catch his wrist. I don't mean to; my hand jerks out and grabs him.

Our eyes meet. Whatever Lorne reads there, he grins.

He swerves the wheel, pulling off on a small side road. All the roads have been winding and narrow since two minutes from the airport. This one is only a single track through the trees.

It's dark here beneath the pines. When Lorne stops the car and kills the engine, it's silent, too.

Wild thoughts fill my head—the worst things you see on the news that happen to trusting and adventurous girls.

"What are we—"

"I thought since Ivy will be back at the hotel, maybe we should…" Lorne gives me a significant look. Actually, he gives his groin a significant look, which makes me do the same. It's quite apparent how much he enjoyed touching my bare leg.

I'm flattered. I was worried I wouldn't know what to do—looks like I might not have to do much.

But also, I was hoping for something a little more romantic for my first time.

I bite my lip, wondering if that's okay to say to Lorne. Wondering how he'll take it.

Some guys are patient when it comes to sex.

But some get mad.

CHAPTER 2
ELENA

LORNE'S HANDS ARE ALREADY AT HIS ZIPPER.

He pulls it down, reaching inside. I make a squeaking sound.

"*Eep!*"

He glances up, blue eyes quizzical beneath his untidy mop of hair.

"What's wrong?"

"I…you know, I've just never…I haven't…" He stares at me while I stammer.

Then he cocks his head as something computes. "Are you saying you're actually a virgin?"

My cheeks burn as I stare down at his pristinely vacuumed floor mats.

"Yeah," I mutter. "I told you that…"

Lorne's laughter jerks my head up.

"I'm sorry," he says, still chuckling as he tucks himself away. "I didn't take all that stuff seriously. You know, all the girls put that *dedicated homemaker, pure as the driven snow* bullshit on their profiles. I didn't think you'd actually never…"

I shake my head.

"Not even, like, a blow job or…?"

I don't think he's judging. I think he's gauging what I might be willing to do.

I am willing. But there's no way I'm going to be able to fake my way through this.

I shake my head. "I've never even had a boyfriend."

The silence is painful. But Lorne doesn't look angry. In fact, he's staring at me in wonder.

"That's amazing. And you're really twenty-seven?"

"Yes." I try not to sound annoyed. "Everything I told you was true."

And I told you almost everything.

"Me too," Lorne says, maybe a little too hastily. I don't want to be suspicious. But if I'm not suspicious at all, am I an idiot?

Trust has to be earned, just like love.

Still laughing to himself, Lorne says, "You'd never see that around here."

Lorne makes a lot of statements about things you'd "never see" where he lives. He seems to delight in my difference.

I hope that remains true when the novelty wears off.

"No big deal." He restarts the engine, backs out, and returns to the road. His hand is relaxed now, draped across the top of the wheel.

I'm studying the side of his face in little bursts, making sure he really doesn't mind.

Lorne doesn't seem angry. Actually, he almost seems...excited?

The edge of his mouth is tugging in the right direction, and the energy in the car feels encouraging. When he turns on the music, the song he plays has a sensual vibe.

Lorne puts his hand back on my knee.

"I kinda like that you haven't had any boyfriends before."

This time, he lets his hand sit there instead of moving it higher.

That gives me time to relax. I take slow breaths, watching the forest spool by like one long, endless reel, always different but still one organism.

We have deep forests like this in Ukraine—giant pines, huge expanses with barely any people. But I always lived in a city. In a tiny apartment, actually.

Lorne told me all about the house he's building, how there are trees all around, a writing room in the attic, a garden for Ivy…

We're supposed to live in that house.

But a few minutes ago, he said something different.

"You mentioned that Ivy's at a hotel?"

Lorne grimaces. His hands grip the wheel.

"Yeah." His voice sounds different from before, tighter and lower. "The house isn't finished. It's not going to be finished for a few more weeks, actually."

My stomach squeezes. We talked on the phone less than twenty-four hours ago, and he didn't mention any of that.

Lorne notes my discomfort.

"It's been really fucking stressful. I didn't want to worry you, and I thought it was going to be done on time." He hastens to add, "The hotel is beautiful; it's the nicest one in Grimstone. I mean, there's this new one up the bay, but all the locals hate it. Trust me, I got us into the right spot."

He gives me a hopeful look, trying to earn back my approval.

What am I balking at—staying at a nice hotel? Look where I'm coming from—Mina and I shared a bunk bed. I had four cubic feet of closet space.

She's got to be a little bit glad I moved out. And a whole lot jealous.

"That sounds lovely," I say, putting my hand on top of Lorne's.

He smiles at me, but then he takes his hand away at the next light. But maybe that was just to make the turn.

We're heading into the actual town now, which is tiny and picturesque. Lorne told me only a few people live in the cluster of buildings around Main Street. Most built their cabins in the far-flung hills.

"People like their privacy around here."

Including my fiancé, apparently. The house he's building is nearly twenty minutes out of town. Longer, he said, if it's been snowing.

"We didn't pass by the house…" I should have realized we wouldn't. I suppose I'm still fixated on the idea from when I thought that's where we'd be headed first.

Lorne says, "I can take you to see it tomorrow."

"Okay." I shouldn't get so set on things; it's one of my worst traits, Mina always says so. It's not Lorne's fault the house isn't done. He's probably really stressed. We're supposed to get married there in a few weeks. "Will the house be done in time for the wedding?"

"It better be," he mutters. "Ugh, sorry, it's been a fucking nightmare. You'll like the Monarch, though; it's like old Italy in there. The owner's such a character, really dour and ogreish, but he'll treat you like royalty. The restaurant's incredible, and there's a café down the street… Honestly, this might be for the best. You'll have a lot more to do staying in town while I'm finishing the book."

Lorne warned me that he's working against a tight deadline, and he'll need to spend a lot of time writing over the next couple of months.

I can't say that I mind. I'm not used to spending all day long with someone, and I can't get a job myself until I upgrade my visa.

The only question is, what will I do all day? I can't remember the last time I had three days off in a row, let alone weeks, or even—*gulp*—months.

It's thrilling and terrifying.

I scan the rows of shops, knowing I'll probably have time to wander through every single one.

Grimstone is like a gingerbread village, if someone bashed it around a bit and spray-painted the alleyways. The slight dinginess is cheering after Lorne's intimidating car. The tattoo shop looks just as likely to give me tetanus as the ones back home.

"Planning all the cute clothes you'll buy?" Lorne teases me.

I'm embarrassed that he thinks I'm already imagining swiping his credit card. We're both aware it's going to have to be his card—I doubt I can afford a pair of socks in this place. Not without breaking the one and only American hundred-dollar bill I tucked in the sole of my sock, the proceeds of selling my beloved library.

"I don't need a lot of stuff."

"Of course you do! And that's okay, Elena. I told you, I'm not hurting for money. Look, I already got this for you."

He hands me an impossibly shiny credit card with my full name printed on it, *Elena Daryna Zelenska.*

The card is shiny because nobody has ever touched it or used it before. Lorne got it just for me.

It's surprisingly heavy in my hand.

"Buy yourself some pretty things. Stuff like this." He gives my dress an approving nod.

This dress is not actually what I would buy, given the choice. Especially not in October in Grimstone. It belonged to Mina, as did the dress I wore the day I met Lorne.

I guess that's where I was just a little bit deceptive—I never told him I live in jeans. Now I have to deal with the consequences.

"Sure," I say, adding hopefully, "and maybe some pants…"

Lorne is magnanimous. "Whatever you need." He pulls the car to the curb, takes my hand, looks into my eyes. "I want you to be happy here, Elena."

I gaze back at him, this man who's been nothing but nice to me. The man offering everything I've ever wanted…

I smile, squeezing his hand. "I know I will be."

He kisses me softly on the mouth. It's probably the lightest kiss he's given me—he's definitely treating me more gently since the v-word.

We've only ever kissed six times total, counting this one and the one at the airport. The rest were all on that very first, magical day. Lorne flew home early the next morning—he said he never leaves his daughter for long.

I'd like to kiss him back like I'm not an awkward virgin, if such a thing could be managed, but my car door unexpectedly opens.

A bellman holds out a gloved hand. He's wearing the classic short-cropped jacket with braid and brass buttons, even the drum-shaped hat. Lorne was right; this place is old-fashioned.

I gaze up at the Gothic facade of the Monarch Hotel. It towers overhead, by far the tallest building on Main Street, weathered black stone with intricate scrolling around its cavernous doorways and pointed-arch windows.

The carved double doors might have been taken off a cathedral. But we enter a space as cool and dark as a sumptuously draped cave.

Walls, carpets, curtains, and furniture in shades of the deepest peacock green are contrasted by silver candelabras and ebony wood. A stone fireplace dwarfs the check-in desk, the birch logs cold. The windows don't let in much light. Though it's only four o'clock, we've entered immediate evening.

Lorne said old Italy...more like old Transylvania.

I smile to myself.

"You like it?" Lorne is pleased. He squeezes my hand.

A petite and pretty girl with pink cheeks and brilliant, dark eyes greets us from the front desk. "Welcome back, Mr. Ronson! I have a few messages for you."

Lorne steps forward to read them. I interest myself in a jewel-toned stuffed parrot inside a gilded cage taller than myself. Even in my highest heels, the parrot's perch is right at eye level. When I bend in for a better look, its extreme stillness becomes an enraged squawk.

I stumble back. I would have fallen all the way backward if not for the immense hands that catch me at my waist and wrist.

"Allow me, Mrs. Ronson..."

I'm easily steadied, a doll set back on the shelf.

I felt the oversized hands and even sensed his bulk behind me. But I'm still stunned when I turn around.

The man who caught me is enormous, shoulders stretching the limits of what must be a custom-made suit. He's got tar-black hair and even darker eyes, deeply set under thick brows. A permanent shadow stains his jawline. His face is surly, heavy like a boxer's, and his voice is low and rough. But his manners are as elegant as his dinner jacket.

It's me who's clumsy. And embarrassed because I can't tell a living creature from a toy.

"I'd apologize on his behalf, but he does it on purpose," says the Goliath man, tilting his head toward the parrot. "I'm Atlas, by the way."

Stupidly, I say, "This is your hotel."

"It is." There's emotion in those two little words. Pride, maybe. Attachment, most definitely.

He looks like he belongs to this hotel, as if he grew here like one of the immense pillars at the foot of the staircase.

With feeling, I say, "It's beautiful, like a jewel. So's your little devil parrot."

I examine him again now that I know he's alive, the undersized bird with the beady black eyes. He had his head tucked under his wing before. Now he gives me a superior look.

When I glance back at the hotelier, his expression has softened. Probably from looking at the bird. This cage is nicer than some people's houses. Add the array of fruit in the dish and it's clear he's partial to this parrot.

"What's his name?"

"Toulouse."

"Like the painter?"

"Exactly like him—he once broke his leg, and he loves to drink absinthe."

I laugh. The laugh is what makes Lorne turn around.

"Atlas!" He strides forward, holding out his hand, leaving the girl behind at the desk.

"Mr. Ronson."

The hotelier shakes hands with my fiancé, who seemed to shrink the closer Atlas walked. Lorne has to tilt up his head to look at him, almost as much as I do.

Atlas must have been a gargantuan baby to earn his name so soon. Or it's a nickname. I won't be asking. Regardless of what Lorne said, the vibe here is not royalty-peasant. It's more like two lords conversing, and only one of them owns this castle.

I'm the serving maid posing as a princess. And I think Atlas knows it. People who work in hospitality can tell the price of your shoes in an instant. He'll know my red bottoms are fake, just like I know Lorne's sunglasses are real.

But Atlas doesn't give me that look, like *Pretty Woman* snuck into his hotel. He's just as respectful to me as he is to Lorne.

"Would you like me to show you to your room, Mrs. Ronson?"

"I'm sure Lorne can."

"I booked you a separate suite," Lorne says smoothly. "So I have my own space to work."

"Right. Of course." I try to act like it's not a surprise, but I'm sure Atlas notices that, too. His eyes rest on my face like he's determining what sort of wife drives her husband to request his own room.

Did Lorne tell him we're married already? We will be in the next ninety days…before my visa expires.

If not, I'll be shipped back home.

Back to my problem.

So let's hope nothing goes wrong.

Atlas scans my face. Before he turns away, the edge of his mouth quirks up. It almost feels like a message passing between us, a return to the amusement we shared over his parrot, though I'm not sure why.

He says, "I think you'll like your room. It looks out over the rose garden and the ocean."

Grimstone is a coastal town, the shops perched on a cliff too high to hear the waves below. You have to take stairs down to the beach.

Lorne described it all to me, though nothing gave me a sense of the scale: the vast, dark woods dwarfing the tiny gingerbread town, hours away from any other place.

America is a land of wilderness still, like Russia, like Ukraine. You can get lost here. You can disappear.

That's what I wanted. But disappearing sounds comforting when you're still at home, like tucking into your favorite hiding spot. When it's actually happening, it feels like falling down a long, dark hole.

Atlas takes us into a filigreed elevator only a little bigger than his parrot's cage. It sinks several alarming inches beneath his bulk.

"Jesus," Lorne mutters. The elevator barely dipped when he stepped inside.

I really, really don't want to get inside. I don't like elevators. Especially not small, metal ones.

Lorne and Atlas stare at me, waiting.

"Climb in," Lorne says.

Atlas promises, "It's stronger than it looks."

His rumbling bass is oddly calming. And credible. I suppose if Atlas trusts his bulk to this elevator each day, I shouldn't worry.

Sweating a little, I slip in next to Lorne.

Atlas closes the cage door, and the elevator rises slowly and steadily to the top floor.

Atlas leads us down a hallway of botanical wallpaper and iron candelabras. Lorne trails behind, examining the portraits on the walls. They catch my attention as well—black-haired girls in muslin dresses punting on a lily-strewn lake, a stern older woman in a man's dark suit, and a slouching boy with his large, well-shaped hands spread over a piano.

"Did these people stay at the Monarch?" Lorne asks.

I already know that's wrong before Atlas answers, "They're my family."

I noticed the resemblance.

"Is the one in the suit your mother?" It slips out too soft for Lorne to hear. Atlas's nod is likewise too subtle to catch. Unless you were watching for it.

It feels like another secret between us.

I don't want to have secrets. I'm trying to escape my secrets, actually. So I fall back until I'm walking with Lorne instead.

He says, "Told you this place was cool."

"It's gorgeous. Even nicer than the hotel in Lviv."

"Well, that place was a dump."

It was the nicest hotel I'd ever stepped foot inside before today, with a chandelier as big as a car in the huge central lobby. I experience another uneasy twinge of dread, trying to figure out just exactly how poor I am compared to Lorne.

It's very confusing. I wish he had a normal sort of job even though, at first, I was thrilled when he told me he was an author. A *bestselling* author—he said it exactly like that.

I slopped my coffee onto the café table, squeaking out, "I work at a bookshop!"

I said it like it was destiny that Lorne and I met, even though that's ridiculous. I'm not soulmates with the baker if I sweep up his crumbs.

But Lorne acted like it really was the same thing. "It's fate," he said, laughing along with me.

It did sort of seem like fate that we both gave up on the romance tour after an hour and went down to the same café. And sat at the same table. And even ordered the same pastry. It all felt so magical and perfect that first day.

The phone calls afterward were almost just as good. We seemed to have plenty in common. Lorne was so charming and easy to talk to; even just listening to him was nice. I looked forward to hearing his voice, escaping the Lviv sleet and the drudgery of stocking shelves and my aunt and uncle arguing to talk to my boyfriend. My *American* boyfriend.

When he proposed to me just a few weeks later over the phone, I felt a bolt of joy and relief. *This is actually happening!*

I was running out of time. The bookshop I worked at had been sold, ownership transferring in a matter of weeks. Which meant that my looming problem was about to come crashing down on my head.

Lorne saved me just in time. The plane ticket he bought me was a literal ticket to freedom.

And here I am, in the country of my dreams, holding hands with a man who wants to marry me.

So what's this strange awkwardness now that we're finally together? Why do I suddenly feel so nervous?

Atlas reaches my room, the last door at the end of the hall.

"The ones by me were already booked," Lorne notes without much apology.

"I can have you moved closer when a guest vacates," Atlas offers.

Lorne considers. "That would be good."

I ask, "Where's Ivy?"

Lorne's mouth tightens in a way that makes his lips go white. "Her room is next to mine. I'll take you over after we drop off your stuff."

Atlas unlocks the door with an actual metal key, not a card, and enters to open the drapes. The window looks out over a walled garden with a flat expanse of dark and distant ocean beyond, just like he said.

It's a lonely view but peaceful, too, without a single human being in it.

The bed is an ornate four-poster, the ceiling higher than you'd expect.

"This room's nicer than mine," Lorne says, slightly annoyed.

"They're the same square footage," Atlas states. "The rooms on the top floor have vaulted ceilings."

When Lorne still looks slightly piqued, I offer, "Do you want to switch?"

"No." He frowns. "Because of Ivy."

"Right, sorry."

"I'll let you get settled in," Atlas says.

It feels like he's leaving the room because we're fighting. Are we fighting? There's definitely tension.

I wipe my sweaty palms on my skirt, trying to relax.

I'm blowing this out of proportion. I'm acting odd because I'm alone with Lorne in a way we weren't at the airport or even in the car. Now we're standing right next to a bed.

He's obviously thinking the same thing. The scowl melts off his face and he crosses the room, taking me in his arms.

"Alone at last..."

He kisses me, and it's not as gentle as before. Now his hands are running up and down my back beneath my coat.

"That turned me on, what you told me in the car." He pulls me against his body so I can feel his erection through his jeans.

"I'm glad you're not disappointed."

"Are you kidding me?" His hands roam up and down my back and even cup my ass, casual and possessive. "That's fucking hot. I'm going to be the first person to...you know. *Everything.*"

"Pretty much."

He pulls back slightly to examine my face. "What have you done before?"

I'd really rather he didn't ask. First of all, because my total amount of sexual experience could fill a teaspoon, and second, because I don't want him to talk about *his* past partners. I'm nervous enough already.

"I've...been touched down there, once or twice."

Drunken fumbling at a couple of parties, mostly over clothes. I got sick and puked before it went any further.

I'm wondering if I even should have admitted that. Is Lorne going to get jealous now that he's decided he likes me all sweet and innocent?

But he only seems more aroused. His hand snakes up under my hair and seizes the back of my neck. "That's sexy. Did you ever come when they touched you?"

"No." I shake my head, as much as I can when he's holding me like that.

"Have you ever had an orgasm?"

Once when Mina was sleeping, I got close. A tingling that seemed like it might turn into something more. But then it faded away to dullness instead.

"No."

Lorne takes in a sharp breath. His shaggy hair hangs down over his eyes so all I see are his full, pale lips. Gripping me by the back of the neck, his other hand slides up under my skirt.

"I could make you come…"

My skin flushes. This isn't like in the car—then, I was terrified, like I'd just been asked to step onstage and sing an opera. Now, safe and alone in a hotel room, I'm willing to give it a try.

I part my knees, arms wrapped around Lorne's neck. I kiss him, highly conscious of his fingers sliding up my inner thigh, hooking in the gusset of my underwear, pulling it to the side. His fingertips touch my bare pussy lips. I'm not tipsy at a party this time—I'm completely conscious and extremely aware as he slides his fingers back and forth, searching for my clit.

It's small and sort of hidden. I know that much from my own explorations.

Lorne rubs his fingers back and forth, softly at first, then harder, like he's starting a fire.

It feels good, but it's pretty intense.

I lay my hand on the back of his, trying to indicate that slightly less friction might be nice, but much like in the car, he flicks it off.

"Lie down on the bed," he orders.

I lie down on the queen-size mattress, noticeably plush even in this moment. Lorne drops down next to me, a determined look on his face.

"Spread your legs."

I open my knees again, but it's hard to keep them open when he rubs hard. My reflex is to curl up like a crab.

"You're not getting very wet," Lorne observes, his hand working between my legs.

"I'm sorry."

"Do you masturbate?"

"Sometimes." This isn't going well. I'm already disappointing him.

"You need to practice," Lorne says. "You should be able to come when I touch you like this."

My stomach sinks and my face burns. "I'm sorry."

I apologize again because it does seem rude, my pussy barely responding when he's kissing me and touching me like this.

Actually, it's kind of starting to hurt a little, the incessant friction making me irritated and raw. It might be okay if I were wet, but I'm not.

It must be because I'm nervous. Lorne is really good-looking. Brilliant and charming. He even smells good, like soap. What's wrong with me?

"I'll practice," I promise him.

Lorne takes away his hand and sits up on the bed, frowning slightly. "I'll get you some good porn so you know what I like."

"Okay."

That seems…mature, I guess?

Married people have to be able to talk about sex. They should tell each other what they like.

If Lorne shows me, that's even easier. After all, I really don't know what I'm doing. I probably should have watched some porn before I came, like an instructional video.

"We'll wait to have sex until our wedding night." Lorne nods like it's settled.

"Okay."

I can't tell if I'm disappointed or relieved. On the one hand, I feel slightly rejected. But on the other, it's considerate of Lorne to give me space and time. Most dudes would be pressuring me to hop into bed this instant since we're already engaged.

Not that I have a ring. I wonder if Atlas noticed my bare finger. Lorne didn't want to risk mailing one to me through the Ukraine postal system. I wonder if he bought it already or if we'll go shopping together.

A real diamond engagement ring…Mina will combust with envy. None of her boyfriends ever gave her anything like that.

I kiss Lorne, trying to convince him and myself that I can catch up in sex like I always caught up in school, by studying and cramming.

"Thanks for being patient."

"I am patient." He bites my lower lip. "For a little while."

CHAPTER 3
ELENA

"I'LL TAKE YOU TO MEET IVY," LORNE SAYS, ROLLING OFF THE BED, tugging down his untucked shirt, and smoothing his hair in a haphazard way.

"Let me get her gift." I kept it safe in my purse in case my suitcase got lost on the journey.

I take out my father's old camera first, wrapped carefully in my favorite soft shirt for sleeping. Thank god I could bring *that* at least, even if I had to give up my library.

"What's that?" Lorne says as I inspect the old Canon carefully for damage, even though it rode most of the way on my lap. "An antique?"

"It still works."

"As what, a paperweight? Don't they have cell phone cameras in Ukraine?"

"A phone can't take a picture like this can."

"Right, 'cause it would actually be in focus," Lorne snorts.

I get why he thinks this camera looks like a hunk of junk—it's older than I am. But it takes beautiful pictures with a tone and grain unlike anything digital.

Also, it's the only thing I own that belonged to my parents.

"It's sentimental," I say.

Like he just remembered, Lorne notes, "You said you like photography."

I don't just like it. I *need* it.

But I don't want to explain that right now, so I just smile and nod.

The gift for Ivy isn't much—a sketch pad and some watercolor pencils. It was the prettiest notebook we had in stock at the bookshop, the sort that's leather-bound with rough-cut edges and a cord to bind it shut. But maybe Ivy would have preferred something designed for a child, purple and glittery with unicorns on it.

Lorne didn't give many useful suggestions when I asked him what Ivy likes. He said, "She plays outside a lot. But she doesn't really play, not with a jump rope or a ball or anything. She just kind of sits out there. And reads sometimes. Or draws."

I get the sense that while Lorne is an attentive father, he finds his daughter slightly inexplicable.

As I'm gathering up the gift, he says, "Don't be offended if she doesn't talk."

"What do you mean?"

"Sometimes she won't speak. It's why I had to take her out of school and homeschool her instead."

"That's okay. I was a late talker, too."

"She *can* talk," Lorne says, frowning. "She just doesn't want to."

What I really meant was that speech doesn't come so easily to everyone. Even now, sometimes, it feels like my tongue is a cold lump of meat in my mouth and the thoughts in my head have nothing to do with words.

Lorne says, "Her mother's family had all kinds of health issues, all sorts of things wrong with them. Sometimes I think she's just not very smart."

"Ivy?" I'm a little surprised to hear someone talk that way about their kid.

Lorne shrugs. "You'll see when you meet her. She just kind of… stares off into space."

None of this is making me any less nervous to meet Lorne's

daughter, especially since I have almost zero experience with kids. I'm an only child, and Mina and I were the youngest of our cousins.

"What have you told her about us?"

"I said I met you on a work trip. She knows we're dating, but I haven't told her we're getting married yet."

I nod. That's probably for the best, not dumping too much on the poor girl at once. Let her get to know me first before she finds out I'm her new stepmother.

The "work trip" is our cover story.

In Ukraine, there's no stigma against marrying a foreigner. If anything, it's celebrated, especially since the war started—anything to get out, even for those of us who live on the west side of the country, farthest from the fighting.

But I already know from my reading that there's a long history of prejudice against "mail-order brides" in America. They think we're a bunch of gold-digging Barbie dolls, and maybe that's true for some. But a surprising number of the women at the romance tours are also educated professionals looking for a real relationship as well as a better life.

That's what I hoped for—even if I'm neither educated nor professional.

I want real love. And why shouldn't that be with Lorne? My grandmother always told me that any two people could fall in love if they treat each other kindly.

Lorne is kind. He's smart, successful, funny…the feelings will come, all the feelings.

It just takes time. Once I've been here a few weeks, I'm sure I'll feel a lot more comfortable. With Lorne and with Ivy.

"I can't wait to meet her," I say, pasting on my biggest smile and clutching the sketchbook tightly to my chest.

Lorne uses his key to open Ivy's door without knocking. Her room adjoins his, two floors down from mine on the opposite end of the hotel.

As soon as we step inside, an uptight-looking woman, skinny and angular with her hair pulled back in a painfully tight bun, says, "Thank god you're here; she's been a nightmare all morning."

She jerks her chin in the direction of a small blond girl sitting close enough to hear every word.

Ivy, perched in the window seat looking down over Main Street, is so silent and still that it's hard to imagine her moving, let alone behaving as some sort of nightmare.

But Mina also looked sweet and innocent as a kid, with her big brown eyes and cherubic face, while she could have beat the devil himself when it came to trouble.

"And this must be Elena." The woman looks me up and down, mouth pursed, chin thrust forward. "Long flight, was it?"

I haven't had time to freshen up after twenty hours of travel. I'm sure I look like shit.

As if she summoned it into being, a wave of exhaustion rolls over me, and I sway on my feet. It's one o'clock in the morning in Lviv.

"This is my housekeeper, Mrs. Cross." Lorne introduces us. "She watches Ivy."

"Taken years off my life, that one," Mrs. Cross says with another jerk of her chin toward the silent Ivy, who gives no indication that she's heard a word being said or even noticed that two more people have entered the room.

I don't like how this woman keeps talking about Ivy like she's not there. I cross the small space, sitting down on the ornate, high-backed chair nearest to the window seat.

"Hello, Ivy. I'm Elena."

She finally turns her head, regarding me with an enormous pair of pale green eyes, round and unblinking. Her lashes are as white as her hair, and her eyebrows nearly disappear on her face. She's wearing a dress that looks pretty fancy for a Tuesday, like she's going to a birthday party later.

She doesn't respond to what I said, staring at me in a slightly eerie way, so I hold out the sketch pad and pencils.

"I brought these for you—your dad told me that you like to draw."

She regards the objects but doesn't take them. Her hands lie in her lap, pale and still as two dead doves.

I set the gift on the nightstand instead, gently turning it toward her. Her eyes follow the sketchbook. There's no expression on her face. After a moment, her gaze returns to me.

"Do you ever sketch outside? There's a pretty garden behind the hotel…maybe we could see if there's any plants to draw?" When she still doesn't respond, I add, "I like to take photographs. But I haven't taken any here in Grimstone yet."

Lorne answers for his daughter, probably because that's the only answer I'm likely to get. "Another time—Mrs. Cross is going to take Ivy back to the house with her, and I'm sure you'd like to take a shower and nap or something."

"If somebody doesn't keep an eye on those workmen, they'll never finish," Mrs. Cross says with relish, as if she's anticipating cracking the whip over the sluggish construction crew. "Let's go, Ivy, hurry up."

After a pause, Ivy slides off the window seat, slow and dreamlike, and follows Mrs. Cross out of the room.

Lorne lets out a breath of relief. "See what I mean?"

I do, sort of…

Ivy is certainly odd. But I don't get the impression that she's lacking in intelligence. Her pale green stare was unsettling but far from vacant.

"I like her," I say, and by saying it out loud, I find that it's true. I'm curious about this quiet little girl. I'd like to see her sketches.

"That's good," Lorne says, squinting like he doesn't quite believe me.

CHAPTER 4
ATLAS COVETT

THE AUTHOR BROUGHT HIS WIFE TO THE HOTEL TODAY.

He's already been staying here for three months with his daughter. Where this wife was the whole time is a mystery. Or it *was* a mystery until I saw her. Heartbreakingly beautiful, rose-gold hair, faint eastern accent, no ring on her finger, at least ten years younger than him...

He was gone exactly one hour and forty-seven minutes, just enough time for a round trip to the Grimstone airfield. I have a sneaking suspicion that this girl just flew in.

It's none of my business.

But then, everything that goes on inside my hotel is my business.

I spoke to her alone while my receptionist distracted the husband. She didn't seem distressed, only exhausted, dark circles under her eyes and hair a little limp. In a strange way, it only made her lovelier, like how the Japanese kintsugi artists believe a crack enhances the beauty of a teacup.

The separate rooms were odd. The author requested it last minute from Amy while she read him his messages.

The only available room was on the opposite end of the hotel. We're booked solid all month long thanks to Grimstone's Halloween festival. It's the biggest event of the year, busier even than our summer season. It was lucky we had an extra room at all until everybody clears out at the end of October and this place becomes a true ghost town.

I was surprised at the number of bookings. Even more than last year. The festival keeps growing, despite all the nasty shit that's gone down the last few years. Or because of it. I guess nothing makes the Reaper's Revenge more authentic than a real-life murder.

The crowds obviously don't care, especially the true-crime enthusiasts who take selfies in the patch of park where our sheriff was stabbed so they can post their theories.

I've got a pretty good idea what happened. Not that anyone will ask me. There are advantages to looking like you were spawned in the pit of Tartarus, and one of those advantages is very little casual chitchat from strangers.

The disadvantage is how easy it is to frighten people. I startle Amy just by existing in the main lobby when she returns to the front desk.

"Jesus! Don't scare me like that!"

"By standing here?"

"Standing so still." She gives me a mischievous look. "And looking so intimidating while you do it."

Amy Archer is my newest employee, brought on part-time for the busy season. She works as a maid at the Onyx resort the other three days of the week. She's too pretty for a receptionist—the businessmen won't stop flirting with her, and it slows down the line. But she's clever and innovative, reorganizing the front desk and streamlining the check-in system without being asked.

She's also cheeky, way too curious about the guests and her boss, but I like that she has the balls to tease me. It's not too difficult to shut her down with a long and silent stare. Keeping her quiet is a challenge.

"I guessed Mrs. Ronson would be pretty, but goddamn! She looks like a snow queen!"

Amy does have a knack for bringing an image to mind.

I see our newest guest as if she's standing by the stone fireplace all over again, tall as a Viking queen in her white fur coat with the ice-blue dress beneath. Her eyes were almost the same shade of clear arctic blue. Her thick ropes of hair were every sunset color, the twisted strands as bright as metal.

Elena.

"Makes sense." Amy taps her pen noisily against her teeth. "Ronson could get anybody; he's hot and loaded and famous."

Indeed.

And yet the author chose someone half his age from a foreign country. Whose suitcase is held together with duct tape.

"How is our newest guest settling in?"

Amy's vivid, dark eyes snap to mine. The wicked little smirk playing at the edges of her lips gives me the uncomfortable sensation that I've exposed myself.

"Sleeping off her jet lag, I guess. Her husband ate alone at dinner."

Lorne Ronson takes most of his evening meals in the restaurant on the ground floor of the hotel. His daughter rarely dines with him. I haven't seen much of the little girl, who mostly stays shut up in her room on the fourth floor or else is dragged around by that bitter-faced assistant who hustles in and out of here on the author's errands.

"The tag on her bag was from Ukraine," Amy notes, watching my reaction. "I wonder how they met?"

I doubt it's escaped Amy's notice any more than mine that while Mr. Ronson has been telling us for a month that his wife would soon be joining him, the woman who arrived today was bare-handed and seemed oddly cautious of her supposed husband.

"Borders are no impediment to relationships these days," I say.

"I wonder if he met her on a book tour," Amy muses. "I bet he travels all over."

"Have you read any of his books?" My receptionist often keeps a novel tucked away in her desk for slow afternoons.

"Just one," says the ever-honest Amy. "I didn't love it."

"Why not?"

"It was too gruesome. And the ending…" Amy shivers. "It was too much for me. I'm here alone half the time. I mostly read romance novels."

That tracks. Amy is always imagining romances between our hotel guests. She was certain that Mr. Portnoy in room 202 would extend his stay after his persistent breakfast buffet flirtation with the widowed Mrs. Bennington from 413. But he checked out at the end of the week and returned to Massachusetts still single.

"Kind of ruined the whole celebrity crush thing for me, though," Amy says.

"What do you mean?"

She pokes out her tongue slightly, one eye closed like a pirate. "It just…gave me the icks. I didn't think he was as hot after."

That makes Amy a party of one because the rest of the female hotel staff are infatuated with the author. I'm pretty sure Olivia's been sneaking him free lattes.

"Guess it just wasn't for me." Amy gives a jaw-cracking yawn, covering her mouth with her hand. "Sorry, didn't sleep for shit last night. Aldous had some girl over."

Aldous is Amy's twin brother and a concierge at the Onyx resort. Since I've already heard more than I want to about the number of women he brings home from work, I say, "You're welcome to leave. Your shift ended an hour ago."

"I know. I stayed so I could clean up that payroll spreadsheet for you."

Amy has wisely made herself increasingly indispensable since I brought her on board. I only promised her employment through October, because winter in Grimstone is dead and the hotel operates with a skeleton crew. But I already know I want to hire her on full-time next year. She's even started taking over some of the night shifts.

I haven't had someone I could trust to do that in…way too long.

Amy makes the right decisions in a pinch, in the moments when there isn't time to ask. That's rare.

"Are you walking out alone?" I ask.

She shakes her head. "Aldous is waiting for me. He's not *completely* useless." She says it with a mix of sibling fondness and resentment that I can only imagine is ten times more potent in twins.

Retrieving her coat and purse from the staff room, Amy exits with a cheery wave. "Good night, Atlas!"

Everyone calls me Atlas, even my employees. When a name fits you like mine does, there's no chance of anyone using *Mr. Covett.*

I've been overgrown since before I was born. When my mother couldn't fit behind the wheel of a car even with the seat pushed all the way back, the doctor induced her early. I still came out at eleven and a half pounds, thirty-one inches, requiring a three-month onesie.

Dane got two measly years as my "big brother" before I surpassed him. He doesn't hold a grudge about it, probably because he's a respectable six foot three and has witnessed firsthand how the extra inches only earn me bad jokes, clothes that won't fit, and charley horses on airplanes.

Maybe that's why the Ukrainian girl caught my eye—in those sky-high shoes, she was at just the right level to do it. Can't say that of many women. I've practically got to get down on my knees to find my tiny receptionist.

But it wasn't actually Elena's height that drew me in.

It was the expression on her face, curious and intelligent. She moved carefully through the lobby of the hotel, examining the clock, the mirrors, and finally Toulouse…I followed without thinking.

Speak of the angel.

Elena has emerged. She pads down the curved staircase in sneakers and jeans. With her face scrubbed clean and her rose-gold hair pulled back in a ponytail, she looks both younger and more Eastern European.

She walks in a cautious sort of way, like she's creeping around someone else's house in the middle of the night. That's probably exactly how it feels to her. It's one o'clock in the morning, and the hotel is silent, aside from the ticking of the carriage clock.

The clock is the heartbeat of the hotel, echoing softly down the hallways, bouncing off the tufted sofas, emerald rugs, and velvet drapes.

Elena pauses at the foot of the stairs, squinting slightly in the gloom. I keep the lamps low at night purposefully. It encourages the guests not to linger and to shut the fuck up so noise doesn't carry through this ancient place.

I could direct Elena. That's what I'd usually do. But I hang back in the doorway, watching.

She guesses correctly, turning left in the direction of the Reinstoff restaurant.

There's a perverse thrill in following her down the hallway, close behind without her knowing. I'm acquainted with every brick and board in this place, every place the floor groans. I'm quiet as the grave as I follow her, shoes muffled by the thick carpet. I reach out and brush the back of my fingers down her silken ponytail without Elena noticing.

Then I fall back, blood thudding through my veins.

It feels like I stole something.

I *am* stealing something…a close-up look at another man's wife. *Supposed wife.*

I still haven't seen a ring.

Elena reaches the restaurant, stopping short when she sees the darkened windows and closed doors.

I step out where she can see me.

"Mrs. Ronson…are you hungry?"

Even though I moved heavily on purpose to give her warning that I was coming, she spins around, hands up, eyes wide.

But she relaxes when she recognizes me, which is…surprising.

"It's you."

The way she says *you* almost makes it feel like she was waiting for me.

I know she wasn't. But it feels that way anyway.

"The restaurant is closed."

Elena shrugs her acceptance. "I know it's the middle of the night. Only..." She gives me a brief, sideways smile. "In Lviv, it's lunchtime."

I want to ask her how she learned to speak English so well. It's impressive, the speed and smoothness of her speech.

But that would be inappropriately personal.

So all I say is, "I have the key to the kitchen. Come inside, I'll make something for you."

"Oh, no..." She backs away, horrified. "You don't have to—"

"I insist."

I take out my ring of keys, the correct one already sliding into place between my finger and thumb. I could find any one of the twenty-seven master keys underwater and in my sleep, just as I'll always know the precise tone of the tumbler sliding home.

This hotel is mine. I know it like I know myself.

I pull the doors wide and place my hand against the small of Elena's back to guide her inside.

Now *this* is inappropriate. If I have to touch her anywhere, I should use her upper back or elbow.

But I touch her there and only there because I have to test what my eyes seemed to promise: that the curve of Elena's back is the exact shape of my palm.

My hand fits flawlessly. Like that's what it was made to do.

I lead her through the forest of upturned chairs, all the way back to the kitchen. *Then,* I take back my hand.

I pull the cord on the overhead light, bathing the forest-green cabinets and oaken butcher block in a firefly glow. Elena slides onto the nearest stool, crossing one long, jean-clad leg over the other. Her sneakers are the shade of gray that takes years to accumulate. Her eyelashes have flecks of reddish gold in them. With all that makeup washed off, I can see her skin.

I'm aware of exactly which of my iron-clad rules I'm breaking right now.

First of all, I have never flirted with a hotel guest before. Especially not a married guest.

I wouldn't say that I'm flirting right now. But I'm alone with a beautiful woman in the middle of the night, and if I were to examine the reason, it's not customer service.

Second, I never make exceptions for hotel guests. Rules are there for a reason—make one exception, and god knows what they'll get me to do next.

But how could I let the poor girl starve? I'd eat my own arm if nobody fed me after a flight from Lviv.

I open the fridge like that will absolve me.

"Ham sandwich?"

"Please," Elena says behind me.

I haul out the ingredients, spreading them across the butcher block.

"Do you often cook for your guests?" Elena has a restrained way of speaking. But I detect a teasing note.

I scan her face. Those arctic-fox eyes give nothing away.

"I've never cooked for a guest."

The tiniest hint of color comes into her cheeks. "Why am I so lucky?"

"Because there's nowhere else to get food at this time of night."

Usually, that means the guests are stuck with the snacks in their in-room minibars.

Elena's getting a ham sandwich because…I want one anyway. I love ham sandwiches.

I cut the slabs of bread thick, toasting and buttering the bread, adding a little yellow mustard and a large amount of shaved ham and sharp cheddar.

Elena lights up when she sees the finished product, reaching out with both hands and ripping in like she's starving.

"Sorry," she mumbles, mouth full. "I haven't eaten since… sometime yesterday. Was it yesterday? Time zones are strange."

I make myself a sandwich just as large and sit down next to her to eat it.

We're quiet, taking huge bites, chewing and swallowing. This is how I prefer to eat. Food is high on my priority list and talking gets in the way. It's not so bad later in the meal, but in the early part, when I'm hungry as a wolf, I like to focus.

Elena doesn't speak until she's devoured every scrap of bread and meat. Then she drinks half the glass of milk I poured for her and wipes her mouth on the back of her hand. "I would have worked all day for that sandwich."

"I did feel like it was one of my best."

She smiles slightly. "Do you cook for *yourself* often?"

I nod.

"Here?"

"I live here."

"And this whole place belongs to you?"

I try to hide the current that surges through me whenever I think of my hotel. "Yes. The Monarch is mine."

Elena watches my face and sees that surge. Her own expression is envy and wonder. "I can't imagine owning something so huge…all these rooms…everything inside of them…"

"It's more like it owns me."

She snorts as if she thinks I'm being falsely modest but is willing to concede the point. "Yes, it must be endless work."

Driven to explain properly, I say more than I should.

"It's not just that. My family has run this hotel for generations. Covetts have been conceived, birthed, engaged, married, and even murdered inside its walls. I spent most of my waking hours here as a child, and I always knew I would run it someday. So I belong to it more than I would to a parent or even a spouse. I've been wed to it since before I was born."

"Oh," Elena says softly.

She falls silent, and I think what I said was too honest and too much.

Then she admits, "I envy you."

"Why?"

"Because I don't belong to anything."

The words slip out before I can stop myself. "Not your husband?"

That was a mistake. The mood shifts in the kitchen now that I've mentioned him out loud. Elena moves on her stool so we're no longer sitting so close.

"Fiancé, actually." She lifts her bare left hand to show me what I already saw. "We're not married yet."

That *yet* nips at me like an annoying little dog. *Yet, yet, yet, yet, yet, yet, yet!*

"When's the wedding?"

"As soon as his house is finished. We're going to be married in the garden."

I've already heard all about this house the author is building, not only from him but from anyone in town who's been hired to work on the project. It's six months overdue and double the original budget, apparently because of Lorne Ronson's bizarre demands. He's gone through three different contractors, including a friend of my brother's named Tom Turner, the second to be fired.

"He had me rip out half the work from the first guy and change it all around. First he wants the window here, then over there…plumbing in rooms with no sinks…closets that make no sense… I do exactly what he says, and then he fires me! I'm telling you, the guy's a fuckin' loony."

I don't mention any of this to Elena, not only because Tom is newly sober and not the most reliable narrator but also because it's none of my damn business.

This girl is engaged. To one of my guests. Who happens to be a handsome, successful author.

So what in the hell am I doing sitting here chatting with her?

I push back the stool, heaving up my bulk. "I hope the work will be finished soon."

Taking my cue, Elena likewise slips off her stool. "Me too."

I give her the kind of nod I'd usually give a guest, measured and professional. "You can leave your dishes there; I'll lock up."

She answers back just as politely. "Thank you again for the food."

We part ways as if the entire interaction was professional.

And maybe it was, mostly.

Except for that moment when our eyes met and she said, *It's you.*

Her voice whispers in my ears all the way back to the front desk.

It's you...

It's you...

It's you...

CHAPTER 5
ELENA

Before I even open my eyes, I know I'm not at home.

It's the silence that tips me off. My uncle's place was never quiet. If the three small children who lived in the apartment above weren't thundering overhead, then I'd be woken by my cousin Ivan singing in the shower, my aunt Sofya banging the frying pan against the stove, or Mina yakking away while she got ready for work, oblivious as to whether I was awake or interested.

The size of the bed is another clue. I stretch beneath the blankets, my feet extending all the way outward without hanging off the end of the mattress, my arms spreading wide without touching a wall on either side.

When I sit up, the room is full of daylight, the soft gray kind filtered through clouds. The drapes are still wide-open; I forgot to close them last night. The clock on the mantel tells me I still managed to sleep in until 10:28.

I can't believe I'm in America.

I've never even visited. Now I live here.

Or I will very soon. It doesn't feel quite like "living here" when I'm still staying in a hotel.

Not that I'm complaining—I don't think I've ever slept in a room this nice. It's an entire suite, with a pretty, jade-colored sofa sitting before an actual working fireplace and a reading chair next to the window. The bathroom has a whole entire clawfoot tub, as well as a shower, and two sinks to choose between when I brushed my teeth last night.

I've never had *one* sink of my own to use. Now I have two!

Most of the white blooms have fallen away from the rose garden outside the huge picture window, only a few bruised petals still clinging to the thorny bushes. It's still a stunning view, especially with the flat expanse of slate-gray ocean beyond.

This room looks like it belongs to a princess.

I *feel* like a princess.

Which, I suppose, makes Lorne my Prince Charming.

He's definitely charming. When I pick up my phone, he's already sent me a text message:

> Good morning, sleepyhead! I came by earlier, but you were still out cold. The breakfast buffet finishes at ten, but you can have food sent up from the kitchen anytime. Charge everything to your room. I want to get some work done this morning—let's meet at 3 to go see the house!

Lorne uses a lot of exclamation points in his text messages. I wonder if he uses that many in his books. Probably not. That wouldn't really work in a thriller.

I need to read his books; I'm embarrassed that I haven't. I tried to order them through my store's system, but I needed manager approval. And by then…well, I couldn't exactly ask Boyka to do it.

Ugh. Don't think about that.

It doesn't matter. I'm here now. Any American store should have Lorne's books. Especially in Grimstone—they probably carry his whole catalog, since he's local.

I'll have plenty of time to check if I'm not meeting Lorne until the afternoon.

I text back:

That sounds perfect

I try adding an exclamation point: That sounds perfect! But that makes me feel false and annoying, like a little kid jumping up and down, so I delete it and simply add:

See you at 3:00

As I tuck my phone away, I wonder if I should have added the exclamation point after all.

Mina would probably tell me that I should. *"You're too cold, too closed off. That's why nobody flirts with you. Men want to know you're interested. They want fun and excitement!"*

I don't feel cold and closed off.

What I really feel is like the rest of the world moves at a faster pace. Like everybody else is a dolphin, flipping and zipping through the waves, and I'm just a slow-moving ray.

I don't know how people come up with witty jokes so quickly or clever comebacks when someone insults them. Sometimes it takes me a minute just to know how to answer a question.

I'm not stupid, but I like to process.

That's why I love books so much—they're a whole entire world I can absorb at my own pace, sinking into them like a warm bath and soaking.

Photography is the same. I go out with my camera and walk around as slowly as can be, taking in everything I see. When I finally snap an image, I've captured it forever, to take home and examine as long as I like, as often as I like.

The bookshop was the perfect job for me. The only question anybody ever asked was, *"Where's this book?"* which I could answer easily because I knew the store so well.

I loved it there. Until it stopped being the perfect job.

And anyway, it paid peanuts.

When I had to get out of Lviv, I found myself in a real dilemma—I was broke as a joke, without the cash for a plane ticket, let alone to set up a whole new life.

The romance tour was a silly, desperate plan, doomed to failure.

But then Lorne appeared, an actual real-life white knight, and swept me off my feet.

The whole time it was happening, I couldn't believe it. I kept thinking, *He'll get tired of me, he'll pick someone else, he can't be serious, he must be exaggerating, he'll change his mind, something will happen, something will go wrong...*

But it didn't.

Every email, every phone call, there he was, warm and charming. Even more inexplicable: he seemed to find me just as amusing, just as interesting. He never missed one of our planned times, like they were scheduled in stone. And everything he told me seemed to check out.

He made it all so easy. Before I knew it, he was proposing.

It was crazy, after just a month of talking. Lorne said, *why wait*? He explained that he couldn't travel back and forth to see me, not with his daughter in the mix.

"And besides...I already know. Don't you?"

There was no reason to refuse. It was exactly what I wanted. I just didn't expect it to happen so fast.

We exchanged documents, filed forms. Lorne had an excellent lawyer who greased the skids. A little more than three months from the day we met, I flew into Grimstone to meet my newly minted fiancé, my K-1 visa tucked in my purse.

Just in time.

It actually happened, the fantasy that every little girl imagines. It happened to *me*! My Prince Charming came along, and he's sweeter and more handsome than I would have dared dream.

That's got to be why I feel so weird right now, standing in this luxurious hotel room in the country where I always wanted to live.

I must be feeling *too* lucky, too undeserving…

Because that's the only thing that could explain the sick, sinking feeling in my gut.

———————

As I walk in the direction of the Reinstoff, I can't help thinking of Atlas. I've been looking for him without meaning to since the moment I stepped out of my room.

He's probably still sleeping if he worked all night.

But then there he is, as soon as I enter the restaurant, standing back by the kitchen, his thick arms crossed over his chest and his scowl firmly in place. I spot him easily because he's enormous, the top of his head almost brushing the ceiling where it's low.

And he, with the same eerie speed, spots me.

His dark eyes fix on mine. He goes completely still, and that's exactly what happens inside of me: my heart stopping dead in my chest, no breath in my lungs. It's like time can't move on if neither of us blinks.

When the hostess touches my arm, I flinch.

"Would you like a table?"

She must have asked at least once before. She's got that look on her face, that strained patience.

"Yes," I mutter, ducking my head. "Sorry."

When I fuck up, I feel especially tall. I lumber to my table, an awkward giant.

The hostess tosses down my menu and stalks away.

"Don't take it personally," says the pretty, black-haired waitress. "She got dumped this morning."

I blink up at her, feeling the oddest sense of familiarity. Then I see those laughing dark eyes and I remember that this is the receptionist.

"They make you wait tables as well?"

"Not usually." She tucks back a slightly sweaty strand of hair that's come loose from her ponytail. "But two girls called in sick, and as you can see, we're slammed."

Nearly every table is occupied, the emptiest belonging to a little blond girl sitting alone by the window.

"Oh, that's Ivy." I stammer a little trying to explain. "M-my fiancé's daughter. Could I join her?"

"Of course," the receptionist/waitress says, already scooping up my menu. I check the classy brass name tag pinned to her breast and learn that her name is Amy.

I approach Ivy from the direction she's already looking, so I cross into her sight line before I come too close. Her gaze fixes on my face without any sign of recognition.

"Ivy, I'm Elena, your father's friend. Do you remember me? Could I sit with you?"

The pause drags on before she slowly nods. Her movements don't seem reluctant—more like sleepy. Like she hasn't quite woken up for the day, even though it's getting close to noon.

I slip into the chair across from hers.

"Pancakes?" I smile at what she ordered. "That's my favorite, too."

I'm proud of myself for remembering the correct word to use. At home we call them *Oladushki,* and we make them with kefir yogurt. Keen to try the American version, I catch Amy's eye.

"Can I have the same thing?" I pass her back the menu.

Amy grins, showing her small and pretty teeth. "Excellent choice."

As Amy punches in our order, I say, "She seems nice," to Ivy, aiming for something friendly. I'm feeling nervous all of a sudden. I really want Lorne's daughter to like me.

I wish I knew what happened to Ivy's mom. Or how long ago she died. Was it recent? Ivy looks pretty melancholy. But Lorne doesn't seem recently bereaved. He talks about Linda like it was all in the distant past. Not that he talks about her much.

"Do you like staying at the hotel?" I ask Ivy. "Or are you looking forward to your new house?"

Asinine questions. They don't deserve any better than the slight lift of her shoulders. *Shrug.*

I realize, too, if Ivy's going to answer silently, I should only ask one question at a time. Or maybe ask less in general. Ivy flinched the last time I talked with too much brightness injected in my tone.

Speaking more softly, I say, "I was glad to meet you yesterday. I hope we can be friends. Would you like that?"

Ivy's pale green eyes rest steadily on my face while I'm talking. But when I ask that last question, they slide away and she sighs, looking distinctly unhappy.

Poor kid. She probably knows I'm dating her dad. Maybe she even suspects what's about to happen. I really wish I knew how long ago she lost her mom.

Before I can do anything else to fuck this up, Mrs. Cross comes speed walking between the tables and seizes Ivy by the upper arm. "There you are! I've been looking everywhere! I told you to stay in the room. Now we're going to be late for the contractor—"

"Excuse me," I say, my pulse jolting. "Please let go."

Mrs. Cross freezes, her whole body going rigid. When she turns her neck to look at me, I almost expect to hear a creaking sound.

"I know you aren't familiar with Miss Ivy's needs, but let me assure you, *I am.*"

If words could cut, I'd be lying here in sixteen pieces.

Also, I really don't want to make an enemy of Lorne's housekeeper.

But her bony fingers are digging into Ivy's arm hard enough to dent, and I see several faint blue bruises already dotting the same area of flesh.

"I said let go of her." It snaps out of me, no need to think this time.

Mrs. Cross twitches away her hand.

"Of course," she says, stepping away from Ivy, drawing herself up to her full height. "*You know best.*"

That might have been intimidating. Except, when I stand up, I'm a good four inches taller than Mrs. Cross. In my sneakers.

"Let's not fight," I say, low and soft. But not exactly friendly... more like a warning. "Didn't you say you're already late?"

The woman's mouth makes a puckered shape. She spits out, "We were supposed to meet the contractor at the house an *hour* ago, but Little Miss has been hiding. So let's *go!*"

She points dagger eyes at Ivy, though she's not quite brave enough to grab her again.

Ivy doesn't make any move to rise. I put my hand on her shoulder anyway, holding her in place.

"Why don't you leave her with me? Then you can be more... efficient."

Mrs. Cross narrows her eyes to slits. I think the offer appeals to her, but also, it's my idea. She'd prefer it if it were hers.

"I'll be gone a long time."

"I can stay with her until three. Lorne's taking me to see the house—if you're still there, we could bring Ivy along with us."

"No." Mrs. Cross shakes her head sharply. "He won't like that."

Something flickered into her expression when I said Lorne's name, disappearing too fast for me to catch. I've noticed that Mrs. Cross doesn't use his name. She calls him Mr. Ronson or, more often, doesn't speak a name at all, like it's too sacred to speak aloud.

She doesn't explain why my fiancé wouldn't like driving out to the house with his daughter in the car.

I wait her out, my hand on Ivy's shoulder.

One thing you learn when you don't like to talk that much is that other people are *compelled* to do it. They have to fill the emptiness. Which makes silence a powerful tool.

Mrs. Cross only lasts twelve seconds.

Grudgingly, as if she's doing *me* the favor, she grunts, "Fine. I'll be back before three."

Ivy's shoulder loosens under my hand.

"Great," I say, trying not to sound sarcastic.

Taking my seat across from Ivy once more, I ask, "Is that okay? If you stay with me today?"

This time the nod comes faster.

The urge to shit-talk Mrs. Cross as soon as she's gone is almost irresistible. I rein it in by saying, with the same hateful false brightness, "What should we do today?"

Ivy winces, raising her hands and plugging her ears. She slumps down in her chair, staring at her half-eaten pancakes, fingers firmly blocking out the world.

Well, shit.

Not off to a great start.

Atlas saves me by appearing beside her. "It's because the restaurant's noisy. It's busy today. She likes it when it's quieter."

I notice how softly he speaks when he stands close to Ivy. He can't completely smooth away all the gravel in his voice, but he's done his best.

The result is…extremely dangerous. Like fingertips dragging down my spine.

I take a hasty gulp of my orange juice.

Don't think about how good he smells…

Too late. I already inhaled a breath laced with Atlas's smoky, woodsy scent. It reminds me of the pure oud oil I smelled in a department store once that cost a month's salary. He smells as expensive as the old-world velvet dinner jacket he's wearing to the breakfast shift. This guy really takes showmanship to another level. Only it doesn't feel like a show. It feels like this is who he is and nothing could be more natural.

Atlas bends at the waist, saying to Ivy with extreme gentleness, "Nobody's out in the garden this morning."

I melt a little in my chair. I can't help it. I'm a sucker for a really good voice. And the image of the enormous Atlas bending over the tiny, pale Ivy is pretty adorable.

Ivy takes her fingers out of her ears half an inch.

I lean forward and ask her softly, "Would you like to go out to the garden?"

Her nod is immediate, her eyes fixed on mine.

It's not much, but it feels like success. I sit back in my chair, smiling.

"Thanks," I say to Atlas, turning my smile on the person who deserves it most.

He gives me that nod that somehow allows him to serve his guests without ever seeming subservient. It demands respect even as it gives it.

But as he turns away, he says, low enough for only me to hear, "I don't like that Cross woman."

CHAPTER 6
ELENA

BY THE TIME THREE O'CLOCK ROLLS AROUND, I'M KIND OF WISHING I had more time with Ivy. She's a surprisingly peaceful presence, while I feel nervous at the idea of another long car ride with Lorne.

I spent almost two hours out in the garden with his daughter that didn't feel long at all, bundled up in coats and scarves, crunching over grass bleached white with frost. That was what made the rose garden so beautiful even without any blooms: the lacelike patterns of frost printed onto the leaves and stems like tattoos.

Each pattern was different. Pressing our thumbs against the frost and melting it away to the green beneath was endlessly satisfying.

I talked a little but not too much at once, which seemed to suit us both. Ivy never spoke at all. Twice she touched my arm to show me something. And once, when a rabbit dashed across our path, she made a sound of happy surprise that gave me more warmth and amusement than the rabbit itself.

Snow began to fall, impossibly light and dry little flakes that dusted down on us like cool icing sugar. I worried if it got any thicker, I'd lose Ivy entirely, already a ghost child on the frosty grass in her white coat.

"We're snow angels!" I said, grabbing her hands, spinning us both around.

I had on Mina's white fur coat. Faux fur, of course, a little dirty from all the times Mina threw it on the floor.

The fur didn't look dirty outside. Out in the garden with Ivy, in her fancy white wool coat, it was easy to imagine that we were mother and daughter and I was wearing chinchilla.

Aside from both being blond, Ivy and I don't actually look alike. But it's still more than she resembles Lorne, her actual dad. When we're all a family, a real family, nobody will know that it didn't start the typical way.

That was the first moment, spinning around with Ivy in the icy rose garden, that the reality of having a daughter finally hit me. I guess I'd imagined myself more like a cool aunt or older sister. The fact that Lorne's daughter was already nine years old made me think she'd be well on her way to grown.

But when I met Ivy and saw how small she was, how shy and how vulnerable, I realized this is very much a little girl still in need of a mother. And I'm the one she's going to get. So I'd better do a damn good job.

It wasn't a bad feeling. It was more like standing at the bottom of a mountain, realizing it was taller and steeper than I thought but feeling ready for the climb.

Ivy seemed a lot more relaxed without Mrs. Cross around. I wonder if I should say anything to Lorne about those marks on Ivy's arm. He's told me what an incredible employee Mrs. Cross is, how she's indispensable to him, *practically a second mother…*

But he also told me how much Mrs. Cross adores Ivy, how close they supposedly are. In reality…there's a lot more tension than I was expecting.

I don't want to overstep, but I feel like I should say something.

Which is part of what's making me so nervous right now, waiting for Lorne.

At least I can tell him that I started one of his novels. I'm only a few pages in, but it's already scaring the shit out of me, which I think is the point.

I've got to finish it because I don't want to admit to Lorne that I'm a bit of a baby. The scariest books I read are fantasy novels, and *romantic* fantasy at that, where the most terrifying thing you're likely to encounter is a villainous fairy prince who turns out to be secretly sexy or, at worst, some dragon penis.

Lorne's book is about a girl being stalked by a serial killer, but it's from the serial killer's perspective. It's creeping me out, stepping inside that guy's head.

I took Ivy along to the bookstore with me, only six shops down from the hotel. I was amused when we arrived because I'd asked Amy where to find it and she'd taken the time to write down instructions, which turned out to basically be, *Walk out the front door and turn left.*

As I'd hoped, the tiny shop had an entire table dedicated to local celebrity Lorne Ronson. His glossy, dark thrillers seemed especially intimidating in towering piles almost as tall as me, with lurid images of bloody daggers, peering eyes, and sinister houses splashed across the covers.

It seemed like the height of assholery to swipe Lorne's credit card to pay for his own books, but buying all seven would have wiped out most of my cash. If I don't use my fiancé's money, I'll soon have none left.

After I pushed Ivy to pick out a couple books for herself, she disappeared so long I got worried, finally returning with a stack she could hardly see over.

"Is your dad okay with this?" I pulled Stephen King's *Firestarter* off the pile.

Ivy slid her eyes toward the gruesome covers of Lorne's thrillers just one table away.

I laughed. "Fair point."

But now, I'm not sure if Lorne will see it that way. I should probably ask him on the drive to the house. Before or after I mention Mrs. Cross and her nasty pinching fingers?

Ugh. What's the right way to do this?

I'm waiting out front of the hotel after returning Ivy to Mrs. Cross. Lorne texted me twenty minutes ago to come down, but he hasn't arrived yet himself.

It's a little chilly. I wrap my arms around myself, wishing Mina's coat was made of a polar bear pelt.

And then…I feel Atlas behind me.

It's surprising how quietly he moves for someone so massive. He's good at slipping through the shadows of this place. He practically gave me a heart attack last night, the way he melted out of the darkness.

One moment I'm alone, and the next his looming bulk is right behind me. I must have been waiting for him because now that he's here, I relax.

I turn my head only enough to see a slice of his dark-suited shoulder, still watching the road. Lorne will pull up any moment.

"You're not going to sneak up on me this time," I say.

Atlas makes a sound too deep to be a laugh. "If I want to sneak up on you, you won't know a thing about it."

The thrill that runs up my spine is part terror, part something too outrageous to be named.

I've often felt there's another Elena…a sneaky little shadow who lives inside my head. She likes all sorts of things she's not supposed to like and whispers terrible thoughts.

That Elena *wants* to be chased through a dark hotel by Atlas. She wants to feel those huge hands seize her body and wrap around her throat.

Which is wrong on many levels.

Starting with, I'm engaged. Even if I don't have a ring.

So I face forward again, straightening my shoulders, eyes trained on the road. "I'm waiting for Lorne."

Atlas's irritation is a storm cloud over my shoulder. Softly, he sneers, "Is he taking you to see his castle?"

His disdain confuses me, as does his word choice.

Castle?

No time to ask—Lorne's car pulls up to the curb, jerking to a stop as he hits the brakes too hard.

"There she is!"

Lorne jumps out of the car, leaving his door hanging wide. He jogs around to kiss me, sweeping me into his arms and lifting me off my feet. It's very romantic. The grunting sound he makes is slightly less romantic. Guys always underestimate how much I weigh.

He kisses me anyway, a long kiss, holding me up with his hands cupped under my ass.

It's a lot more enthusiasm than I expected, more than he showed when he picked me up at the airport. It kind of feels like he might be doing this because he saw Atlas talking to me as he drove up.

By the time he stops kissing me and sets me down, I'm sure Atlas is long gone.

I hope he is. But I can't bring myself to check.

———

Leaving the town of Grimstone, it only takes mere minutes before we're swallowed by deep, dark forest. Hundred-foot pines tower on either side of the two-lane road, providing a narrow view of the sky that winds like a river overhead.

I can't shake this fairy-tale feeling. It's the German Gothic style of Grimstone itself and the sudden and magical way I met Lorne, of course…but also, this pervasive sense of something darker and more dangerous beneath the surface.

I look at Lorne, at his lean, handsome face, his hand dangling over the wheel. Soft hands. Writer's hands.

This is a good man. He's not dangerous.

It's got to be something else nagging at me, and I should talk to Lorne about it. He's going to be my husband. We should be able to talk about anything.

"Lorne?"

"Yeah?" He turns, already smiling.

Which issue to broach first?

Cowardly, I pick the easier one.

"Do you have rules for what you let Ivy read or watch?" When Lorne blinks at me, I say, "Because I took her to the bookstore today and told her she could pick out some things." I confess the worst in a rush. "I let her buy a Stephen King novel."

I can't tell if Lorne is mad. His expression goes blank while he thinks.

"She picked out books?"

"Yeah, a whole stack."

"Huh," he says, frowning slightly.

"Is...that okay?"

He shrugs, his smile bursting back. "Sure. Why wouldn't it be?"

I don't know how to say this without sounding sanctimonious, since I'm the one who bought her the book.

"She's only nine. I thought it might be too scary for her..."

"If she even reads it." Lorne shrugs like he thinks she won't. "Besides, there's nothing wrong with being scared." He glances at me sideways, lowering his voice. "Don't you like to be scared?"

Is he flirting?

Fuck, I'm so bad at this.

My laugh is nervous. "Sometimes."

"What scares you the most?"

Lorne's voice is soft, caressing, even. It *sounds* like he's flirting. But his eyes are cool, darker than usual in the gloom of the pine trees all around. He's not touching my thigh like he did before in the car. Both his hands grip the wheel.

I press my cold hands between my knees.

Arm across my throat, pressed against the metal wall of a tiny box, that old sweat smell...

I crush the thought like a bug under my heel.

"Small spaces," I say. "I hate them."

A light kindles in Lorne's eyes, hot like a blue gas flame. "What happens?"

"W-what do you mean?"

"What happens when you're trapped in a small space?"

My throat tightens and my skin goes cold just thinking about it. "My heart beats faster and faster. And…I start to sweat. But I'm cold. Shivering."

"When did that start?" Lorne is keenly interested. He almost sounds excited.

I'm feeling more and more uncomfortable. "I…It's always been that way."

He studies my face, dissatisfied. Like he knows I'm holding back.

I know it's important to be honest with the people you love. And I will be. Over time.

But this is probably the *last* thing I'll tell Lorne, when we're eighty years old together in bed. When it will be so long ago and far away, it won't even matter.

I haven't even told Mina what happened.

Nobody knows. And maybe, maybe…nobody ever has to.

"What's your biggest fear?" I say instead, trying to keep the fun, getting-to-know-you vibe going.

"Mm…" Lorne sounds careless. "Being naked, I suppose— onstage or something."

He shrugs like it's not something he considers often. Which is funny because his whole job is thinking up terrifying situations.

I can never quite seem to predict what Lorne will say in conversation. For all the time we've spent talking, I wouldn't say I know him extremely well. Not yet.

If Lorne would have said, *My greatest fear is something happening to Ivy*, then I would have had a really useful segue for what I need to bring up next.

But he didn't say that. So I fidget around a bit while he's messing with the music and then mention, as casually as I can, "I spent some more time with Ivy today."

"Oh yeah?" Lorne looks up, so pleased that I hate to sour it.

"Yes. And it was nice, really nice. We played in the garden, went to the bookstore—I told you that…" Hating myself for stalling, I force out, "I noticed some, ah, bruises. On Ivy's arm?"

Lorne's face has gone still and blank again. Impossible to read.

My mother always told me, in difficult conversations, state the facts, not interpretations.

"Mrs. Cross grabbed Ivy by the arm at breakfast. And I noticed there were bruises already. In the same place."

Now Lorne reacts, but only by squinting and pouting his lips slightly, which doesn't tell me much.

Driven to soften the blow, I continue, "I'm not saying she meant to hurt Ivy. But maybe when Mrs. Cross is angry or frustrated…"

"Well," Lorne slips smoothly into the conversation, "she can be very frustrating."

I pause. "Ivy?"

"Yeah." Catching the look on my face, he says, "I mean, maybe not today. I'm glad if she was good with you. But sometimes she's a fucking nightmare, I'll be honest. We're lucky to have Mrs. Cross."

The road grows steeper, winding higher into the mountains. The sky's already darkening though it's not even four o'clock, thick gray clouds blotting out any hint of sunset color.

Lorne does not seem concerned by what I just told him. So I guess I shouldn't be, either.

I know people who spank their kids. But those people also adore their kids. With Mrs. Cross it was more like…animosity. She seems to *dislike* Ivy.

And in a small way, it appears that Lorne…finds that understandable?

"What's wrong?" He's watching my expression, not the road.

"Nothing." My hands twist in my lap.

He grabs them, unknots my grip, twines his fingers with mine. "Come on, tell me."

His grip is tight.

I should drop this.

No, not quite yet.

I try once more.

"If Mrs. Cross gets stressed with all the things she has to do, I could watch Ivy."

Lorne tilts his head, a tiny movement like a ticking clock. "You really liked hanging out with her, huh?"

"Yes, I did."

It's true. My hours in the garden with Ivy were the most peaceful I've spent since I boarded the plane. I don't mind that she doesn't talk. I'd rather not talk half the time, either. She has other ways of communicating—a glance, a happy chirping sound, a ghostly little hand plucking at my sleeve.

"Okay. If you don't mind." Now Lorne's tone sounds like, *You have no idea what you're getting yourself into.*

I hope I'm not making a huge mistake.

Grinning that bright white grin, my fiancé says, "So are you excited to see our new house or what?"

Our new house...

I'd been thinking of it as Lorne's house. But he said *our house* so naturally, like that's how it always is in his head.

Excitement expands in my chest scarily fast.

I *really* want a house.

Of all the things I drooled over in storybooks, nothing captured my imagination more than big, beautiful, private houses.

Nobody I know owns their own house, let alone the type of house that populates the pages of fiction, with a ballroom, a library, an attic, hidden passageways, secret compartments, a hedge maze or a private garden...

A house like that is its own world tucked away inside the real world, separate and safe in a way an apartment could never be.

That's what I fantasize about in the deepest chamber of my heart, even more than I wished for a Prince Charming. A place I can make completely my own. Where I feel safe and happy, away from the world.

When we turn the last bend up the winding mountain road, I see that Lorne isn't just my Prince Charming.

He comes with an actual full-size castle.

Lorne is loving my reaction.

I'm stunned. Like, "somebody just hit me on the back of the head with a baseball bat" stunned.

I can't believe he's building a castle…

A huge castle. With turrets and ramparts and towers. Everything but a drawbridge, really.

It's too much. This can't be real.

"You doing okay there?" Lorne grabs my arm to steady me.

We're crossing the churned-up patch of land that stands between us and the massive stone entryway. Planks have been laid across the mud, but it's still not the smoothest journey, the slush making the wooden boards slippery.

Plus, I'm completely freaking out again.

I can't believe he has a castle.

"So…do you like it?" Lorne watches me, hands stuffed in his pockets, waiting for the good part of my reaction. Because he just gave me the best surprise ever. I should be so excited.

"*O Bozhe,*" I say softly, because that's all I can manage. "You didn't describe it like this."

"You had to see it for yourself," Lorne says with satisfaction.

The immense stone castle stands in the forest like it's stood there for a thousand years. The parts of it that aren't quite finished only add to that effect, like the west tower is crumbling instead of half-constructed. The soot-black walls and pointed Gothic archways are faintly familiar—I suppose it resembles all the oldest buildings in Grimstone, that old-world aesthetic.

Dracula's castle…

Actually, it looks a bit like the Monarch. I wonder if that's what inspired Lorne. He must have seen the hotel every time he drove down Main Street, long before he stayed there himself.

But something holds me back from asking. Maybe I don't want to mention Atlas, or maybe I'm worried it might offend Lorne in some way. I'm sure he wants to think of his castle as completely unique.

There are no other houses around. Nobody to see or hear us for miles on either side.

I shiver, wrapping my arms around myself. It's pretty lonely out here. I wanted to be away from the world, but this is *really* far away…

But that's okay. I won't be alone. I'll have Lorne and Ivy and, sometimes, (sigh*)* Mrs. Cross.

He's still waiting for my response.

"I'm stunned."

Lorne smirks. "Clearly."

He takes my hand, leading me up wide stone steps into an entry-way that yawns like a mouth.

"No electricity yet," he says, hitting the flashlight on his phone. "That's the main reason we can't move in. The rest of it is getting pretty close!"

He sounds a lot more pleased talking about it today than he did yesterday. Maybe the contractor had good news. Or maybe it's just impossible not to beam with happiness when you walk inside your very own castle.

I'm sure I'll feel that way, too. Eventually.

Right now, I feel like someone took out all my bones and filled me with air. I'm light and floating but highly unstable. I have no idea where the wind will blow me next.

This is too surreal.

Lorne's flashlight sweeps across the entryway. This one room alone is bigger than my uncle and aunt's entire apartment in Lviv. The light glints off a plastic-wrapped niche partway up the wall, too small to be a closet—a space for a statue, perhaps?

It's hard to see anything in the gloom. The piles of boards and ladders and paint cans are difficult to navigate.

Lorne leads me through cavernous room after room, only a small circle of the tantalizing space illuminated by his phone. He's describing everything around us—"This will be the formal dining room, up here is Ivy's room"—but mostly I have to take his word for it. All I see are shadowy pillars, fireplaces that might be doorways and doorways that might be fireplaces, and my own image jumping out at me from unexpected mirrors.

"I should have brought a real flashlight," Lorne says. "I forgot how dark it is in here. The workers have a generator…it must be out of gas."

"Where is everyone?" I ask timidly, not wanting to poke a sore subject all over again.

Lorne scowls. "They stop working every time it rains."

"Even inside?" I glance up at the roof, confused. It seems intact. Most of the castle is close to complete; some of the rooms are even furnished, though in a jumbled, plastic-wrapped way.

"Oh, they think there's some flood risk here." Lorne waves his hand dismissively. "Don't worry about it; it's all total bullshit made up by the last contractor I fired. He's half the reason the work's not done—he's been spreading rumors around, trying to scare away my workers."

"What kind of rumors?"

"Ridiculous nonsense." When I pause, waiting, Lorne says, "That accidents happened, the site is haunted, the castle is cursed…

You wouldn't think grown men would believe that horseshit. And most of them didn't, so now he's come up with the flooding bullshit."

"…Okay."

I believe Lorne. But I wish he hadn't put the image in my head. My mother was a geotechnical engineer, so I have a great respect for flooding and landslides.

And the weather in Grimstone is mercurial. I don't think I've seen a scrap of sunshine since we arrived. Rain is spattering down from iron-colored clouds that boil across the sky.

Inside the castle, the dark is even deeper, the walls thick and the windows high and narrow. I know that's a feature of Gothic architecture, but I wish Lorne weren't being quite so authentic. It makes me feel shrunk to a doll's size, looking up at those small patches of sky.

Lorne seems to know his way, even in the dark. He must come here often to check on the work. Confidently, he leads me down a long hallway with curved walls like a tunnel. Here, there's no windows at all, and I'm starting to get nervous. Our feet thud dully over the unfinished floor.

At last, we reach a pair of double doors that Lorne throws wide. "The marital suite."

He pulls me into the center of a near-circular room. I realize we must be at the base of the unfinished tower—that was the windowless hallway, passing from the main body of the castle into here.

The space feels enormous, the floor under my feet even more hollow. Lorne turns me around, the cell phone flashlight making shadows rear up on the walls like wild horses. I spy yet another fireplace, which I'm sure will come in handy this winter, and a distant bathroom with a glint of a tub. Also, an extremely large bed.

Lorne doesn't say anything and neither do I, but we're staring at the mattress where I'll have sex for the first time in a few short weeks.

With Lorne.

Right now, the bed is wrapped in plastic to protect it from dust. Even the headboard and footboard are wrapped, giving the whole thing a ghostly shroud. It's…a little creepy.

To me, at least. Lorne grabs me and kisses me with an unexpected amount of tongue, pressing my face between his hands so I can't move as his wet tongue delves in and out of my mouth.

When he pulls back, my chin feels moist. I kind of want to wipe it off, but that would be rude.

"Does this make you excited to move in?" Lorne says, low and husky.

Uhh…

I look into Lorne's eyes, dark and flickering in the unsteady light.

Over his shoulder, a void yawns, larger and darker than the fireplace, an inky black deeper than all the black around it.

"What's that?"

"That," Lorne says softly, his hands dropping down on my shoulders, "will be your brand-new walk-in closet."

He propels me closer, steering me like a ship until we're all the way up to the blank, empty space.

"Want to take a look?"

Lorne's fingers dig into my shoulders. He's still holding his phone, too, but pressed against my arm, so it's not illuminating inside the closet. I can't tell how large it is inside. Or if it has any shelves.

"Next time." I swallow. "We need a proper flashlight."

Lorne's still holding me by the shoulders. For one sickening moment, it feels like he's going to shove me inside that ink-black space. My brain plays tricks on me, telling me it's not a closet at all but an elevator shaft with an endless fall down, down, into the earth…

But that's ridiculous.

It's just a closet.

And my fiancé isn't going to push me inside. He drops his hands to his sides.

"You're right. Let's head back."

Lorne starts striding for the door. He's still holding his cell phone, pointed at the floor, the light swinging back and forth with his arms. I have to hustle to keep up with him as he cuts a straight path back through the house. I mean, *castle.*

It's hard to keep pace with him in the dark, especially as we weave through tarps and ladders, piles of lumber and cans of paint.

Lorne never hesitates.

He seems to know his new home *very* well.

CHAPTER 7
ATLAS

THE AUTHOR PICKS UP HIS WIFE—OH, NO, EXCUSE ME, *FIANCÉE*, that fucking liar—after making her stand twenty minutes in the cold. Watching him kiss her is unpleasant.

Actually, it's worse than unpleasant.

It's enraging.

It shouldn't be. The girl is nothing and no one to me. But I don't like the way they look together.

For one thing, he's not quite tall enough for her. I know that sounds biased, but I'm telling you, the proportions are off. He's a fit guy, but he's long in the torso, short in the legs, and Elena is all legs. They don't look right when they stand together.

And he's so goddamned pretentious.

The way this fuckin' guy dresses. There must be some shop that makes tweed jerking-off jackets for professors, Nobel laureates, and *wri-tahs!*

I didn't like him even before Elena showed up. It's not just the overly familiar attitude or the bad brunch tips. It's something in his eyes during conversation when the other person is speaking. Some private amusement, like he's writing a scene in his head and not really listening.

But now that Elena's here…my dislike is curdling into something darker.

I don't like the way he treats her, like she's something he bought on vacation. Some exotic piece of art he'll take home to his fucking castle once it's finished, to lock away where no one else can see her.

He sure as hell didn't think about feeding her when she arrived. I did that.

I loved watching her devour her food like a wild animal. I loved seeing her in her normal clothes, face scrubbed clean, as opposed to the painted doll that arrived on the arm of the author.

I could tell she wasn't actually comfortable in that dress or those shoes. Her fingernails likewise gave her away, bitten short and unpolished. Posh women prioritize their manicures.

Did she dress up for him? The thought makes me jealous.

That must be what she thinks he likes: the short skirt, painted face, false lashes, sky-high heels...

What would she wear for me, to please me?

Not that dress.

I imagine Elena knocking on my door late some night, naked as Venus...

Yeah. That's what I'd request.

The mental image cheers me up momentarily, but then I remember that Elena will not be knocking at my door because she's about to marry somebody else. She's with him right now, the two of them all alone up at his creepy castle.

Who the fuck builds a castle, anyway?

It's like he's trying to show me up. I used to have the biggest place in town. Well, except for the Onyx resort up on the north end of the beach, but nobody counts those interlopers.

My hotel's still better. For one thing, it's symmetrical. I've seen that jumbled shit he's building up there—I couldn't help myself; I drove up once to see what had everybody yakking. Or more accurately, my brother drove me. Dane's become chipper and helpful ever since he fell in love, which is disturbing. He used to be grumpier than me.

His girlfriend, Remi, source of this newfound cheerfulness, was sitting in the back seat. I offered her shotgun, but she refused to take it, and I sure as hell wasn't going to argue. I can hardly cram my legs in Dane's car even with the seat pushed all the way back.

"Why don't you get an SUV already?" I grumbled.

"I tell him that all the time!" Remi chirped, right in my ear. She was not using a seat belt, leaning so far forward that her face was sandwiched between ours. "He's too tall for a car!"

"So's his much taller brother."

"Not *much* taller," Dane muttered. He squinted up the road, trying to decide the correct route to the castle. "I'm not getting a bigger car just to chauffeur you around."

"You want to see this place, too!" Remi poked him gleefully in the ribs. "Tom says it's fucking bonkers!"

Even with that expectation firmly in place, we all fell silent when we saw it looming over the trees—the dark and chaotic building, larger than any of us expected.

It had a Frankenstein look, the work of several different architects stitched together by multiple contractors. We'd all heard about the drama. Nothing happens in small towns without weeks of judgment and exaggeration.

"Yikes." Remi sniffed. "Can't buy taste."

She had a right to her slight air of superiority since she'd just renovated and flipped the Blackleaf house for a pretty penny. It looked like a completely different place by the time she was done with it, showing a level of aesthetic skill you'd hardly expect from someone with electric-purple hair.

Lorne's castle wasn't tacky, exactly. It was more…disturbing. Something not quite right in the angles, the proportions.

I wonder if Elena's liking it.

I can imagine her eyes lighting up, her cheeks flushing as Lorne shows her around. That whole big place, not built to host a bunch of guests and strangers but for her alone.

Okay, maybe I'm a little jealous.

Maybe a lot jealous.

I storm through the hotel in a hell of a mood.

Amy's the only one brave enough to talk to me. "Something wrong, boss?"

"No."

Yes.

I saw something I want, and I can't have it...

Over Amy's shoulder, a small blond figure sneaks down the stairs. The girl makes a neat turn, heading left, in the direction of the restaurant.

"You look pissed off," Amy observes.

"More than usual?"

"Yeah." She grins. "And that's saying something."

Now Mrs. Cross comes furiously hustling down the stairs. When she reaches the bottom, she looks both ways and then turns right.

I smile to myself.

"That's more like it," Amy says, missing the intrigue unfolding behind her back and crediting herself for my change in mood. "Can I get you a coffee, boss? Gin and tonic? Completely professional shoulder rub?"

"What previous boss told you there were workplace-appropriate shoulder rubs?"

"I give everyone shoulder rubs!" Amy says innocently. But then she taps her fingernail against her teeth, musing, "Though I did end up shagging some of those people later."

"Let's stick with the coffee."

"You got it, boss!"

As Amy skips away, I can't help but wish I could hire her on full-time right now. She really does make my days easier. She's like a little house sprite, popping up at just the right time to make herself useful.

And she brews my coffee perfectly, black as sin with one cream, no sugar.

While she's making it, I head in the direction I last saw Ivy disappear. Technically this area is for staff only, as the hallway passing behind the kitchen contains the dumbwaiters we use to send food up to the rooms. It's remote enough that there's usually no need for a sign to keep guests away, but Ivy has wandered far avoiding her keeper.

Unfortunately, she finds herself at a dead end. I see her, small and pale as a white rabbit and just as twitchy, crouching next to an urn not large enough to conceal her.

Close by, Mrs. Cross mutters, *"Where is that little bitch?"*

Ivy's pale green eyes meet mine, the fingers stuffed in her mouth chewed and raw.

"In here," I say, pulling up the shutter of the nearest dumbwaiter.

In the quickest move I've seen her make, Ivy hops inside the small space. I close the shutter just as Mrs. Cross rounds the corner.

Mrs. Cross reminds me of the meanest teacher I ever had. Just like Mrs. Feinman, Mrs. Cross seems to be that inexplicable type of adult who detests children but has chosen to work with them full-time.

She worships the author, her master. But the soppy adoration that spreads across her face whenever she gazes at Lorne Ronson does not extend to his daughter.

"Oh!" she says when she sees me, smoothing back the glassy surface of her hair that's already pulled painfully tight against her skull. It's her face she should have wiped, milky sweat running down her temples. "Have you seen Mr. Ronson's daughter?"

"She was out in the garden earlier."

Mrs. Cross takes that statement exactly the way I intended and hustles out the back doors.

Before I can tell Ivy the coast is clear, a much different figure appears at the end of the hall. Unlike the skinny Mrs. Cross who strides along with her shoulders up to her ears and her head thrust forward like she's walking into a strong wind, Elena has the posture of a queen and curves that could feed my eyes for days, let alone my hands or my mouth...

She's back from the castle.

My eyes immediately check her left hand. When I see it's still bare, I feel a hot and ugly rush of pleasure.

She's hurrying a little herself, hunting about. When she spots me, her face softens with relief.

"Atlas! Have you seen Ivy? Mrs. Cross said she ran off."

As she approaches, I say, "You're getting warmer…"

Elena pauses, anticipation coming into her eyes at this age-old game. Watching my face, she takes a step backward.

"Colder."

She bites her lip to hide her smile. And takes two steps forward.

"Warmer. Warmer…"

She closes the gap between us, ten feet away, now five…

"Warmer…"

She stops right in front of me, our bodies inches apart. When she looks up into my face, I'd hardly have to move at all to kiss her.

"Very hot."

Elena flushes and drops her eyes. It was fun playing along, but now we're standing too close to each other for her comfort. She tries to step away. I plant my palm against the wall, trapping her in the small space between my body and the dumbwaiter.

Her body tightens, her skin flushes, even her scent changes. It's so sudden, I notice it like a spritz of perfume in the air—her fear mixed with something else.

That *something else* does *something else* to me. It rolls over me like sickness, like famine…

I want her.

Elena whirls around, our bodies pressing together as she snarls, "Let me out!"

She's furious, and even though every inch of me screams to continue pressing itself against every inch of her, I step back and say with apology, "Of course. You found the prize."

I open the dumbwaiter, revealing Ivy curled up comfortably in the cupboard-sized space.

"There you are!" Elena gasps. She helps Ivy climb out, though Ivy seems like she'd rather stay, gazing longingly back into the cool, dark space.

I probably shouldn't have shown her that. Kids love hiding spots, and that's not a place she should play.

"Thanks," Elena says, holding Ivy by the hand but not quite meeting my eye.

"Anytime." *I'll kidnap the kid myself if it gets me another five minutes with you.*

This attraction to her is some kind of illness. I'm already hot and weak-kneed knowing that she's about to walk away from me.

The last half second ticks away. She shifts her weight, starts to turn—

"What did you think of the house?" I say in desperation.

Elena pauses, not quite turning all the way back to me. She scans the carpet, lashes fluttering against her cheeks. "It's…overwhelming."

I love that tepid response. It would have killed me to hear her gush over her future home.

But as she continues on her way, holding Ivy by the hand, my satisfaction collapses into something uneasy…

Because Elena looks afraid.

CHAPTER 8
ELENA

LORNE KNOCKS ON MY DOOR AT 8:22 SO WE CAN WALK DOWN TO dinner together. He said he'd come at 7:00, but as I'm learning, my fiancé gets pulled into his work and forgets to check the time.

Even though my father used to say stealing time from other people is one of the rudest things you can do because it is the scarcest commodity that any of us have, I'm not that annoyed. It means I can calm down after a somewhat intense day and zone out in front of the mirror, trying to make a zen process out of failing to recreate the makeup Mina can do so effortlessly.

Unfortunately, I do not have her steady hand with eyeliner, nor her ability to blend powders and shadows with da Vinci levels of precision. I end up washing off my first two attempts, the third reasonably successful only because I keep things simple, just a little gloss and blush and mascara because those are harder to fuck up.

When Lorne arrives at last, he's wearing a fresh button-up shirt, and he's combed his hair neatly backward, exposing the angles of his face, leaner now than when I met him. That day at the café, he was at the end of a two-week vacation, eating and drinking his way across Europe. Now he's been working out every morning in the hotel gym.

He's also wearing an expensive-looking pair of black-framed eyeglasses, which makes it all the more difficult to read those cool blue eyes.

I think he's in a good mood, so I ask, "How did your writing go?" and trust that the answer will be positive.

"Excellent," Lorne says, slipping his arm around my waist and pulling me closer. "I was feeling extremely inspired after our visit to the house."

"That's great."

I'm not entirely sure what type of inspiration I gave him.

I want to love my future home, but in truth, I found the half-built castle a little creepy. I'm sure it was just how dark and jumbled it was inside and the unexpected and overwhelming size of the place, but the visit didn't increase my excitement for our move-in date. The only things it increased were my nerves and my growing unease that I don't deserve any of this.

Now that I've seen with my own eyes how wealthy Lorne is, I'm more confused than ever how he happened to pick me out of all the women in the world. He's got to be Grimstone's most eligible bachelor, even if he has a kid already.

Apparently, he's thinking something along the same lines because his eyes move from my face to my body, and he frowns slightly.

"Is that what you're wearing to dinner?"

I cringe at his tone, shrinking away from him. I put on the second-best dress in my suitcase, the nicest being the one I wore on the plane. Both belonged to Mina originally, and while they're a little tight on me, I still thought I looked nice.

"Yes," I venture. "Is it not…quite right?"

"It looks a little cheap." Lorne tweaks one of the flimsy straps. "Haven't you bought any new clothes yet?"

"I only went to the bookstore today." After a moment I add, "I'm sorry."

"Well, do it tomorrow," Lorne says. "No offense, but I'd prefer to make it less obvious that you're not from around here."

The way he says "not from around here" sounds a lot more like "a dirt-poor refugee," but that's probably just my insecurity warping his tone. Lorne doesn't care that I'm broke; he's told me a dozen times, "*I've got more than enough for both of us.*" And he obviously doesn't care that I'm from Ukraine, since he's the one who traveled to me.

Still, I don't feel nearly as pretty as I did ten minutes ago when I surveyed myself in the mirror, pleased with the results of my work. Now I'm uncomfortable in the tight polyester dress, tugging the hem down to cover more of my legs.

"Could you come shopping with me, maybe?" I ask tentatively. "I don't know much about American fashion…"

Especially not the rustic, woodsy style favored in Grimstone. I never knew so many types of plaid existed, or so many shades of denim. Are there subcultural rules I'm unaware of? Are fringy jackets only for single girls?

"Wish I could," Lorne says. "But I'm not taking a day off work until this book is done."

"Okay." I try to focus on my fiancé's impressive work ethic and not on my terror of accidentally buying a bunch more clothes Lorne doesn't like on *his* credit card. "I'm sure I can figure it out."

"Take Mrs. Cross, why don't you?" Lorne offers.

That would be a great idea if Mrs. Cross weren't the only person in Grimstone with worse style than me. She dresses like an eighteenth-century schoolmarm mixed with a fascist prison warden.

Also, I'm kind of starting to loathe her. The vicious chewing out she gave to Ivy after I found her in the dumbwaiter (I mean, after *Atlas* found her) had me biting my tongue and wondering again if I should say something to Lorne.

But that didn't go very well last time. I think I need something a little more concrete than "the woman who watches your daughter kind of seems to hate her."

And now I'm thinking about Atlas again. Specifically, the thrill that shivered down my spine when he fixed those wicked black eyes on mine and growled, "*Warmer*," and I realized he was playing with me.

It was irresistible, the urge to creep closer to him, to test the parameters of the game…

Heat flushes my cheeks, and I shove that thought away, hoping that Lorne won't notice.

"Good idea," I say without actually committing to ask anything of Mrs. Cross. Style aside, I don't want to owe her a favor.

"Great." Lorne nods like it's settled. "Let's get down to dinner, I'm starving."

He takes my hand and leads me down the hallway.

"Is Ivy meeting us?"

"She eats earlier. By the time I'm done working, it's practically her bedtime."

Lorne told me he's not an early riser, and he often works late into the night, which I suppose is the perfect time to write thrillers. But I'm a little surprised that he doesn't eat dinner with his daughter. She seems to spend more time with Mrs. Cross than with him. Is that normal for a single parent with a demanding job? I don't have any friends with kids, and everything is so different here that I really can't judge.

I must look judgmental anyway because Lorne says, "Trust me, she likes it better that way. She hates eating in the restaurant; most of the time she just wants a PB&J up in her room."

I nod. But then I ask him, "Will we all eat together at home?"

A brief hesitation. Then Lorne says, "Sure. Of course."

That sounds nice. I try to picture a family dinner at our new house, me and Lorne and Ivy sitting around one of those grand American farmhouse tables, laden with all the delicious dishes I'll learn how to cook when I have a kitchen of my own. If the house is ready by Thanksgiving, I could make one of those epic browned turkeys I've seen so many times in movies.

Of course, I'd probably need about a year to learn to cook a turkey properly.

This is what I dreamed of: the things that looked so luxurious, a completely different kind of life with so much of everything for everyone…

A real house, a real family, holidays like you see in the movies with gifts and decorations and mountains of food…

But now that I've actually seen the house (*castle*), all I can picture in my head is that dark cavity in the master bedroom that Lorne said was a closet, that seemed to go down and down and down…

I push that thought away, too. It's just a closet, and I'm way too old to be afraid of the dark.

We've reached the Reinstoff. Like much of Grimstone, the restaurant has that quaint German style that makes everything look like a Grimm's fairy tale with folk-painted walls, shuttered windows, and a thatch-and-beam roof. Even though the restaurant connects to the Monarch, it feels like a witch's cottage.

The waitresses wear pretty dirndl dresses, and the bartender has on leather lederhosen, though he doesn't seem happy about it.

I look around for Amy. She's either back at the front desk where she belongs or she already finished her shift.

We're served by one of the usual waitresses, a shapely blond in a pink-and-gold dirndl. Lorne gives her such an appreciative look that I'm wondering if I should have borrowed one of those milkmaid costumes to wear to dinner instead of Mina's dress.

"Good evening, Mr. Ronson!" she chirps, displaying a stunning white American smile. Do all the waitresses have to be so pretty? This girl looks like a goddamned beauty queen. It's unnecessary.

"Good evening, Olivia." Lorne smiles back at her warmly.

Beneath the table, my nails dig into my thighs.

Looking only at Lorne, supermodel-turned-waitress Olivia asks, "Would you like to hear the specials tonight?"

"I'd love to." Lorne rests his chin on his palm, like he hopes it takes all night.

Olivia rattles off half a dozen dishes that probably would have sounded mouthwatering under normal circumstances. The ingredients jumble in my ears as I watch my fiancé grin up at this gorgeous girl.

I'm not normally this jealous, especially not over something so... innocuous. But my skin is burning, and my stomach feels like it's turning in on itself.

I try to tell myself that Lorne has been staying at the hotel longer than me, so of course he's made friends with the waitresses. It's not Olivia's fault she hit the genetic jackpot. I'm just feeling insecure because I realized today my fiancé has a castle, and now the fact that I gnaw my nails like a beaver and can't dance very well and failed half my math classes are starting to feel like pretty big liabilities.

Especially because my fiancé still hasn't given me a ring.

Lorne says, "Bring us two rib eyes. That sounds delicious. Fondue to start. And the Bordeaux, of course."

The waitress says, "You got it, Mr. Ronson. Coming right up!" in a flushed and giddy way that shows that she absolutely knows who Lorne is, professionally speaking, and probably has a bit of a crush on him.

Lorne is a lot more intimidating here in America. In Lviv, he seemed like just another cute tourist, nervous and out of place. Now that he's back in his hometown, he's almost a different person. Direct. Confident. A little demanding sometimes, even.

He even looks different. A lot different, actually, with the combed-back hair and shaved face and newly hardened physique.

Objectively, he's only gotten hotter, his grooming cleaned up, his chest and shoulders filling out his shirt. Olivia certainly noticed.

But it makes me uneasy, like a mirror with a crack in the middle, my mental images not quite aligned.

It doesn't help that at that exact moment I glance up and see Atlas staring at me.

Great. He probably saw that whole thing.

I bite my lip hard, afraid of what he might be reading on my face.

Atlas's expression, meanwhile, is impossible to read. At this moment, with those thick, lowered brows and that iron jaw and the burning, black rage in his eyes, you might assume he's plotting a murder. But I've known him just long enough to understand that he mostly always looks like that.

Unless he's talking to me alone...

Then his face softens. Like when I stood so close that heat radiated from his barrel-sized chest, and I smiled up at him because we were playing a game and it all seemed so innocent.

But then he smiled that wicked dark smile and said, "*Very hot,*" and I knew it wasn't innocent at all. Not for him and not for me. And I tried to flee.

He trapped me there, and that was when I came closest to sinning. Because I *hate* being trapped in small spaces. I hate it worse than anything. It terrifies me until my heart beats so fast, I think it will explode in my chest.

But somehow, in the heat of Atlas's body, against his thick arm, I wasn't just afraid...I was also turned on. Lust flared like a furnace, fear and desire feeding each other like gasoline and flame.

And that's when I snarled at him, "Let me out!"

Atlas stepped back, surprised, touching his chest, bowing slightly, using his "thank you for being a guest here, ma'am" voice on me again.

And there was Ivy, perfectly safe inside the dumbwaiter, filling me with so much relief and gratitude that I didn't feel angry anymore, just foolish for overreacting because I was trapped (*that's all it was, I was trapped*).

That's what I tell myself. And it mostly works.

Except that I keep thinking about it, over and over.

The thickness of his arm pressed against my cheek, his whole body blocking me in, solid like a wall but warm and alive, smelling like—

Never mind what he smells like.

Worry about why he's looking at me like that.

I thought I parted with Atlas on reasonably good terms. Now

he's staring at me like he wants to devour me. But I shouldn't think about him at all. I should be listening to my fiancé.

Lorne is talking about fondue.

My eyes flit back to Atlas. The chef has come out of the kitchen to talk to him. He crosses his arms over his chest in unconscious imitation of his boss, but that only makes plain how much bigger and broader Atlas is.

Lorne is still talking about fondue.

I look at Atlas again. At his square jaw. His coarse black hair. The way his eyebrow rises slightly as he murmurs something to the chef, who snorts, nodding, and heads back into the kitchen.

I'm going to go to hell if I don't stop this.

Another glance at Atlas.

Don't look at him. Stop feeling this...

"Are you listening to me?" Lorne demands.

"Yes. You were talking about the fondue."

"That's right," he says, slightly mollified.

Thank god he doesn't inquire further, because I heard nothing else during his eight-minute speech. Lorne is good at making words; it's his job. As I learned on our phone calls, he can talk for ten, fifteen minutes without needing much but sounds of assent. Since he's witty and knowledgeable, it wasn't boring, and that's when I most thought I was in love, during those hours of listening to his hypnotic, sweetly funny voice over the phone.

Other times I wasn't certain. Because love takes time to grow. And this all happened so fast.

The waitress brings the wine back so quickly, it feels like she must have ordered it before she even visited our table. She's still flirting with Lorne as she pours, laughing and touching his shoulder multiple times. She doesn't look at me at all, like my side of the table is empty.

I take my glass, saying, "Thank you," as carefully as I can, like everything happening is normal and meaningless. Even though it all feels spiky and strange.

Lorne clinks his glass against mine. I can feel Atlas watching us. Watching me.

He's being outrageous, standing there staring. He's, like, seven feet tall. Why doesn't Lorne notice?

Lorne looks only at me, studying my face like he can peel down the layers to my thoughts.

"What's wrong?"

"Nothing." The lie is automatic.

"Okay," Lorne says. "Then take a drink."

I lift the wine to my lips mechanically, though the dark and bloody color repulses me. That's what wine looks like, I guess. Usually, I order vodka. When I'm allowed to give my own order.

I don't care if it's petty; I'm a little bit bugged.

I gulp down the wine. It tastes metallic.

"What's wrong?" Lorne expects an answer this time.

"Nothing. It's just…" I try to make my laugh self-deprecating instead of accusatory. "I realized the waitress might know you better than me."

Lorne sits back in the booth, scoffing. "Oh, come on."

But he's watching me so carefully that I can't believe there's nothing between him and this waitress.

At bare minimum, Olivia has a crush.

At least a crush…

I sit very still, wondering if I have the right to ask him if he ever slept with her. Like…even before we met.

Lorne squints at my face. "I don't know any of these people!" he says, throwing up his hands. "I spend all day writing. I barely even see Ivy. I told you, I'm on a super tight deadline."

Yes, your days are packed…but what about your nights?

Lorne leans forward, giving me his full and undivided attention. His expression gentles until he looks much more like the man I met on the ground floor of the Ambassador Hotel.

"Elena," he says, his eyes soft, his voice melting. "You can't seriously think I care about any other girl."

I relax slightly, settling back into the booth. I didn't realize how tense I'd become, all bunched up in my shoulders.

Breathe, babe, you're acting ridiculous. What did he do? Smile at the waitress? Give her his order?

Our order, actually. Lorne didn't ask me what I wanted.

I know he comes here all the time. He knows what's good.

Still…I kinda wanted a salad. On the side or something.

Aren't you being a little petty? He's bringing a castle to the table, and you're bringing a suitcase half-full of books.

I don't even know how people do things here. Maybe they weren't flirting at all. Maybe it's totally cool to giggle and stroke someone's arm, like just as friends.

But I don't think so.

When I don't know what to do, I stare at the other person. That's probably why I don't have that many friends.

Mina was cool with it. She always seemed to know what was going on better than me. In life and in my head.

Thinking about Mina brings on what I would classify as my first legitimate bout of homesickness. I've called her twice, but she didn't answer—probably stuck at work. It's hard to sync up our schedules with the time difference.

I miss her. I miss feeling comfortable.

I blink very hard, because if I cry right now, it's going to look so over the top and manipulative.

Lorne, as it turns out, is good at staring back. He has not said a word and continues to say nothing as I continue to tear up despite maximum blinking.

Please don't let Atlas be watching this…

I close my eyes and take several deep breaths.

When I raise my head, I say small and softly, "Everything is fine, I'm sorry. I'm very tired. I haven't adjusted to things here, the time, the food…"

It's all excuses. I trail off confusedly. I really am tired, waves rolling over me, eyelids droopy. My head hurts.

"Are you okay?" Lorne says. His voice sounds distant and echoey.

All the noise is muffled: the clinking of plates and forks, the conversations of the other diners that seem to blend together into no language I've ever known. The lights grow brighter, then darker.

I sag sideways in the booth.

Damn…now I'm not even going to get to try the fondue…

Lorne grabs for me, but I topple over too fast. I fall out of the booth, dropping for a dizzyingly long time, everything gone silly and slow…

Black moths fluttering everywhere…

The sharp stone edge of the elegant molding heads straight for the center of my skull.

Until a pair of arms lifts me out of the air, arms so thick and warm, I don't need to hear his voice or notice how high I'm hoisted to know who caught me.

"Atlas," I murmur, slipping away.

CHAPTER 9
ATLAS

THE AUTHOR ISN'T HAPPY WHEN I WON'T GIVE HIM HIS WIFE *(fiancé, you fucking liar; you haven't even bought her a ring)*.

"Sorry," I tell him, standing like a brick wall in front of the door. "When a guest falls unconscious on hotel property, it is the Monarch's policy that they stay overnight in the infirmary for observation by our medical examiner."

The *sorry* is a denial, not an apology. Whenever I especially want to tell someone to fuck off, I speak to them as the hotel. Because I am the Monarch, and it is me. It's my castle, my fortress, and sometimes…my prison. For me and, tonight, for the unconscious Elena.

And there's nothing Lorne Ronson can do about it. I've already secured positive relations with the new sheriff. Lorne's attack dog is Mrs. Cross—excellent for terrorizing nine-year-olds but less effective against me.

He can't do anything, not tonight. And he knows it.

His lips go pale and thin, his newly sharpened jawline tight with impotence. He's been working out every morning in the hotel gym since OIivia started flirting with him. The results are starting to show in his trimmer physique and in the free lattes Olivia's been sneaking him.

She knows damn well I'll fire her if she fucks him. And *I'll know* if she fucks him—very little happens inside this hotel without me noticing.

Which is why I intend to find out what the hell just happened to Elena.

All types of people pass through my hotel—the best and bravest, the cruelest and most selfish. And sometimes…the dark and deeply depraved.

Some struggle against their demons and chase the better version of themselves.

Some embrace their inner devil.

And some play saint or sinner without feeling anything inside.

As Lorne Ronson's face hardens, I note something flat and cold in those pretty blue eyes that gives me a chill.

"Fine," he says. "I'll come get her in the morning."

I stare at him without nodding, without agreeing to anything.

I saw how Elena passed out. I caught her before she hit her head, yet she still fell unconscious.

I don't trust this motherfucker.

And I *will* protect Elena while she's staying at my hotel.

Lorne holds my eyes as long as he can. But in the end, he looks away, stalking off like he had the last word.

I watch him all the way to the stairs, then head back inside the infirmary, closing and locking the door. Our medical examiner is prompt because I'm the medical examiner. My brother isn't the only one who went to med school—he's just the only one who likes doctoring enough to do it full-time.

I walk over to where I made Elena comfortable on the cot, pondering in what shade of gray it would lie for me to examine her.

I've done it plenty of times before, even on unconscious hotel guests.

This feels…different.

Probably because of how rawly sensual she looks in the soft, silvery light, curled on her side, hand against her cheek, face flushed, hair tawny. I try to ignore her beauty, but I might as well try ignoring an oasis in the middle of the desert. She draws my eyes, my thoughts, and every ounce of my longing.

I touch her throat, her pulse steady under my fingertips. Her breath comes softly through parted lips.

My shoulders relax. She's going to be fine.

And *I'm* going to be professional.

Completely professional.

I lift her head gently a few inches off the pillow, cradling it in my hands, examining her skull. I'm sure she didn't hit anything, but I check carefully anyway.

I feel nothing but silken hair, smooth skin, sweet breath on my face. No damage.

Options include a blood test sent to the drug lab, an IV bag of saline in the meantime, and maybe a call to the police.

But that could all be overkill. Elena might just be tired from her flight, dehydrated and jet-lagged.

I decide on the saline bag for certain if she doesn't come to in five minutes, and drug testing if she worsens or wants it after she wakes up. Assuming she wakes up.

She'll be fine.

She's got to be fine…

Elena rolls over, letting out a sigh. Now she's facing upward, back arched, head tilted back, the skirt of her jade-green dress pulling up her thighs…

Oh, fucking Jesus.

She's better than fine.

She's…the most luscious thing I've ever seen.

The dress hugs her in all the right places, sketching curves of exaggerated proportions that promise untold pleasure to the hands, the lips, and of course, the eyes—if, for example, it were necessary to take off her clothes to examine her more closely…

The skirt has ridden so far up her thighs, I'd only have to tilt my head to know for certain if she's wearing underwear.

I already have a guess…

I swallow hard.

I'm a doctor and a decent person. Yeah, that's right, a decent person. Look, see how I'm behaving myself.

Thoughts are just thoughts. Filthy, naughty thoughts.

I rub my hands against my thighs and then stuff them into my pockets, like that will keep them out of trouble.

But Elena's still lying there helpless on the bed.

The urge to touch her again is almost irresistible.

There's no one around. No one to see.

Just looking at her as long as I want without interruption is turning me on. I can take all the time in the world, memorizing the thickness of her thighs, the deep pink of her lips, the heartbreakingly ragged state of her cuticles.

Gazing down at her feels like drinking cool water. It satisfies a thirst deep down in my cells, filling me up until I'm saturated.

But now that I'm no longer thirsty…I'm fucking hungry.

Ravenous, even.

And Elena looks like a ten-course feast.

I've noticed that most of her clothes aren't quite the right size. Her jeans seem passed down from some larger male, and her dresses look bought for someone slightly smaller.

This green dress hardly covers her mile-long legs, acres of creamy skin exposed to my gaze. Her breasts test the limit of the cheap, flimsy top.

But it's her lips that hook me and drag me closer. Those dark, dusky-pink lips…

When she's talking to me, my urge to watch her mouth battles with the need to gaze into those arctic-fox eyes. Usually, her eyes win.

But right now, her eyes are closed. Her mouth is all I see.

I drop to one knee by the bed, a prince at the side of Sleeping Beauty. Except I'm no fucking prince.

That's a story from the olden days, when you could kiss an unconscious woman.

I'm not going to do that. I could lose my medical license. Also, it's fucked up.

But still…

I guess I want to do a fucked-up thing. So much that I can hardly breathe from wanting.

I brush rose-gold hair off Elena's forehead. The strand is a ribbon, the skin beneath warm and velvety. Before I can stop myself, I've bent and taken a deep breath, inhaling with my nose buried in her hair.

I smell her soap and her perfume, her skin and her scalp, and even her soft, sweet breath, all mixed up together in the scent that is Elena. I've caught hints of it before, but now I've reached the source, like some poor fool who stumbled upon the forbidden base of a rainbow. I've dunked my head and breathed it in.

What it does to me is irreversible.

It's the moment when a duckling spots its mother and all the tiny wires in its brain fuse with the undying imperative: *follow this creature wherever it goes.*

It's the drug you try once and you're a slave to the craving.

I breathe her scent into my lungs, and she owns me forever.

I feel it happen like a manacle snapping around my wrist, and I wrench myself away from her, stumbling all the way across the room until my back is pressed against the door. Blood thuds in my ears, and my heart races with the magnitude of what I just felt.

What in the seventh layer of hell was that?

Only…it didn't feel like hell.

It felt like the most delicious, most desirable, most tempting—

Fucking knock it off!

I stare at the sleeping Elena with a mixture of lust and horror. Mostly lust. Then mostly horror.

I'm not one of those "fall in love" people you hear so much about. Actually, I was against it. Firmly. Sensibly. Permanently.

Or so I thought.

And this, this cannot be love.

It feels more like a meat hook in my spine, jerking me around.

I don't want to be in love. I don't even want to be involved.

Elena's engaged to another man. Not only a hotel guest but a famous author who lives right here in Grimstone.

Without meaning to, I've already crept halfway back across the room. To think of her is to look at her, and to look at her is to draw closer...

What am I doing? Do I just want her because I can't have her? *You could have her.*

I sink down on the chair next to Elena's cot, which is not really a cot but a comfortable twin-sized bed with side rails. The bedding on it is nicer than mine.

I sit very still, looking at her.

They're not married yet.

The devil inside me speaks with cold, calm clarity. Whispering what he wants.

Thousands of guests have passed through these doors. But she's the one I want.

He wants her, too—the author. As carelessly as he treats her, he spent a lot of effort bringing her here. And a lot of money.

It's not his money that concerns me.

It's the way he looks at her when she's not looking at him. When he thinks no one's watching. Then, his face is full of cold calculation. And deep anticipation.

Something's wrong with Lorne Ronson. I feel it, deep down in my bones. The author has something rotten inside of him.

And he's mistaken. Someone is watching. *I'm* watching. I'm watching her...which means I'm also watching him.

As I pull a blanket over Elena's sleeping body, I allow myself to drag the back of one finger gently down her flushed cheek.

She doesn't wake until nearly three o'clock in the morning.

When she comes to, she's groggy and her mouth is dry, despite the pint of saline I put in her arm. I bring her a glass of ice water and help her sit up in the bed to drink it.

"What happened?" she asks confusedly.

"You passed out at dinner."

She presses the heel of her hand against her forehead, wincing. "My head feels like a pumpkin."

"I can take you to the hospital in—"

"No," she says quickly. "I'm fine. I was probably just…hungry or something."

Maybe.

Her eyes drop to the crook of her elbow, to the small bandage from the IV line, which I removed while she was still sleeping. She touches the gauze, frowning.

I hurry to say, "I gave you some saline. I have my medical license. I could take a blood sample as well in case—"

"In case what?" she bites at me, eyes flashing. "You think I do drugs?"

"I wouldn't give a shit if you did."

"Oh." Elena settles back, cheeks still pink with offense and embarrassment. "Then what did you mean?"

I give a slight shrug. "It wouldn't be the first time someone tried to slip someone else a roofie under the roof of my hotel."

The problem is that the most obvious culprit is Elena's fiancé.

She flushes all over again, snapping, "You're not saying that Lorne—"

"I'm not accusing anybody. I'm asking if you want me to take a blood sample and send it to the lab."

I'm speaking calmly, but my body is rigid, blood rushing in my ears. Because I do, absolutely, one hundred percent think her husband—*I mean, fiancé*—is capable of slipping her a roofie.

The only reason I'm not saying it out loud is because I also think there's a two percent chance that OIivia might have done it if she got jealous enough.

Also, attacking Lorne will only make Elena defensive. Which is happening already.

"That's not necessary," she says, swinging her legs over the railing of the cot, attempting to stand. "I'm fine, I don't need—"

She's already toppling over, going nowhere, of course, except right into my arms.

"You're not fine, you—"

"Get your hands off me—"

"Get your ass into bed!"

I tip her back onto the mattress, putting one huge hand on the center of her chest to hold her there. Maybe I should pretend it's difficult because she looks furious at how easily I hold her down.

"You fucking—!"

She lets out a string of what I can only assume are Ukrainian swear words. I wish I had a translator handy because it sounds like I'm missing some seriously spicy shit.

"Look," I say with what I hope is ninety percent gentleness and only ten percent aggression. "I've got nothing against your fiancé." *Nothing I can admit out loud.* "But you passed out in my restaurant, and hotel policy says you need to stay here overnight. What you do after that is your choice."

Elena isn't buying that for a minute. "It's *your* hotel! And your stupid policy!"

I press her into the mattress, a thousand watts of fury between our eyes and a thousand degrees of heat between her body and my hand.

"Exactly."

Then I drop down into the chair next to her bed and cross my arms over my chest, making it plain that she's not going anywhere tonight.

Elena stares at me, outraged. "So you're a jailor as well as a doctor now?"

"Guess so."

She glares between me and the door, measuring how little space she has to slip past my bulk in the tiny box of the infirmary.

Then she slumps back against her pillow, scowling, arms crossed over her chest as if she's imitating me.

But really, she's just pissed.

CHAPTER 10
ELENA

WHEN I WAKE UP, ATLAS SLIDES A TRAY OF HOT FOOD TOWARD ME. "Peace offering?"

The warm apple pastries, crispy bacon, and fresh coffee would buy a lot more than this level of forgiveness. Atlas should have saved this in case he runs over my foot with his car.

I rip apart a pastry. "Yeah, all right, I forgive you for forcibly taking care of me."

I'm not sure how much of that Atlas can understand because, with half an apple pie already stuffed in my mouth, it comes out more like, *"Yahawbigh, I fobi boo bor borciby taggingare of be."*

Atlas looks suitably charmed. "I'm glad to see your appetite hasn't been affected."

"Fuck you, I'm tall." I swallow before I say that so it comes out nice and clear.

"Yes," Atlas says drily, "I understand how that works."

I know he truly does understand, because he brought me four apple pastries and eight strips of bacon instead of the half slice of toast that my uncle thinks is all a girl should eat for breakfast. I'm not joking—once, I asked him for a second piece of toast, and he turned and said with real horror, *"Another* piece?" like I'd asked him for a second mortgage.

How generously Atlas feeds me is in the top five things I like about him so far.

Locking me in here with him last night is not.

Sternly, I say, "You're going to cause trouble for me."

"You're already in trouble," Atlas replies in his low, blunt way. It makes everything he says come out extra menacing, which I am not appreciating in this moment.

"You don't know what you're talking about."

"Oh yeah? How long have you known this author?"

I shove aside the tray and push myself out of the bed. This time I'm strong enough to stand. My head swims a little, but that might just be anger.

"That's none of your business."

Atlas stands up, too, which is a lot more intimidating. But his voice comes out surprisingly soft.

"I know it isn't."

It's the gentleness of his voice that makes me look up at him. Where I expect to see anger and stubbornness, I find…understanding.

But also…he's the size of a house.

I'm bigger than most women—five foot ten in flats and not willowy.

Atlas is the only man who's ever made me feel truly small. I'm little next to him, like a fox next to a bear. The feeling of shrunken-down vulnerability is strangely intoxicating.

He touches my arm. His palm spans almost the entire space between my elbow and shoulder; his fingers wrap all the way around. He's holding gently, but there's no real chance of shaking him loose.

"This isn't business." He looks into my eyes. His are oddly beautiful in his broad and brutal face, deep set and almond shaped with irises as dark and glinting as a cut gem. "I care about you."

"What?" I'm shocked and far too elated. "You're not supposed to. I'm engaged—"

"Where's your ring?"

"He hasn't…" My voice hitches, and I say way too fast, "He's getting me one."

Atlas's snort of disdain tells me everything about what he thinks of that. Sensing weakness, he demands, "Do you love him?"

"I—" Fear and pressure become another flash of rage. "Now you're a detective, too? I won't be interrogated! Or trapped in this room!"

Atlas is just as angry as me but better controlled. "I'm only trying to protect you."

"It's not your job to protect me!"

He stands there, blocking my way, nearly as broad as the infirmary, immovable as a mountain. "Yes, it is."

A sudden knock on the door makes me jump. My throat tightens up.

Lorne is here.

———————

My fiancé can either sense the heat in the room or see it in our faces. In response, Lorne becomes quiet and careful. Which somehow makes him seem more menacing.

"What's going on in here?" He glances between us, smiling slightly. I'm still not sure I like his face shaved clean like this. It makes his lips look strangely naked.

"Nothing's going on." I snatch up my purse from the nightstand where Atlas considerately placed it. "I was surprised when I woke up here."

The lie comes easily. Truth and safety walk hand in hand, and some of us have rarely felt safe enough to tell the whole truth.

But Lorne has noticed my mostly devoured breakfast. He frowns.

"Sorry, baby, I wanted to be here." He slips his arm around my waist and pulls me possessively close. "Your friend here wouldn't let me visit."

Atlas looks down at Lorne's hand, gripping my hip like a pale spider. Now he's frowning, too.

"Let's go," I say.

Before Lorne can move, Atlas says, "Olivia tells me you asked her to keep a bottle of wine in the back."

The accusation is obvious, if unspoken. Lorne is ready with one of his own. He bites back, cold and just as angry, "I thought it would be safe there."

The two men glare at each other.

I push between them, forcing Atlas to stand aside. "I was tired, that's all. You're making something out of nothing."

Atlas looks like he wants to say more, but I touch him lightly on the chest, a gesture hidden from Lorne by my body. "I'm fine," I say softly. Then I drop my hand and step back.

Lorne takes my elbow. "Let's go, Elena."

He steers me out of there like I was the one slowing us down.

———————

Before we're even back to my room, Lorne lets out his anger.

"Who the fuck does he think he is?" He turns on me suspiciously. "What did he say to you?"

"Nothing. We barely spoke."

But Lorne saw the empty breakfast tray. He knows I must have been awake at least long enough to eat.

"He's got a thing for you," he says accusingly, as if it's my fault. Maybe it is my fault.

"That's not true."

The lies keep stacking up. I don't want to fib to my fiancé, but Lorne's shoulders are stiff with rage, a vein pulsing in his temple. I'm terrified of what he might say or do if I admit the worst of it.

I care about you…

Even the memory of what Atlas said brings a flush to my face. Lorne seizes on my reaction as evidence.

"Then why are you blushing? Are you attracted to him?"

"No!"

Lies, lies, lies.

Lorne grabs my upper arm, his fingers digging in. His breath has a sharp, acidic scent as he hisses in my face, "I see the way he looks at you."

Frightened and frustrated, I snap back, "How about how Olivia was looking at *you*? Maybe *she's* the one who slipped something in my drink so she could bat her eyelashes at you uninterrupted."

"Who?" Lorne says with convincing confusion. His lip curls as he sneers, "Oh, the waitress. All the waitresses flirt with me."

That doesn't make me feel any better.

But it does seem to please Lorne in some perverse way. He relaxes a little, letting go of my arm. Though that might owe more to the fact that the woman in 602 just exited her room, throwing a concerned glance at our tense position.

Lorne tilts his head, smiling at me in a way that makes the back of my neck prickle. "I like that you're jealous."

I'm not sure it's jealousy I'm feeling, exactly…more a sense of hurt and disrespect.

But I guess I'm a huge fucking hypocrite because I've disrespected Lorne, too. Not by flirting right in front of him but definitely with the naughty thoughts in my head. Not to mention a particularly graphic dream I had last night…

I shove that thought aside, like I have to repress all thoughts of Atlas. Especially when Lorne is watching.

Calmly and deliberately, I say, "I didn't come here for Atlas. I came here to be with you."

Mostly true.

Now Lorne's face finally softens, his smile returning, the steel going out of his eyes. "You're right. I'm sorry, Elena. I was just so worried about you all night. Are you really okay?"

It's the first time he's asked me that question. The first time he's checked in with me at all. His expression seems sincere and searching, but my heart closes up like a clam.

"I'm fine," I say. "I really think I was just tired."

Another lie. The dizziness that swept over me was not a normal level of exhaustion. I've never passed out like that in my life. But I don't want any more conflict. And I *especially* don't want Lorne or Atlas pressuring me to visit the hospital or, worse, contact the police.

That's the one thing I definitely can't risk.

No worries of that happening with my doting fiancé. Lorne is already snapping back into productivity mode. "Glad to hear it because I do need to get back to writing. I already missed an hour of my morning."

Sorry to inconvenience you.

"No problem," I say. "I'll go take a shower."

"Wish I could join you." Lorne lifts his eyebrows suggestively.

He leans forward to give me a quick kiss.

His lips feel nice, but the acidic flavor in Lorne's mouth has lingered. He doesn't taste good.

Perhaps thinking the taste comes from me, Lorne pulls back, wrinkling his nose. "You'd better brush your teeth, too. See you at dinner!"

Before he's taken more than a few steps down the hallway, he turns and reminds me, "Don't forget to buy some new clothes."

"I will," I promise, though I'm more nervous than ever to go shopping in Grimstone.

I unlock my hotel room door using the old-fashioned brass key engraved with 609. When the door swings wide, my hand flies to my mouth.

Bloody letters four feet high drip down the walls, shouting: *GET OUT!*

CHAPTER 11
ELENA

AFTER THE FIRST MOMENT OF SHOCK, I CAN SEE THAT THE WORDS are written in paint, not blood. Still, I feel a little sick staring at the lurid red letters. They're messy and lopsided, the product of a crazed and deranged mind. Or somebody with terrible penmanship.

But as I step closer to examine them, I think maybe the material was the problem. This isn't paint either.

I lean forward and sniff. *Tomato sauce?*

Now I'm suspecting Olivia all over again. It would be easy for a waitress to get her hands on tomato sauce. Though, I guess it would be equally easy for anybody who's visited a grocery store.

The question is, why? I've been here two days. How do I have an enemy already? And how did they get into my room?

My stomach churns, realizing this person must have snuck inside sometime between 8 p.m. and this morning. Did they know I was in the infirmary? Or did they break into my room expecting to find me sound asleep in bed?

I snatch up the phone receiver, suddenly afraid to be alone in my own room. But I hesitate, fingers hovering over the buttons. My first impulse was to call Atlas. This is his hotel, his wallpaper that was ruined. And if I'm honest with myself, at the first bolt of fear, I craved his massive, reassuring presence.

But I should probably call Lorne first. He's likely opening the door to his own hotel room right now, or else settling down at his desk, opening his laptop.

He might be annoyed at the interruption. I already made him miss an hour of work this morning.

And after all, it's just some tomato sauce. This could be…a prank.

But as I look at the dripping letters, I don't think so. Somebody wants me out of here.

I dial the front desk.

"Front desk, Amy speaking," a familiar voice chirps.

"Hi, Amy, it's Elena Zelenska in room 609."

"Of course!" I can hear Amy's smile. "What can I do for you, Elena?"

"Someone's vandalized my room."

———————

The heavy tread in the hallway and the low, firm knock tell me that Atlas has come. I get the sweep of relief I was craving even before I open the door.

The feeling of security doubles once Atlas is inside, taking up most of my living room. Even the giant bloody letters look smaller and less intimidating next to him.

Atlas stands there staring at the message for several minutes, scowling. Then he checks the door, the windows, and even looks inside the closet. Finally, he examines the chairs in the living room, peering at one seat in particular that seems dirty.

"I'll have the lock changed on this room," he says at last. After a pause, he says, "Would you like me to give your fiancé a spare key again?"

I flush, sensitive to the implication. "Lorne didn't do this."

"I never said he did."

Well, your eyes sure did.

But why would Lorne do this? Is he getting tired of me already? Regretting that he brought me here?

He still hasn't given me a ring…

On the other hand, would he be so jealous of Atlas if he wanted to be rid of me?

Possibly. Men are prideful, covetous of their toys even if they don't want to play with them anymore.

But Lorne wouldn't do this. He loves me. He was worried about me last night. He came to see me first thing this morning.

And if he wrote all over my wall, wouldn't he have come inside the room with me to see my reaction?

Atlas is still watching me.

Flustered, I say, "Maybe it was Mrs. Cross. I'm pretty sure she hates me."

"She could have taken your fiancé's spare key," Atlas agrees. Though maybe just to throw a little of the blame back onto Lorne.

I'm still considering the flirty waitress, but I don't say that to Atlas because I don't want to accuse his employee. Especially when I might be just a wee bit prejudiced against the stunning blond who captured my fiancé's attention so effortlessly.

Instead, I say, "Sorry about your wallpaper."

Atlas makes a low, grunting sound. "I've got rolls of it stored away. Trust me, I've had guests smear way worse shit than that on the wall. Literally."

"In a place this nice?"

"The wealthiest guests treat the rooms the worst. Then bitch the most if I charge them for it."

I laugh. "That sounds right. I worked at a fancy steakhouse once—the tips were better at my breakfast shift at the Greek café."

"How many jobs have you had?" Atlas asks curiously.

"Quite a few." I duck my head, embarrassed to admit "I dropped out of school pretty early."

"How early?" Atlas asks, still curious, without judgment or disdain.

Gazing down at the carpet and wishing I'd never brought it up in the first place, I mumble, "Fifteen."

"You didn't like it?"

"No. I mean, I liked some of my classes, but that's not why I left. I had to move in with my uncle and aunt. I guess I could have switched schools, but they don't have much money. I felt guilty, thought I should get a full-time job to help out."

"Where were your parents?"

"Dead," I say, expecting awkwardness to ensue as it usually does when people feel compelled to offer their pithy sympathy. "It was a car accident."

I was in the car, too, lying across the back seat asleep on the way home from the movies. Which is why I got off with a sprained wrist and two cracked ribs while my parents were…obliterated.

Sometimes I wish I were hurt worse. Maybe then I wouldn't feel so guilty.

"I'm sorry," Atlas says. "My parents are gone, too."

"Oh." I'm not glad to hear that, but it does create a certain kind of understanding between us. I definitely don't have to worry about Atlas spouting off platitudes like *they're in a better place now* or *everything happens for a reason…*

Instead, Atlas says, "What did one orphan say to the other?"

"What?"

"Get in the Batmobile, Robin."

I snort. "That's awful."

"Yeah, well. Blame my brother for that one."

"You have a brother? Does he live here?"

"He's got a house outside of town. You might run into him sometime or other—he's a doctor, too, the best in Grimstone. The only one in Grimstone, but he'd be the best even if there were a couple others."

I snicker softly, recognizing the pride and affection in Atlas's voice even while he tries to play it down.

"And what's your job now?" Atlas asks. "Or what *was* it?"

"I ran a little bookstore in Lviv. Perfect fit for me."

"You were sorry to leave?" Atlas says, smiling.

"Yes." I'm remembering my last look at the cozy little corner shop with its brick walls, blue-shuttered windows, and window boxes of geraniums that I planted myself.

After all the time I worked there, six days a week, opening in the morning, locking up at night, I almost felt like I owned the place. But, of course, I didn't.

"The shop was sold," I tell Atlas. "So I was going to lose my job either way."

"One of those big-box chains snapped it up?"

"Even worse—a developer. It probably won't be a bookstore at all anymore."

"What a shame," Atlas says. "I'm sorry you lost your favorite job."

"It's not so bad. I always wanted to come to America."

"How's it living up to your expectations?"

I consider. "Pretty much everything I knew about America came from movies and books. So I have to admit, I've been a bit disappointed by the lack of varsity jackets and palm trees."

Atlas gives a rough chuckle that does dangerous things to me. "I might still have my old varsity jacket tucked away somewhere."

"Really?" The image that puts in my head is even more dangerous—a youthful, sweaty Atlas engaged in physical activity is not something I should be imagining. Yet I can't stop myself from asking, "What sport did you play?"

"It's more like which one *didn't* I play. And the answer's swimming—I sink like a stone. Football was my favorite."

"I pity the opposite team."

"Don't bother—they're all dead," Atlas deadpans. Then winks at me.

My stomach explodes in butterflies.

Oh shit…

I'm a complete sucker for a good wink. Atlas's was so sly and sexy, it just about knocked me off my feet. It was more than a wink—it's another naughty secret between us.

I don't want to make secrets with Atlas. I don't want to feel this attraction. I flew halfway across the world to marry *Lorne*, my fiancé. This is wrong. I'm being a bad person right now.

Clearing my throat and not quite looking at Atlas, I say, "I better get going. Thanks for coming up here, and I'm sorry again for the damage."

Atlas frowns, either at the abrupt change in mood or at my apology. "It's not your fault someone broke into your room. If anything, I should be apologizing to you. Do you want me to move you to another suite?"

That might make me feel a little safer. But I already know the hotel is fully booked, so I don't want to cause trouble for Atlas. And besides, I love this room with its vaulted ceilings and view of the garden. It doesn't feel dangerous anymore, as if the presence of Atlas not only secured the space but forever banished the possibility of future intruders.

"I think I'll be fine here. Especially if you change the locks."

"I'll do it this afternoon," Atlas promises.

"Thank you."

There's no reason for us to keep standing here, but we both do, gazing at each other instead of the view spread out below the grand picture window. It's hard not to look at Atlas—he dominates the room, his features dark and intense, jaw like granite and black eyebrows like furious slashes on his face.

He smiles at me because I haven't moved.

I smile back at him because neither has he.

"Where do you have to go?" he asks.

"Oh." My smile wobbles on my face. "Lorne said I should buy some new clothes. But I don't really know what to get. Or where to shop…"

I trail off, hoping Atlas might have a good suggestion despite the fact that there isn't a store on the planet with off-the-rack clothes that size. His suits must all be custom-made.

Atlas slips a business card out of his breast pocket, along with a sleek silver pen. He turns the card over to write on the back. When he passes it to me, *The Dapper Dress, Vivian,* is written in his clean, precise script.

"Vivian is a friend. Tell her I sent you."

I'm not sure if I'll actually have the balls to name-drop Atlas to this Vivian person for a discount, but I'm grateful for the recommendation either way.

I flip the card over to the front side, noting that Atlas's full name is Atlas Westerbrook Covett and wondering, despite my virtuous intentions, whether the phone number listed is his personal line.

"Thank you," I say again.

Atlas doesn't move, looking me right in the eye. "I want you to call me. If anything else happens."

He closes my fingers around the card, his huge hand completely enveloping mine. The butterflies in my gut are still swirling, with no intention of settling down.

"I mean it, Elena. Passing out last night, and now this—"

"That could be coincidence," I say, though I don't really believe it.

Firm as a mountain, Atlas shakes his head. "I don't think so."

I agree with him, actually. And the thought that someone is out to get me should terrify me.

But somehow, with my hand inside of Atlas's and his dark eyes fixed on mine, I don't feel frightened.

For the first time in a long time, it feels like everything's going to be okay.

CHAPTER 12
ELENA

I TAKE A HOT SHOWER, SWEATY FROM A NIGHT OF DEEP, POSSIBLY drug-induced sleep in which I drifted through twisted dreams that mostly featured Atlas. The temptation to remember those dreams, and maybe touch myself in the shower while I do it, is almost overwhelming. Especially with the hint of Atlas's cologne lingering in my room. Instead, I turn the faucet to freezing and punish myself with the icy spray until I'm no longer horny and my teeth are chattering.

I'm not going to cheat on my fiancé. Not even in my head. Not even with Atlas.

Wrapped in a towel, I pick through the meager selection in my suitcase. With few choices remaining, I settle on jeans and an oversized Dynamo Kyiv jersey that belonged to my father once upon a time. The bright blue and yellow makes me miss home and probably doesn't fit in at all in Grimstone, but I'm feeling rebellious.

I'm not seeing Lorne until dinnertime, so he won't know if I wear something that makes it obvious that I'm "not from around here."

Heading downstairs, I pause at the fourth-floor landing. Following an impulse, I walk right past Lorne's door and knock on Ivy's.

"Who is it?" comes Mrs. Cross's irritated voice before she

wrenches open the door. She can't hide the curl of her upper lip when she sees that it's me.

"Good morning!" I make my greeting extra cheerful just to see if she'll keep scowling. She does. And she also doesn't invite me into the room. I step inside anyway, waving to Ivy, in her usual seat by the window. "Hi, Ivy."

I'm pleased to see the sketchbook I gave her open on her lap. It looks like she might have even used some of the pages, though she's not drawing at the moment.

Ivy doesn't reply to my greeting or wave in response. But that could be because Mrs. Cross is roaming the room, aggressively straightening stray pillows and twitching the curtains back into place. Ivy flinches every time Mrs. Cross gets close. She sits stiffly in the window seat, her face anxious and unhappy and maybe paler than usual, though it's hard to tell on someone with the complexion of Casper.

Scanning the room for anything else out of place, Mrs. Cross's eyes fix on my bright blue and yellow jersey. Her nose wrinkles up. "What's *that*?"

"A sports costume," I say, thinking that should be obvious even if she's not familiar with the team.

"What's a *sports costume*?" Mrs. Cross demands, eyeing my Dynamo jersey like it might swing her around the room and make her dance the *hopak*.

"You know, jerseys, track suits…" Defensively I say, "I've seen Americans wear them, too."

"Not like *that*," Mrs. Cross sneers.

If there was even a one percent chance of asking her to accompany me shopping, that fractional possibility evaporates.

And anyway, that's not what I'm here for.

Carefully monitoring Mrs. Cross's expression, I mention, "Someone broke into my room last night."

Her head jerks up. "What?"

"Someone broke into my room," I repeat, wondering if that was surprise or a nervous reaction, "and wrote 'get out' on my wall."

"Get out?" she repeats, like she's turned into Toulouse, the parrot.

I can't tell if she's genuinely confused or only buying time.

I glance over at Ivy, who's sitting very still, watching us. Maybe I shouldn't have mentioned any of this in front of her, but it's too late to back off now.

"Have you told Mr. Ronson?" Mrs. Cross asks cautiously, folding scrawny arms over a narrow chest.

"I didn't want to interrupt his work."

"Good." She gives a stiff nod. "You shouldn't."

That's the first approving thing Mrs. Cross has said to me. It would be amusing, except for the fact that she's Lorne's employee and almost a part of the family. I really should figure out a way to make friends with her.

Especially if she's not the one who wrote on my wall. From the suspicious look on her face, it's almost like she thinks I did it myself. Like I'm trying to make trouble.

"I told Mr. Covett." Calling him that feels odd, but *Atlas* seems too intimate. "He's going to change the lock."

I'm still waiting for a reaction—perhaps frustration or disappointment—but I forgot that I'm shit at reading faces. I never know when people are lying. Not even Mina, who used to tease me about my gullibility. "*You just believe whatever people tell you!*"

What's everyone else doing, reading minds?

I can't read Mrs. Cross's mind. She seems irritated at the mention of Atlas, but since most things seem to irritate Mrs. Cross in one way or another, I'm not sure that it means anything.

"Who still uses keys these days?" she sniffs.

I glance at Ivy, who seems to be shrinking into herself, curled up on the window seat, legs drawn up to her chest, large, round eyes peering over her knees.

Stung with sympathy, I say, "I was about to go shopping. Do you want to come with me, Ivy?"

I deliver the last sentence directly to Ivy. She glances nervously between me and Mrs. Cross, then gives a quick nod.

Mrs. Cross's mouth purses. She's torn again between her desire to be rid of Ivy and her dislike of capitulating to my requests. But I'm winning the war, because this time it only takes six seconds.

"Fine," she snaps. "Put on your boots, Ivy."

Ivy hurries into her bedroom. When she emerges a minute later, she's wearing a pair of lace-up boots and her white wool coat. Her legs are bare beneath the hem of another fancy-looking dress.

"Do you want to put on pants instead?" I ask her. "It's pretty chilly outside."

Ivy just stares at me.

"No problem." I let it drop. "I don't think we'll have to walk far."

The shop's address is on Main Street, and walking the entire road couldn't take more than ten minutes. Ivy won't freeze, even with bare knees.

As we cross the main floor of the hotel, I find myself looking for Atlas. Even when he's not visible, his presence permeates. The hulking stone pillars, the cavernous spaces and smoke-scented velvet sofas seem as much a part of him as his old-world suits.

But Atlas is nowhere to be seen. Which is probably for the best.

The doorman tips his hat as he holds the door open for us. "Good morning, Ms. Zelenska."

"Thank you." I'm a little flustered at being recognized and remembered. Nobody holds the door for me in my normal daily life. Nobody calls me *Ms. Zelenska* and tips their hat to me.

As soon as we're out on the sidewalk, Ivy slips her hand into mine. I glance down at her, pleased and surprised. Her hand is so fragile, it makes me feel protective of her. I switch sides so that I'm walking on the edge closest to the road, even though there isn't a single car driving up Main Street at the moment.

We stop to look in every window we pass. The display windows are one of the most charming aspects of Main Street, each a work of art. Some are traditional, like the arrangement of rainbow-colored candy in Sweetie's or the autumn garlands that adorn Darkly Blooming. But some are delightfully odd, like the neon hearts and vintage tattoo guns in the window of Black Heart Ink or the hundreds of paper moths that flutter on near-invisible wires in Pen & Palette.

As on our visit to the bookstore, Ivy seems thrilled to be outside the hotel and away from Mrs. Cross. Her expression is animated and her stride is buoyant from the moment we step outside. She makes her happy chirping sound as she watches the toy train zipping around the adorable miniature model of Grimstone in the window of Toytopia.

The Dapper Dress is right next door. The mannequins in the window wear long white gowns and seem to be riding broomsticks, with carved jack-o'-lanterns in place of their heads. Ivy stares at them wide-eyed, hesitant to step inside.

I'm hesitant, too, because the dresses have an artsy, bohemian look to them, like they were hand-embroidered by a hippie, which means they're probably expensive as hell.

Too late to back out now—the bell overhead jangles loudly, bringing a tiny, dark-haired woman bustling out from the back of the shop. She's curvy and shrewd looking, her bright eyes flicking from my jersey to my sneakers to Ivy in an instant.

I'm hoping the fact that Ivy's dressed like an American Girl doll will somewhat make up for the fact that I look like a football hooligan.

The woman breaks into a smile that crinkles up her face in the nicest sort of way, saying, "Hello, hello! You must be Elena. Atlas told me you were coming."

Warmth spreads through my chest and my shoulders relax. I feel ridiculously grateful that Atlas called ahead, sparing me the awkwardness of having to beg for a discount. I know it should be a dream come true, shopping with someone else's credit card, but I'm stressed.

"I'm Vivian," the shopkeeper says, holding out her hand to shake. Though her hand is hardly any bigger than Ivy's, her grip is strong.

"Elena Zelenska," I say, though she already knows that. "I moved here recently, and I need some new clothes. Things that are good for the weather here and for...fitting in."

"That's easy enough," Vivian says. "Except maybe the 'fitting in' part. Everyone knows who's local here, especially after Halloween when all the tourists clear out. It's an insular place. But not unfriendly."

"Oh," I say, slightly crestfallen.

"Well, don't lose heart." She laughs. "You already made friends with Atlas, and he's the grumpiest guy in town. Keep it up and you'll be mayor by Christmas." She looks me up and down once more, this time with an appraising expression. "Size twelve, are you?"

"Uh..." I have no idea what that means. At home, I'm a forty-six.

My eyes dart to the tag on the closest shirt. It says "S." What number is S? Also, the shirt is $59.99. *Oj, this is so expensive...*

This was a mistake.

"I...I'm sorry..." I'm backing toward the door.

Vivian steps forward, smoothly taking my arm, leading me deeper into the store. "Don't worry," she says, "I've got lots of things that will look lovely on you." She winks. "And most of them are on sale."

She nods, pulling items off the racks with scary speed and draping them over her arm. "This will suit your coloring... You might like this one... Oh, this just came in..."

She leads me back to the dressing room, pulling still more items along the way.

Ivy remains at the front of the store, enthralled by a display of birthstone necklaces. She examines them one by one, leaning close without actually touching anything.

"Thanks for helping me," I say.

Vivian waves off my gratitude with a flap of her hand. "Anything for Atlas."

"Is he…a close friend?" I hate myself for the insinuating question and for the twist of jealousy in my gut as I sneak a sideways glance at Vivian's pretty features and compact curves. Does Atlas prefer petite women? His receptionist is tiny, too…

But Vivian only snorts. "He's my cousin."

That's a data point that shouldn't matter but absolutely does.

I'm scanning her now for signs of resemblance. The beetle-black eyes could have tipped me off, but the difference in height was distracting. "I saw the photos of your family inside the hotel."

"Did you see the portrait of dear old Grannie on the fifth floor? She poisoned Pop Pop, you know," Vivian says, like she's relaying a perfectly normal piece of family trivia.

Amused, I shake my head. "Atlas didn't mention that on the tour."

"Pop Pop should have known better," Vivian sniffs with very little sympathy. "She'd been married three times before, and all three bit the biscuit in suspicious ways. But men are fools in love." After a moment, she adds, as if it proves that women can be fools in love, too, "Grannie was married to Pop Pop longer than any of the others—fourteen years."

I'd like to ask her what Atlas's grandfather finally did to piss her off, but we've reached the dressing room.

"Come out and show me so I can see how it all fits," Vivian demands.

Obediently, I start working my way through the pile.

I've only had a chance to try on a couple of items before the bell jingles once more, signaling that someone else has entered the shop.

Vivian says, half-amused and half-annoyed, "Don't you trust me? I told you I'd take care of her."

My heart kicks into double speed even before I hear Atlas's

deep growl. "I'm not here to check up on you—I'm here to see the results."

I don't want to examine my suspicion that Atlas only let me walk over here alone so no one would see us together.

I also don't examine the impulse that governs what I do next.

I was midway through pulling on a pair of boring wool slacks, but I shuck those off and grab something sleek and silky off the hanger.

My heart races as I zip it up—or at least zip it as far as I can on my own. I step out of the dressing room, pretending I want to take a look at myself in the three-way mirror.

As soon as I emerge, there's no pretending. Atlas turns to look at me, and I clearly and deliberately present myself to him in the dark teal gown that clings to my curves like no dress has done before.

"Fucking Jesus" is his eloquent response.

Vivian says, "I knew it," with deep satisfaction.

The dress drapes off my body, cool and sleek and impossibly luxurious. I don't know where I'd wear something this nice, and I don't even dare peek at the price tag. Because when I see the hunger on Atlas's face, the way his dark eyes glue to my curves, I already know I'm going to buy it.

Ivy's still on the other side of the shop, examining the jewelry.

With a sneaking sense of how utterly inappropriate this is, I turn to show Atlas the low back of the dress, and the even lower zipper I couldn't quite reach on my own.

"Will you finish zipping me up?" I lift my hair in my hands, exposing more skin.

Atlas steps close behind me, in the exact position we first met. I feel his mass and his heat before those huge hands find the delicate zipper resting just above my ass. He pulls it up the last few inches, the backs of his fingers brushing the bare skin of my lower back.

The dress cinches a little tighter around my waist. The brush of

Atlas's fingers has made my nipples stand out in hard points against the thin silk.

I turn around anyway, letting my hair fall down around my shoulders once more, looking up into his face. "Better?"

His throat rolls as he swallows. He bends his head until it's close to my ear, saying so quietly that not even Vivian can hear, "I would have thought it was impossible, but yeah...you look even better now."

Pleasure rushes in like a breath of air. I turn my head, not realizing how close it would bring our mouths. Gazing at him from the distance of a kiss, I experience the kind of madness that might compel me to throw myself into the arms of another man with my fiancé's daughter standing ten feet away.

What the fuck am I doing?

I take a step backward instead, face hot, eyes fixed on the floor like that will obliterate the overwhelming presence of Atlas, impossible to ignore no matter how much I refuse to look at him.

"Thanks," I mutter, turning to flee back into the dressing room.

Atlas seizes my wrist, dragging me back effortlessly until his lips press against my ear once more. His huge hand rests on the small of my back, palm burning against my bare skin as he growls, "Don't you dare wear that dress for anyone but me."

CHAPTER 13
ATLAS

ELENA SPENDS THE NEXT HOUR TRYING ON EVERYTHING IN VIVIAN'S shop that could possibly fit her. At first, I act casual, like I just came to check in, but soon I can't resist slipping in a few items myself.

When Ivy tires of the jewelry, she joins Elena in trying on hats and gloves, sweaters and skirts. Vivian's children's section is much smaller, but Ivy seems particularly delighted with the items that are miniature versions of the women's clothes. She chooses a button-up cardigan, a pair of embroidered jeans, and two dresses that are all smaller versions of what Elena has set aside.

Elena agonizes over each item, obviously torn between what she personally likes and what she thinks is "normal" in Grimstone—all balanced against her fiancé's demands.

Watching her try on clothes is a maddening form of torture. Each outfit brings out some new facet of her attractiveness—the ski sweater that highlights her Siberian cheekbones, the jeans that hug the curves of her ass, the leather bomber that makes her look like a badass bitch. It's driving me nuts knowing that it's the author who will get to enjoy it all, day after day, night after night, long after Elena has checked out of my hotel.

Watching her and Ivy try on matching outfits should slap me in the face with that particular reality. But all I can seem to notice is the adoring expression on the little girl's face as she holds up a T-shirt printed with butterflies for Elena's approval.

She's like a different kid when Elena's around.

I get it—I'm a different kind of man. The kind who obsesses over a smile or a glance or the chance to sneak a stolen half-hour with another man's bride.

Elena adds everything Ivy wants to the purchase stack, but she's much more hesitant with the items for herself. She pares down her purchases to a meager selection of some of the clothes she seemed to like the least.

"That's all you're getting?"

She flushes. "That's more than my whole wardrobe back in Lviv."

"I thought you didn't like this one?" I hold up a stiff, dark dress that came down to the knee and didn't flatter Elena in the slightest.

She won't meet my eye. "It's fine. It'll be useful."

Meaning, she thinks the author will like it.

"You're not getting that one?" Vivian points to the teal gown, carefully replaced on its hanger and hung on the rack with the rest of the rejected clothes.

"I don't think I'll be attending any balls anytime soon." Elena keeps her tone light, but I catch her last, wistful look at the dress.

Vivian rings up the purchases, giving Elena the deep discount usually reserved for employees.

Elena still flinches at the total. But since more than half the items she's buying are for Ivy, she boldly swipes what looks like a shiny new credit card.

"One moment," Elena says as Vivian wraps up the purchases. She hurries up to the front of the store where the birthstone necklaces are displayed.

"May fifteenth, right?" she says to Ivy, bringing back the emerald necklace the little girl looked at longest.

Ivy nods, eyes alight with hopeful longing. Elena fastens the clasp behind Ivy's neck and steps back to examine the effect.

"It matches your eyes."

Ivy hurries over to the closest mirror and stands there motionless, gazing at the tiny, glimmering jewel on its silver chain.

"I'll pay cash for that," Elena says, taking out her wallet once more to retrieve a hundred-dollar bill that looks like it was folded up tiny at some point in its life, still marked with creases though it's since been smoothed flat. "I want to buy it for her myself," she murmurs when she sees me watching.

I'm wondering if that's all the money Elena has. The hundred-dollar bill was the only cash in her wallet.

Purchases safely wrapped in tissue and hung over her arm inside a pale pink bag, Elena has to drag Ivy away from the mirror.

"Come on, little love. I'll take you for ice cream. Thanks again, Vivian!"

"Anytime," Vivian says, banging a fresh roll of quarters against the edge of her change drawer.

Elena turns to me last of all. She seems to want to say something particular, her fox eyes searching my face, her lips slightly parted. But in the end, all she says is, "Thank you, Atlas."

It's all I need. The sound of my name on her lips is almost as good as a kiss.

The bell jingles as the two girls depart, Ivy's thin, pale hand linked with Elena's.

When they're gone, I tell Vivian, "Pack up the rest of the clothes. Send them over to the hotel, along with the bill."

Vivian raises one thin, black eyebrow. "Customer service has reached a whole new level at the Monarch, I see."

Refusing to be baited, I fold my arms over my chest and give her my most glowering stare. Unfortunately, that doesn't work as well on people with the last name *Covett*.

Vivian lifts the skirt of the teal gown and lets the silk flow through her fingers like water. I shiver, remembering how it painted Elena's curves.

With a wicked glint in her eyes, she says, "Even this one?"

"*Especially* that one."

———————

By late afternoon, I've had the wallpaper and the locks replaced in Elena's room. She could have asked me to move her closer to the author, but she didn't, and that gives me a fierce satisfaction.

She hasn't returned with Ivy. I find myself picturing the pair slipping in and out of the shops together, buying ice cream and sweets, maybe carrying their prizes down the rickety wooden steps to the black sand beach below. As I imagine them out in the fresh fall wind, bits of colored leaves blowing into Elena's hair, the hotel has never seemed stuffier or drearier. I'm tempted to sneak out again to join them.

But that's ridiculous. It was already risky walking over to the Dapper Dress. What if Ivy tells her father?

Speak of the devil.

Lorne Ronson leans his elbow on my reception desk, chatting up Amy.

Unfortunately for him, Amy hasn't come to like him any better. In fact, she likes him worse. It's the shitty brunch tips. Amy is a whiz with numbers—it only took a glance at his bill for her to snort, "Thirteen percent! With the money he makes!"

Still, she has her best fake smile pasted on her face while Lorne Ronson drones on and on about something he clearly finds fascinating.

When Amy sees me watching, she widens her eyes ever so slightly in silent annoyance. Lorne, oblivious to her boredom, notices immediately when her attention shifts. He turns and plasters a fake smile of his own across his face as he strides forward.

"Atlas! Just the man I was looking for."

Goddamnit.

"How can I help you?" *Out a fucking window...*

Now Lorne fashions his features into an expression of concern no more genuine than the smile.

"Your receptionist just told me that someone broke into my wife's room."

The fact that he's still calling Elena his wife makes my skin crawl. I must not have hidden it as well as I thought, because something flickers in Lorne's eyes in response. He's wearing a dark suit today, more formal than usual, hair combed back. I can't help but think he's trying to intimidate me.

"I've already had the locks changed," I say.

His eyes narrow slightly. "I haven't received the new key."

"Maybe it would better to keep the spare at the front desk."

"Why would that be better?" Lorne demands, attempting to stare me down.

Since his last name *isn't* Covett, that's not going to work. I fold my arms and give him a return stare that makes his left eye twitch behind those stupid fake glasses.

"Because it would minimize the chance of loose keys floating around between children, housekeepers, and...anybody else."

We both know that the *anybody else* I'm referencing is standing right in front of me. And he doesn't appreciate the implication.

There's a new edge to his voice as he says, "You've taken quite an interest in my wife."

"Is she your wife already? I hadn't noticed a ring."

A brick-colored flush tints his face, even the whites of his eyes. "She'll be my wife in a few more weeks."

Weeks.

It sounds like a death sentence. The idea of Elena married to him forever, shut away in his creepy castle instead of here with me...

No. Every bone in my body rebels.

"If she makes it that long." I didn't mean to say it out loud, but I don't regret it, either.

Lorne Ronson goes still, an odd blankness falling over his face, his eyes seeming to deepen and darken like boreholes.

"What's that supposed to mean?"

I know I should stop, but instead I step closer. "It's funny, don't you think? All these things happening to your *fiancée* when she's been here less than a week. Does she even know anyone in Grimstone? Besides you, of course."

Lorne snarls, "All these things happening in *your hotel.*"

"That's right. It is my hotel. And I'm going to make sure Elena's safe while she's here. Safe from anyone who might want to hurt her." I lay only the slightest stress on the word *anyone*, but he knows exactly what I mean.

Lorne's not flushed anymore. He's reached a new level of rage that drains the blood from his face until his lips are pale as worms, his eyes flat and lightless.

His voice comes out in a low hiss. "Don't mistake your role here, *Atlas.* You own the hotel, not the guests. Elena belongs to me. You hold the door for her."

I don't think I've ever been so close to punching a guest. My fist is a lead weight on the end of my arm, and I am *aching* to smash it into the middle of the author's face.

But all I say is, "Then I guess we'll see who protects her best."

CHAPTER 14
ELENA

LORNE KNOCKS ON MY DOOR AT 6:40, EARLY INSTEAD OF LATE FOR a change. When I open the door, he pushes his way into the room, his body tense with nervy energy. He seems irritated when he spots Ivy sitting Japanese-style on a cushion next to the low coffee table, testing out her new watercolors.

"What's she doing here?"

Ivy stiffens and sets down her brush, biting the edge of her thumbnail instead. Her eyes dart between me and her father.

"I thought she could come eat with us." I'm wondering why I feel so uncomfortable inviting my fiancé's own daughter to dinner.

"Where's Mrs. Cross?" Lorne snaps.

"I have no idea. I took Ivy shopping with me, and we've been together ever since. We checked out the shops, visited the park, walked down to the beach…"

I trail off, noting that Lorne doesn't seem interested in our afternoon activities. He's pacing the room, not looking at me, barely listening.

When I stop talking, he looks up. "You got new clothes?" He's finally noticed the outfit I spent an hour putting together.

I had a lot more options than I expected once the rest of the clothes were delivered. My closet and drawers overflow with Atlas's generosity. I might have tried to refuse, but everything was hung up when I got back to the room, tags already cut off.

"Do you like it?" I turn in a circle so Lorne can get the full effect. "I went to Dapper Dress."

Lorne's lips tighten. He barks, "Why did you go there? Did Atlas send you?"

My eyes dart to Ivy's. Her eyes widen, and she gives the tiniest shake of her head.

I try to swallow through a bone-dry throat. "It's…the only dress shop on Main Street."

"Right." Lorne relaxes slightly. "Atlas's cousin owns it—that dumpy Vivian woman. Did you meet her?"

I've noticed that Lorne uses insulting labels that don't quite match the person he's describing. Vivian isn't *dumpy* any more than Atlas is *ogreish*.

"I met her," I say quietly. "I thought she was pretty."

Lorne makes a dismissive sound that sets my teeth on edge. "She's not pretty. *You're* pretty."

I don't like being complimented at another woman's expense. And I don't understand why Lorne's so wound up. There's an aggressive edge to everything he says and to the way he strides over to me and picks at my clothes, rubbing the material between his fingers, testing the quality.

"Feels expensive." He nods his approval. Then lets his hand slip from my shoulder to my left breast, groping a feel. With a smirk, he says, "*Very* expensive."

"Lorne…"

I try to move away from his hand. Ivy's right there. But he pulls me closer instead, sliding his palm down to my ass and grabbing a rough handful of flesh that almost makes me cry out.

"He likes you, you know," he hisses in my ear. "Atlas."

My blood goes cold. Does he know Atlas came to the shop? Does he know about the extra clothes?

"Let go of me, please," I murmur, hoping Ivy won't hear.

Instead, Lorne's other hand snakes up under my hair and grips the back of my neck. Fingers digging in painfully, he accuses, "Are you wearing this dress for him or for me?"

I try to pull away from him, but he only grabs a handful of my hair and yanks my head back until tears spring into my eyes. It hurts, but what's really disturbing me is the hardness of Lorne's cock digging into my hip. He seems angry and jealous, but also... he's enjoying this.

His nose nuzzles the side of my neck while the roots of my hair scream. "Answer me."

"For you!" I gasp out. "Ivy and I dressed up for dinner."

Ivy's name seems to remind Lorne that his daughter is in the room, sitting just a few feet away, watching us. She also happens to be wearing a soft gray dress that matches mine, which should make it all the more apparent that neither one of us is trying to lure Atlas.

Lorne straightens, letting go of his handful of ass and loosening his grip on my hair. But he doesn't release me entirely; his hand falls to the back of my neck and rests there.

"Cute," he says. "I like when my girls dress up for me."

That explains why Ivy's closet is full of a bunch of itchy dresses that are too fancy to play in. I get a bleak view of my own future, closet stuffed with clothes I don't even like, purchased to please my husband.

But I do like the clothes Atlas sent me. Especially the teal silk gown.

"Don't you dare wear that for anyone but me..."

A sick mixture of guilt and pleasure squirms in my gut.

Lorne's right to be jealous.

Atlas likes me.

And I'm afraid I might just feel the same.

———————

Dinner is our first meal together as a family. Lorne spends most of the time talking about his new book, which sounds even creepier than the serial killer thriller I still haven't finished. I tried to pick it up earlier in the evening while Ivy was sketching, but set it down again immediately, bothered by the interior monologue of the murderer, who sounds a little too much like Lorne.

But that's probably true for all authors—I mean, they can only write what they know. Of course Lorne's characters have...certain similarities to him.

I try to draw Ivy into the conversation by asking her yes or no questions, easy stuff like, "Wasn't that black sand cool down on the beach?" but she won't even nod, shrinking down in her seat until her pale green eyes barely peek out over the tablecloth.

Lorne acts like she doesn't exist. Which is strange, considering how effusively he talked about her before. "*She's my best little buddy, my treasure, my angel...*"

The differences between the Lorne I met before and the Lorne I know now are starting to add up, increasing the uncomfortable sensation that I'm sitting across the table from a stranger. One I'm not sure I like nearly as much as the man I met at the café.

When Atlas enters the restaurant, Lorne puts his arm possessively around the back of my chair. A glance passes between them that is much less than friendly.

I don't dare look at Atlas myself, not with Lorne right here.

The way he behaved upstairs was upsetting. He didn't hurt me—not in any serious way. But his grip on my ass and my hair was painful. And it made it so much worse that he would do that in front of Ivy.

On the other hand, I shouldn't be flirting with Atlas. I shouldn't be looking at him or even thinking about him. I'm engaged. *Even if I still don't have a ring.*

And if some part of me wishes it was Atlas I met at that café instead of Lorne, that thought isn't just disloyal. It's stupid and dangerous.

The name on my fiancée's visa is Lorne Ronson. If I don't marry him, I'll be sent right back home. Back to my problem. Which is going to become an even bigger problem any day now. So I can't go back to Lviv. No matter what.

Besides, I like it here in Grimstone. I like Ivy and I like Lorne—when he's not yanking on my hair or making me feel insecure about…pretty much everything.

Miserably, I stare down at my half-eaten dinner. The schnitzel is crispy and buttery, but I don't have much appetite.

It's my fault that things aren't going well with Lorne. I need to focus on my fiancé and forget about Atlas.

That's hard to do when he's standing a few meters away, pretending to monitor the Reinstoff but really keeping watch over our table.

I refuse to look at him all through the rest of dinner, though I can feel his dark eyes burning on my skin.

————————

Strangely, Atlas staring at me seems to have put Lorne in a better mood. Maybe it's because I kept my eyes fixed demurely on my plate.

After we drop Ivy off at her room, Lorne walks me back to mine.

We pause outside the door with its shiny new lock.

"Atlas wouldn't give me the key," Lorne says sourly.

I would never admit the wisp of relief I feel knowing that Atlas and I have the only keys. Plus the maids, I suppose.

"He's probably worried about liability," I say vaguely.

Lorne scoffs. "I don't think so."

I don't ask what he means because I really don't want to talk about anything that has to do with Atlas. I turn the key in the lock. Lorne grabs my arm. "Aren't you going to kiss me good night?"

"Of course," I say, turning obediently and tilting up my lips.

Lorne grabs my chin between his thumb and index finger. He holds my face steady, pinching too hard, cool blue eyes boring into mine.

"Open your mouth."

I blink in confusion. Then slowly, hesitantly, open my mouth.

Lorne spits in it.

It's so sudden and shocking, the glob of spit hitting my tongue. It feels acidic, electric. I jerk back, but Lorne holds me pinned.

"Now swallow," he orders, his eyes coldly opaque, reflecting nothing back at me, not even my own face.

The spit sits on my tongue. The idea of swallowing makes me want to vomit. But he's obviously not going to let go until I do.

Fighting every reflex, I swallow his saliva. My stomach heaves, but I hold it down.

Lorne smiles. "Good girl."

My skin is crawling, my stomach rolling. I want to flee into the safety of my room, shut and lock the door. I'm more grateful than ever that Lorne no longer has a key.

But my fiancé still hasn't let go of my chin. He's gripping it so tightly, I'm worried there will be twin bruises in the morning, like a pair of butterfly wings.

Softly, he says, "I like how you behaved yourself at dinner. I like how you're dressed tonight. You look classy and expensive. You look like a real wife and mother."

Those are all things I want to be—classy, fancy, a good wife, a good mom for Ivy. But somehow, Lorne's compliments aren't pleasing me. Actually, they make me feel a low, cold dread, a river running below my thoughts.

Still, I whisper, "Thank you."

Now Lorne leans closer so his eyes stare into mine from only a few inches away. His handsome face is all I can see, leaner than ever against those soft, pale lips.

I want to feel that feeling I've read about so many times, like I'm falling into his eyes, like he's looking into my soul. But I can't see anything in Lorne's eyes, and I can't even begin to guess his thoughts.

Those blue eyes are flat as glass. With his hair combed smooth and his chin tilted down, he almost looks like a snake.

Especially when his voice hisses out, "My sweet, darling love, don't forget who brought you here." His fingers bite into my chin and his eyes hold me pinned, clear, cold, and piercing. "And you were keen to come, weren't you, Elena? You were in a hurry."

He knows! He knows! He knows!

Panic yaps in my brain, things that are impossible, things that cannot be.

No one knows. Not yet...

As always happens when I'm most afraid, I go completely still. It's not really a choice, and thank god it cuts off the noise.

Everything goes quiet, and my perception slows. I see one thing and one thing only: Lorne's face staring into mine. And in those bright, blue eyes, I notice something. A disturbing blankness. I don't know how I didn't see it there before. There's no light, no warmth. Only the flat, cold gaze of a predator.

Then Lorne blinks and it's gone, but I saw it there like the sheen of a wolf's eyes by a campfire. Flickering in and out again like a ghost peeking through his eyes for a moment.

Lorne sees the change in my expression.

His face changes, too, hardening, becoming carved and masklike. In a flat, harsh tone, he says, "You already made your choice, Elena. There's no going back, you know that."

He lets go of my chin but only to seize my left hand. He's taken something out of his pocket, flipping open a box...

With strange, slow horror, I see the diamond, bigger and more dazzling than my wildest daydream. Nightmare. Daydream.

Lorne forces the ring onto my finger. He's rougher than he needs to be; it should have slipped on easily.

There's no speech and no proposal. He already did that weeks ago over the phone. *A hundred years ago.* Who was that girl who said yes? Who said it happily, eagerly, with excitement? She thought all her dreams were about to come true.

The stone is so heavy, it twists the band until the ring hangs down on my hand. I turn it around, feeling nothing between my fingers.

I'm completely numb. I feel nothing, nothing at all.

Except a sensation rushing beneath my feet, down where nobody can see. A river, dark and endless. Whispering under the ground...

Get out, get out, get out.

Lorne hasn't let go of my hand. His fingers clamp around my wrist like a manacle. I can still taste his spit in my mouth.

Carefully and quietly, I say, "I know who brought me here. I'm very sorry, Lorne, if I've done anything to offend you."

His order is swift and immediate: "I don't want you talking to Atlas anymore."

The tiny hairs rise on the back of my neck, but I stand very still. I don't blink, and I hold my face expressionless.

"No problem." My lips are numb. Lorne doesn't seem to notice. "I won't."

Lorne leans even closer.

My heart slows and slows.

He presses his lips against the center of my forehead. They're soft as rotting fruit.

"Good night, my love," he says, pulling back slowly. His eyes fix unblinkingly on my face.

I pray the tiny smile I force is convincing.

"Good night, my love."

CHAPTER 15
ATLAS

I CAN'T SLEEP.

Many things are bothering me.

First and foremost, who broke into Elena's room?

The obvious answer is Mrs. Cross. She surely resents Elena's presence as the new woman in Ronson's life, as well as Elena's alliance with Ivy.

But would she risk angering her master? Especially with such an ineffective taunt?

I'd expect something sneakier from her. Something stolen from Lorne and planted in Elena's room...some drama concocted with Ivy...

Mabe it was Ronson himself. I know he's fucked up; I've seen it in his eyes. Is he tormenting Elena? Testing her? Trying to scare her to drive her deeper into his arms?

I don't think it was Olivia. All she'd admit to when I grilled her the other night was flirting and free lattes.

"I just poured the wine he gave me! Where the hell would I get roofies?"

Which points the finger right back at the author for drugging Elena. Or someone else with access to the kitchen.

I can't stand not knowing what's going on under my own roof. There are rats running around inside my house.

And maybe something a lot worse than a rat…

I've been looking into Lorne Ronson. The Grimstone gossipers like to think they know everyone's dark secrets, but they may have been blinded by their desire for a homeborn celebrity.

Because our hometown hero moved away for eleven years. And what he did while he was gone…doesn't quite match his story.

I turn it all over in my head, everything I know, the scraps of information I've gathered. I'm putting a puzzle together with only some of the pieces.

Four times in the night, I scale the stairs to the sixth floor and walk down to the end of the corridor to stand outside Elena's door, listening.

I've never put cameras in the hotel. I use a staff I trust and my own eyes to keep track of what's happening.

But now, for the first time, I'm wishing I had more.

I want my eyes on Elena always.

She's a guest in my house, and I will protect her.

Even from another guest.

———

When she comes down in the morning, she's pale as milk.

"Are you all right?" I say, touching the outside of her arm.

I was close to her room, to the stairs, all night long. Now I'm thinking I should have stayed on her floor. I could move the guests around, sleep in the room next to hers—

She pulls me into a sheltered space.

"Please, Atlas," she begs, snapping me straight to attention. "I can't talk to you anymore."

That's worse than a slap to the face. I'm jolted to this exact screaming millisecond.

"What's wrong? What happened?" I have my hands on both her arms now, holding her steady. But she steps back, shrinking away.

"I'm making him angry. He's jealous."

"What did he say? What did he do?" She's tense and shaking. I rub the outsides of her arms to calm her. "It's all right, Elena. You can tell me. I'll help you."

Her body trembles like a note so high it could break glass. Someone comes down the stairs, and she shrinks away farther still.

With her eyes on the carpet, she says, "I mean it, Atlas. I'm here to marry someone else. It's wrong of me to look at you or speak to you that way."

God, I fucking *wish* she'd look at me right now.

I want to touch her again, but I know she doesn't want me to.

Carefully, I say, "Usually, I'd be on your side with that. But under the circumstances…I'm going to have to respectfully disagree."

Her eyes flick up; she can't help it. "What circumstances?"

"I'm crazy about you. And you can't trust him for shit."

Elena flushes deeply, her eyes shining with something so bright and brilliant, I think that I've already won.

But then she falters, shaking her head.

"You don't know what—"

Another fucking guest comes down the staircase. Her mouth closes, cutting off whatever I *don't know* like someone hit a mute button.

And that person, a rabbi named Joshua Stein, is an eagle-eyed hunter. He hurries over to speak to me, making Elena disappear like a startled deer.

———————

Three hours later, I'm not looking for her. But I am unusually motivated to take a walk in the rose garden.

Sometimes you can just feel where someone will be. And I don't like to give credence to things I can't prove…but sometimes I'll act on them anyway.

I *know* where to find Elena. It's a pull, a drag below my skin, gravity tugging on my bones.

I walk through the rows of bare, thorny branches, everything cold and asleep. Except for her. I turn down a row, and there she stands, bright as a vision, too vivid to actually be real.

The sun burns on her hair in every shade of melting orange. She holds her camera up against one eye, red lips laughing at me as she snaps a picture of my face.

"You're following me!" She's accusing, but I know she's glad to see me. It's all over her face when she lowers the camera, her eyes bright with much more than sun.

What shade is that blue? Those are the kinds of stupid things you think to yourself when you stare at the woman of your dreams and can't say anything out loud.

I finally manage, "I hoped you'd be here. Is that a crime?"

"I can't—"

"What? Speak to me while you're staying here as a guest in my hotel?" I say it lightly, and it pulls a smile out of her. But the smile goes to my head. I lose all strategy and rush on with "Are you afraid of him?"

As soon as I say it, her face closes up. She changes entirely, drawing in, pulling away. Inches are everything in conversations. Invisible barriers spring up, and they're all the more dangerous to cross if you can't see that they're there.

"I don't want to talk to you about Lorne," she says, coloring and looking away.

"Then I won't mention him," I promise rashly because that's what she does to me. The smell of her warm skin in the cold fall air is sweet as smoke and apple cider.

If a thousand people walk through my hotel and only one of them smells like this…well, it's hardly a choice at that point.

"Where did you get that camera?" I don't know much about Ukraine, but I'm pretty sure they have technology a little newer than that. The loving way she cradles the battered lens screams sentimental attachment.

"It was my dad's. He was an artist. He always took a photo before he painted anything."

"You like using it?"

"I like developing the photos afterward. The first time I saw it, it was like magic, the way the images appeared on the paper, like ghosts in reverse..." Elena gets that dreamy look of someone remembering the moment they discovered a passion. "There it is, exactly what you saw but never quite like you remember." She smiles at me, the camera lens glinting in the sun, as she shrugs helplessly. "I never get tired of it."

"Where are you going to develop that picture of me stalking you?"

I finally get to hear her laugh. It's just the tiniest bit haughty, which is sexy as hell, especially when she gives me that look. Eyes narrowed, she says, "That's exactly how you look, you know...like a villain in a play."

I shrug. "I've always looked like a bad guy. It's useful—if I do anything nice, it's a pleasant surprise."

Elena stops smiling and becomes serious. "You've done lots of nice things for me. The clothes were too much." She lifts her hand, palm out, like a warning.

I grab that hand and pull her into my arms.

"There is no *too much*."

To prove it, I kiss her exactly how I want. I crush her against me and make her feel what I'm feeling, from her skin all the way down to her bones.

Some people you're meant to kiss and hold. There's harmony in the skin, in the breath. The barriers dissolve, and you slip inside each other's flesh.

Elena knows it now; she'll never forget it, how right it feels when she's in my arms.

But I do let go of her in the end. Because I'm not all the way a bad guy.

My fingertips throb from that last touch of her bare skin. "I meant what I said…only wear that green dress for *me*."

Elena's eyes dart left and right, confirming that we're alone in the tangled labyrinth of rose bushes. Just that look, that silent confirmation that she *wants* to be alone, flushes me with heat.

Low and teasing, she says, "Here in America, you tell someone how to use a gift?"

She's baiting me on purpose. She wants me to grab her again.

That's exactly what I do, but this time I don't kiss her. I hold her tightly in my arms. Tightly enough for her to feel how much harder I could squeeze her if I wanted to.

Her heart races against my chest. Her face glows with color.

"Tell me to kiss you."

I won't do it again until she asks. I'm not going to pretend that I don't want her. And she's not going to pretend that she doesn't want me.

"Fuck it," she says. "One more time."

Since it's only going to be once more, I kiss her deeply and I take my time.

I don't feel guilty, not for a moment of it. It's too obvious that she was meant to be mine.

She pulls away finally with a nervous glance at the hotel windows. Her breath comes out in a silver cloud—it must be colder than it looks.

I can't feel the chill at all. My body's on fire. It might as well be the Fourth of July just from kissing her.

"That was the last time," Elena says. She tucks her camera carefully back into her bag. Her hand is slightly shaking.

And that's when I see something I can't believe I failed to notice before. I was blinded by those fox eyes and the sun in her hair.

Elena has a diamond ring on her finger—as huge and gaudy as the author's castle.

Quietly, she says, "I'm marrying him, Atlas. That's what I'm here to do. And I don't want to be the kind of person who…acts like this."

"Okay, I get it." *I'll never fucking get it. I'm going to continue to respectfully disagree.* "But just answer me…do you love him?"

The time it takes her to reply *is* the answer.

Elena turns away, shaking her head. "Don't…Love grows over time, it's not an on-off switch—"

"That's the stupidest thing I ever heard."

I seize her and kiss her again. I never agreed to this *one more time* bullshit, and I'm not that great of a guy.

She kisses me back, hands slipping under my shirt to touch my bare chest. Without gloves, her fingers are freezing, burning like ice on my skin. She's just as hungry as me, her tongue in my mouth.

But then she shoves me away, twice as mad as before. "Stop that! I told you, I don't want to be a cheater."

It's not cheating, not when it's with me. And not when it's against *him.*

Lorne Ronson is false down to his core. I can feel it. And I know Elena does, too. She just won't admit it because…

She's afraid. Of something…or someone. The shaking hands, the pale lips, the nervousness…what is it? The author or something else?

I grab her hand one more time but now just to hold it, hating the feel of that gaudy ring.

I make her look me in the face as I say, "What's going on? You can tell me, Elena. You can trust me. I want to help you."

Her lips press together, emotions battling on her face, fighting, swimming to the surface. Her eyes tear up, and she turns her head, ashamed. "You don't know me, Atlas. You don't know what I've done."

"Tell me." When she won't look at me, I squeeze her hands and pull her closer, insisting, "Tell me, what have you done?"

She looks at me with her whole face flushed and open, her lips poised to speak. But at the last moment, she shivers and draws into herself and will only say, "I meant, you don't know my situation."

"Elena—"

"No, please." She bites her lips, turns away. She won't look at me at all now. "I'm with Lorne. That's the end of it."

"It doesn't have to be."

"That's how it is." She slings her bag over her shoulder, bowing her head like a penitent. "Some things can't be taken back."

At first, I think she means her word in the engagement.

But as the long night wears on, as I smoke and drink by the fire, I start to believe that it's something far worse than that.

I think Elena did something bad back home in Lviv.

And now, in some shadowy way, perhaps without meaning to or wanting to, she's punishing herself.

But here's the problem:

The punishment she'll get from Lorne Ronson will be more than she can handle.

CHAPTER 16
ELENA

ALL NEXT WEEK, I DO AN EXCELLENT JOB OF AVOIDING ATLAS. I only speak to him twice in passing and only in the most polite, mundane way.

The problem is, I suspect Atlas is *allowing* me to avoid him. And only for a limited time.

It's the sensation that used to creep over me when I'd play chess with my mother. She'd act calm and mild while instigating her sneakiest plots. It taught me to fear when people withdraw unexpectedly, luring me into a false sense of security.

I don't think Atlas has given up at all. He's just waiting.

Lorne is playing the opposite strategy.

He's been twice as attentive since putting the ring on my finger. He compliments me whenever I wear my new clothes and showers me with gifts and chocolates. After he spat in my mouth, he sent six dozen star lilies up to my room. The vases sit everywhere, two to a table, filling the air with the scent of their blooms.

Lilies were my mother's favorite flower. I ordered them for her funeral…and have hated them ever since.

Scent welds to memory. However much I loved the smell once, associating it with Easter and my mother's birthday, moments when my parents looked happy and in love, that one cold morning of their funeral forever bound lilies to the darkest dread and sorrow I've ever known.

I know I've told Lorne that my favorite flowers are roses.

In fact, I'm quite certain I even mentioned how much I dread the smell of lilies.

As the sickly sweet scent of death seeps through my hotel room, it starts to feel more and more like a message…

A reminder from my fiancé to stay away from Atlas.

———————

Lorne is in a great mood all week long. Mostly because the workmen are making progress on the house (*I mean, castle*).

"It could be finished in a couple more weeks!" he tells me as I slip my feet into my shoes, preparing to head downstairs for dinner.

"That's great." I smile back at him, though inside, I'm as frozen and spiky as the rose garden beneath my window. The vines look glazed in metal. The ocean beyond is black as ink.

Sometimes Grimstone is even more depressing than Lviv.

Lorne brought over a whole stack of wedding magazines and set them on the coffee table. Even though the ceremony will be small, he wants me to pick the color of the flowers and the style of the cake so Mrs. Cross can throw us a little party.

He's thoughtful. I should be grateful.

Instead…I'm filled with dread.

"Who are you inviting?" I ask Lorne, after spending way too long wondering if I should.

Something I've learned about my fiancé is that he only likes certain types of questions. Mostly ones related to his interests and his work. Those he'll answer for hours. *What's your favorite movie? Where have you traveled? Which authors have influenced you?* Questions about friends, family, and his past…not so much.

This query is easily batted aside. "Why invite anybody? I'd rather it just be you and me and Ivy. And the priest, of course."

Lorne leans forward, smiling at me. He's handsomer than ever with his hair combed back, his stylish black horn-rim glasses giving him that extra air of intelligence and importance, especially when paired with his favorite cashmere turtleneck.

Lorne pays a lot of attention to how he looks. And to how other people look. Now that I know this about him, how long he spends on grooming, how carefully he selects his clothes, I have to rethink my first impression of Lorne as a cute, dorky tourist.

No.

Lorne *was dressed* as a cute, dorky tourist. Because my fiancé picks his clothes carefully. Always. And he knows how to dress for an occasion. To make a certain impression.

I've never seen him dress quite like that ever again. Or talk like he did that first day, stuttering and sweet.

It's interesting.

Some things you only notice with time, with distance. When you see what comes after. And how everything changes.

The man sitting across from me on the sofa at this moment is different from the man I met in Lviv. And different from the one who picked me up at the airport. Lorne's changing. Or my perception of him is changing.

If I ask Lorne about his family, I already know what he'll say:

That's boring; you don't want to hear about that. Let's talk about that later. I want to hear about you…

Lorne is never more interested in *me* than when I ask awkward questions about *him*.

I know what will happen. But I ask anyway.

"You really don't have any family to invite? Not a cousin or…"

Lorne's jaw stiffens, his mouth a thin line. "No, I told you. I'm an orphan like you."

"Okay, sorry."

I seem to be tacking apologies onto most of my statements these days. It's almost become automatic.

Now we're seated in a cozy corner of the Reinstoff, tucked away by the fireplace, and Lorne still seems irritated. He might be extra irritated because Olivia isn't serving us. She's standing by the bar looking sulky. Which I'm guessing means that Atlas warned her away.

I try not to let my satisfaction show. Or look at Atlas himself.

He's standing by the pass-through to the kitchen, which is his new way of pretending not to watch me. He has not stopped stalking me through the hotel and staring at me wherever I go. He just does it from a bit farther away now.

If I look at him, Lorne will notice. He watches my face all the time, following my eyes wherever they look. He can also repeat back anything I've said to him, word for word, like a lawyer.

Sometimes it feels like an interrogation when I slip up. When my statements don't match.

But that doesn't happen if I'm careful.

I'm careful not to look at Atlas. No matter how huge and dark he looms in my periphery, a six-foot-six granite block.

I've been well-behaved enough to make Lorne relax. I'm playing the perfect good girl.

It shouldn't be that hard to make Lorne happy. He's quite clear about what he wants, a tough but explicit boss. And since I'm unemployed at the moment, I have plenty of time to meet his demands.

It's not too difficult to dress up for him. Or to run his little errands, even when I bring Ivy along.

How much I enjoy having a bossy partner is a separate question.

Sometimes I can handle it.

Sometimes I'd like to punch him in the teeth.

Cooler heads prevail...for now.

A sick giddiness sweeps over me. I'm tense, so keyed up around Lorne that I'm losing all sense of what's safe and what's normal.

I haven't had a solid night's sleep since he put that ring on my finger. It's like it's cursed. The nightmares have me sitting up in my bed three or four times a night, shrieking into the wadded-up blankets.

Lorne told me to never, never take my ring off in case I lose it. But I disobeyed him, superstitiously slipping it off my finger before bed, refusing to even set it on the nightstand and instead tucking it inside a drawer.

But then I put it back on my finger this morning. Because I spoke to Mina, and she told me that trucks are lined up all along the curb outside the bookshop. Construction crews could be walking through there tomorrow. *Through every last room.*

So I've had to come to terms with certain realities.

Yes, Lorne is picky and demanding. He's jealous and...intense. But how bad is that, really? He's also paying for everything without complaint. He's generous and attentive. He sent me flowers twice this week (though possibly as a threat*)*. How do I balance these things?

I know what my mother would say: *Nobody's perfect. You can't get everything you want.*

Still, I'm not sure Lorne is what she had in mind.

The times when he's kind are beginning to unnerve me almost as much as his moods. When he's extra attentive, when he fawns over me, it's like I'm waiting for whatever's coming next.

The little things he says bother me. Small jabs, but they're like slivers of glass that burrow in deep. The critiques. The ways he brushes aside what I want, what I say.

And when he spat in my mouth...that was more than a sliver. It festers and bubbles under my skin. Why he did that to me. What it means...

"What?" Lorne's smiling, but his eyes are sharp behind his glasses.

I've never worried so much about what my face might be giving away. I never used to even think about it. Now my expression feels stiff and masklike as I try to prevent my emotions from slipping through.

"What?" I say back to Lorne, wooden and stupid.

Something flickers in his eyes. Irritation? Suspicion?

"I don't know," he says. "You look…"

"What?" This time I force a smile.

"Nothing." He lets it drop. The mood relaxes but only a little, a leash without much slack.

I feel drained in a way I can't explain. The food doesn't smell as good, and the noise of the other diners is irritating. All the colors in the room seem dingy and dull.

My head is pounding. I've been having dreams that I'm trapped in coffins, in boxes. Dreams of chains wrapped round my limbs and a long fall out my window into the ink-dark ocean below, where I'm dragged down and down and down…

It doesn't take Freud to explain that I'm feeling anxious. And maybe not entirely excited for my upcoming wedding.

My eyes want to return to Atlas, over and over. I'm tired of fighting them.

"Are you excited?" Lorne speaks so softly you have to listen carefully for the snares.

"For what?" I say carefully.

"To be married." He smiles patiently.

I've already learned not to trust that smile. That question has a hook in it. I can't just answer it—I have to answer it correctly. With the appropriate level of enthusiasm.

I aim for humor. "Is that even a question?"

"I don't know." Lorne's expression goes cold and flat. "Is it?"

I counter with hurt, mostly manufactured because inside I'm empty and dull. "Not to me it isn't."

I let my eyes drop to my plate, demure and almost pouty. I don't like doing it, but some people make you play their stupid fucking games.

Lorne softens as soon as I submit. Now his foot presses into mine under the table, rubbing against my ankle, then sliding up my leg. "I know you're excited."

Then what the fuck are you grilling me for?

I smile back at him, fluttering my lashes. "I wish it would come sooner. The wedding. All of it."

The thoughts in my head get angrier the more sweetly I try to behave.

Time away from Atlas was supposed to make it easier to bond with Lorne. But Atlas is like a pressure relief valve. Without him, the anxiousness in my chest only builds. And more time with Lorne makes it worse.

I don't like the way he looks at me.

Have I made a terrible mistake? *All over again…*

Lorne checks his phone. I sneak a quick look at Atlas.

The jolt I get when our eyes meet is exactly the kind of thing that makes people blow their entire paychecks at casinos. One look and my blood is buzzing.

I glance back at Lorne. He's still reading his messages. I steal another fix from Atlas.

Double-breasted suit today, dark as a coffin, black stubble almost grown into a beard. Dressed like an undertaker and extra glowery, or am I just imagining that because I want him to miss me?

"You watched Ivy again?" Lorne says, confirming something he read in his messages.

"Yes." My eyes snap back to his face before I even register what he said. "All day today."

Ivy's been knocking on my door earlier and earlier each morning, but I don't mind. I like when she joins me for the day. She's peaceful company and surprisingly easy to understand once you get to know her little sounds and gestures.

I'm starting to think I like her more than Lorne. She's definitely easier to please.

She comes over when I'm still in my pajamas, so I let her dress me up like her oversized Barbie doll. She's really into matching outfits, and goddamn if it isn't filling some unknown hole inside of me.

Dressing up for someone is an invitation into their world—to be who they want you to be. When you play that role, you get to see life the way they see it.

Some of the outfits Ivy puts together are odd, but I wear them anyway because it's a look inside her head, how she hopes our day will go, who she wants us to be together, adventurers or fairy queens...

Ivy's world lies on the border of fantasy and reality. Sometimes she's highly present, making eye contact, pointing things out to me. Sometimes she seems pulled into another world, one that lies right on top of ours like the fourth dimension. She'll lie on her stomach for an hour examining the frost on the grass and the way that it melts in the heat of her breath, or she'll spin and spin and spin, staring up at something only she can seem to see.

When I come into her world, she shows me more and more, the sketches of birds and rabbits and toadstools in her notebook, the parts she underlined in *Firestarter*: "*The brain is a muscle that can move the world...*"

Well worth wearing outfits that occasionally make Atlas smile at me in an amused kind of way.

Lorne doesn't see those outfits. I always change before dinner into what he prefers, which is a posh, conservative sort of look. If I wear anything he considers *cheap* or *trashy*, he's quick to point it out.

Lorne's world has much stricter rules than Ivy's. He likes to think of himself as an artist and provocateur, with his gruesome, sexy books. But he's conservative in real life, highly concerned with how other people behave and what they think.

I get that he's trying to help me fit in, but I wish he weren't quite so concerned with public opinion. The last time I brought Ivy to dinner with us, he made her go back upstairs to change just because she dribbled a little soup down the front of her dress. I mean, she's a kid; nobody's going to judge her for spilling. Other than her dad, I guess.

"The more you watch Ivy," Lorne says approvingly, "the faster the work gets done."

Me minding Ivy frees up Mrs. Cross for full-time nagging. Apparently, she's so irritating that the electricians have finished in record time. Whether we'll all burn alive in our beds is a different question.

"Incredible," I say, smile plastered on my face. "How soon can we move in?"

Lorne's voice turns almost reverent. "Right after Halloween."

I have to hold back a shudder.

Grimstone is *way* too into Halloween. This town practically worships the Grim Reaper. A twenty-foot-tall skeletal monstrosity is already taking shape at the end of Main Street.

I don't want those to be my wedding decorations.

But Lorne's going to take it personally if I try to delay.

"That's…perfect," I manage.

My intestines roll like snakes. I throw a guilty glance at Atlas though he's too far away to have heard me.

Why do I feel like I'm cheating on Atlas? I'm not cheating on Atlas. The cheating is when I think about Atlas.

The more you try not to think about someone, the more they haunt your mind.

As if summoned, Atlas appears at my elbow.

Excitement expands in my chest like a hot-air balloon. Now I'm staring down at my plate because there's no way this isn't leaking out of my face, this sudden, crazy, stupid happiness that came along with Atlas.

And why?

Because he's standing right there, a foot away from me. So close, I could almost brush his leg with my elbow.

And that's how I know I'm in very deep trouble.

My skin starts burning from my scalp to my face, down the back of my neck and across my collarbones, all down my arms, from my bare knees to my toes. We're the closest we've been in a week, and my whole body knows it.

"Ninety-six Margaux..." Atlas displays a bottle of wine, small in his massive hands. "Compliments of the house."

Lorne sounds genuinely impressed. "How generous."

Atlas brought the good stuff to our table personally...as an olive branch?

His manners to Lorne are polite and reserved. But then he gives me a look with so much heat, I know why he's really here.

My disloyal heart thrills inside me.

The voice of reason tells me to knock it off.

My heart keeps beating just as hard, just as wildly.

Because the heart wants what it wants...no matter how much trouble it will cause.

Atlas stabs the cork and pops it out of the bottle, as easily as spearing an olive. The flex of his bicep makes a tiny muscle contract in my belly in response.

I very carefully do not look at Lorne. Or anything else. Only my plate. That has to be safe.

The gravity at our table is all wrong, and there's no way Lorne can't feel it. Every cell in my body pulls toward Atlas.

I can't seem to stop it. I can't stop wanting him.

Atlas pours the wine. No one has ever poured wine more slowly. He's doing it on purpose. He knows how good he smells, his warm skin mixing with the scent of the wine, crushed grapes and sex and sin...

Lorne doesn't seem to notice a thing, completely distracted by the long, pretentious process of tasting his wine. He swirls it around. Sniffs it. Makes little slurpy sounds.

I lock eyes with Atlas and take a heady draft. The Bordeaux bursts on my tongue, the taste of temptation.

Atlas lets his eyes drag down my body, admiring my figure in the black velvet dress bought and paid for by him. He raises an eyebrow, pursing his lips slightly until I can almost hear his voice in my head: "*Now, that's just not fair.*"

I'm going to kiss him again, I already know it.

I stare at his lips, imagining how that thick, black stubble will feel scratching against my bare skin...

"Incredible." Lorne smacks his lips, still laser focused on the liquid in his glass. "It's got that freshness in the nose, with just a hint of mineral and black fruit."

I don't have a clue what he's talking about.

All I can hear is the blood thudding in my ears as I gaze up at Atlas.

Atlas steals one more look at me in the tight velvet dress. His hungry eyes roam my body like hands until at last they fix on my face.

With a wicked smile, he says, "Well worth the price."

CHAPTER 17
ELENA

LORNE CAN'T RESIST ATLAS'S BRIBE. HE HAS A TASTE FOR THE finer things in life, and this wine must be particularly fine because he downs the rest of the bottle in less than an hour, making him tipsy, handsy, and a lot more forgiving.

"Atlas ain't so bad," he slurs, setting a sloppy hand on my thigh. "He's got good taste, at least. I like this dress, by the way."

I refrain from telling Lorne that Atlas also picked out the dress.

It must be perfect because Lorne hasn't found a single thing to criticize in my appearance tonight. In fact, he scoots his chair closer and slings his arm around my shoulders.

I spent my last hour with Ivy recreating makeup looks we found on YouTube. She gave herself the "rainbow unicorn makeover" while I attempted the "subtle smokey eye." The results were pretty damn good, and so what if I'm getting my fashion advice from a nine-year-old? Mina can only do so much over the phone.

Lorne obviously likes the results. His fingers brush against the top of my breast.

I take another sip from a glass that's mostly still full.

I don't like wine that much, even super fancy wine that's older than me. *Especially* super fancy wine that's older than me, it turns out. It's a little sour.

Lorne keeps talking about *mouth feel* and *layers* and *bouquet*. He's droning on and on.

I've always liked to listen more than I like to talk. At first, I loved Lorne's charm and wit, how he can easily fill an hour with amusing anecdotes.

But Lorne seems to think he's *always* interesting, and the truth is…sometimes he's not.

The wine isn't helping. It's making his speech mushier and his stories less coherent.

I'm listening less and watching Atlas more the drunker Lorne gets.

Atlas roams the restaurant, barking orders at servers and cooks, his scowl progressively darker. I'm pretty sure he brought Lorne the wine to distract him, but now Lorne is tipsy and openly groping me, and Atlas looks pissed.

I can't kiss Atlas again. What was I thinking? Lorne's my fiancé. I'm marrying Lorne.

I try to block out the walking storm cloud and focus on the man sitting right next to me. The one touching me. The one staring down at my tits.

How can the man on the other side of the room feel closer than the one slipping his hand down the front of my dress?

"Lorne…" I squirm away from him, scooting my chair over a few inches. "People are looking."

"Nobodysh looking," Lorne slurs. He hasn't actually checked. If he did, he'd see Atlas glowering at us, as well as the old lady sitting two tables away.

He scoots closer to me again, like we're slowly chasing each other around the table while glued to our chairs.

Slinging his arm around my shoulders and breathing sour, boozy breath into my face, Lorne says, "Have you watched that porn I gave you?"

"Yeah. Some."

Lorne gave me a brand-new laptop earlier in the week, which seemed like a really nice gesture until I realized he'd filled it with super graphic pornography he expects me to watch.

I started a couple of videos, but they kind of made me feel sick. Especially once I realized that all the girls in the videos were blond and curvy and Eastern European. I guess I should be glad that I'm obviously Lorne's "type," but it gave me a weird feeling...like if a different blond girl would have come to the café five minutes earlier, she'd be marrying Lorne instead.

Plus, the videos were intense. Is that how Lorne expects me to behave in bed after we're married?

I don't have the guts to ask him.

Lorne slips his hand down the front of my dress again, groping my left breast. His wet mouth breathes into my ear. "Have you been practicing?"

I tried touching myself, but the videos didn't turn me on. I'm afraid to tell Lorne that I still haven't had an orgasm.

"Yes," I lie, shrinking under his arm, trying to pull away from his hand, but he catches my nipple between his thumb and index finger and pinches. I yelp, "Yes! I've been practicing!"

"Good girl." Lorn nibbles at my ear.

My skin crawls. I don't like my tits groped in public, and I don't like my ears licked *ever*.

"Stop it, Lorne," I mutter, but he only squeezes my breast harder, his other hand moving up my thigh.

"Why? Is he watching?"

Yes, Atlas is absolutely watching. I can feel his eyes burning on my skin even before I meet his furious gaze.

But telling Lorne that will only egg him on. He's almost pulling my breast out of my top.

"Lorne, stop!" My voice is a little louder now as I try to pull away from him. "You're embarrassing me."

Lorne lets go of my breast, but only so he can grab the back of my neck instead. Flushed from the wine, even his eyes are bloodshot as he presses our foreheads together. "*I'm* embarrassing *you*?" he sneers. "You should count your lucky stars every time you're seen in public with me."

Tears spring into my eyes, from hurt and humiliation and the pain of his fingers digging into the tense muscle at the base of my neck.

"Stop, Lorne! I don't—"

Lorne is jerked out of his seat. One moment his hands are all over my body, grabbing, pinching, groping, his boozy, wet mouth licking at my ear, and the next instant his feet dangle in the air as Atlas lifts him by the throat.

"Atlas, stop!"

I'm shrieking and beating at his arms, but I might as well pound the side of a mountain with my fists. Atlas's face is a mask of rage while Lorne silently chokes.

It's not until Lorne's eyes start to roll back that Atlas snaps out of it. He flings Lorne back down so hard that the chair rocks back on its legs and almost tips over. It's balanced by the limp body of Lorne himself, who slumps forward and vomits down the front of his shirt, dark as blood from all the wine.

"Get him cleaned up," Atlas barks at the closest busser.

The entire restaurant is staring at us, every last server and shocked guest, including the little old lady two tables over. I can only imagine what she thinks of my dinner-table drama.

Tears of shock and humiliation flow down my cheeks.

Atlas tries to put his arm around my shoulders, but I twist away from him. "Get off of me!"

He glowers. "I was only trying to help."

I look at my drunken, throttled, vomit-spattered fiancé, who's sure to be furious at me tomorrow when he sobers up.

"You're not helping! You're making things worse!"

I turn and flee the restaurant.

CHAPTER 18
ATLAS

THAT WAS A STUPID FUCKING PLAN.

My intention was to get the author drunk enough that he'd go to bed early, leaving me alone with Elena.

Instead, I turned him into a horny frat boy. Then I acted like Elena's overprotective dad, and now she's pissed at me.

She's right to be pissed at me. What the fuck was I thinking?

I gave her space all week long because that was obviously what she wanted. But it was torture watching her pick through the breakfast buffet each morning, giggle with Amy at the front desk, play in the garden with Ivy, and stalk the hallways of the hotel with her camera, snapping pictures of anything that caught her interest.

Amy gets to talk to her. Ivy gets to talk to her. But not me.

It didn't seem fair.

I brought the wine over just to get a look at her up close. I'd never seen her in black before. The dress set her off like a jewel in a velvet box, her sapphire eyes, her blushing skin, her legs a mile long...

I was reckless, squandering the bottle I've saved for years because I knew how well it would work. I glugged twelve hundred dollars of that shit into Ronson's glass while drinking in the scent of Elena's skin until I could hardly stand up.

I hoped Ronson would drink himself silly and head off to bed, but of course he couldn't keep his hands off her in that dress. I would have seen that coming if I could have thought about a damn thing besides Elena.

When he manhandled her, I went into a rage. Sixteen years I've been running this hotel, and I've never once laid hands on a guest.

I regret it.

But only because I didn't knock his fucking teeth out when I had the chance.

All right, so I'm still a little angry.

No…I'm fucking furious.

He doesn't deserve her. He doesn't even love her—there's nothing real in his eyes, in his voice. He just wants her. For his own fucked-up purposes.

I don't trust him. He drugged Elena that night; I know he did. He didn't take a single sip of his wine while he pressured her to drink. And Olivia told me the bottle was already uncorked. He probably thought whatever he put in that wine would take longer to kick in and he could get her back to her room to do god knows what to her. Maybe he planned to blame it on jet lag, but the jet lag knocked her out too soon.

Only guesses, but I know one thing for certain: Lorne Ronson is not what he pretends.

How can I make Elena see it?

She tries to avoid me the next day. I allow her to slip past me out the front door of the hotel, and then I follow.

Elena's alone today, no pale little shadow trailing after her. I'm not surprised, since I already saw Mrs. Cross dragging Ivy outside by the arm an hour earlier.

Elena has her camera out, slung around her neck with a strap that looks hand embroidered. She never lets the camera bounce but holds it carefully in her hands. The strap is just for extra security.

She pauses to take a picture of the fountain in the town square, full to the rim with garnet leaves. She snaps pictures of the clock tower and the row of shops, then pauses in front of the twenty-foot-tall sculpture of Mr. Bones, mascot of the Reaper's Revenge. But she doesn't lift her camera for him.

It's a brisk day, the wind blowing in off the ocean chilly and damp. That salty sea air whips through Elena's hair and sends scarlet leaves skittering against my legs.

"Taking your stalking outside the hotel, are you?" Elena says without turning around.

I come out into the square, unembarrassed and unrepentant.

"Whatever I have to do to talk to you."

She turns, her hair lifting and settling around her shoulders. Her camera is raised to her eye, and she snaps a photograph of me before lowering the lens, frowning.

"I don't need you following me. And I don't need you protecting me—especially not from my own fiancé."

"You're right. I'm sorry." I hold up my hands. "That's what I came here for, to apologize."

Elena softens slightly, lowering her camera so it's no longer a protective barrier between us. But she doesn't come any closer.

"Look, Atlas…" Her voice is husky and unhappy, her eyes cast down at the ground. "I really appreciate how you've tried to look out for me. But this thing between us…it's not right. Not when I'm with Lorne."

His ring still hangs on her finger, ugly, heavy, too big for her hand.

I want to argue with Elena. I want to tell her she shouldn't be with Lorne. But that will only push her further away.

"All right," I say. "I'll back off."

She looks at me in surprise, those blue eyes keenly curious. I pretend to be cool even though every inch of me is on fire beneath my clothes.

"Where are you going to develop that film?" I say as if I'm changing the subject.

"Nowhere," Elena says. "Not yet. Maybe eventually I can set up a darkroom again. I used the broom cupboard at my uncle's house. It was cramped, but you don't need much space—just total darkness."

"There's a darkroom at the Monarch," I say, oh so casually.

Elena's mouth falls open. Every part of her seems to perk with anticipation: her shoulders, eyebrows, even the tips of her ears. "There is?"

"You can use it anytime you want."

"Could you show it to me?" she asks eagerly. "Tomorrow?"

It's so hard not to smile.

"How about right now?"

CHAPTER 19
ATLAS

ELENA'S SO EXCITED THAT SHE ONLY SPARES A COUPLE NERVOUS glances as we reenter the hotel together. She doesn't have to worry—the author's still sleeping off his hangover, and Amy will tell me the moment he leaves his room. But I don't mention that to Elena because she's already forgotten Lorne Ronson as I lead her down the back hallway by the kitchen and through a hidden doorway to the basement stairs.

She's practically as intrigued by the hidden door as she is by the prospect of a darkroom.

"You have secret passageways? This place is so fucking cool! Where's your room?" The question pops out of her, but then she seems to second-guess herself, biting her lip like she can bite back the words.

I would love to take Elena to my suite. In fact, it's one of the top three goals on my priority list, but the timing's not quite right.

I learned my lesson last night, rushing in, acting a fool. I have to be more strategic.

I want Elena. I can admit that to myself. And I don't think Lorne should have her—because he doesn't deserve her and because I don't trust him to treat her right.

But she's not going to leave him if she's *more* afraid of something else…whatever that *something else* might be.

I don't know if it's the visa issue or some bogeyman back in Ukraine or just her guilt at breaking off an engagement, but whatever the problem is, Elena's not ready to tell me.

So I've got to work this from the opposite angle.

First, I have to win Elena's trust. She's not going to tell me a damn thing when she thinks we're strangers, so I have to show her what a good friend I can be.

The next bit's trickier. I've got to demonstrate that her fiancé isn't just an asshole, he's dangerous. Lorne Ronson has secrets, and I'm digging them up one by one. The hard part will be exposing him without looking like I've got an ulterior motive. Because I *do* have an ulterior motive, and Elena knows it.

Step three: when Elena is safe and happy and far away from her ex-fiancé, *that's* when I'll give her the full private tour.

For now, we're still on step one. Which means getting to know her on a deeper level so I can show her that I'm the one who will protect and promote what matters to her most.

So I say, with ultimate casualness, "I'll show you where I live. But I think you're a little more interested in this…"

We've come to a plain metal door that unlocks with the smallest key on my ring. This room was used for document storage long before computers. It's fireproofed, the windowless walls lined with lead, but well ventilated. I've already stocked the space with all the necessary chemicals and supplies. Some were difficult to find, and all had to be disguised so they looked less obviously new.

Elena is still suspicious.

"You just happened to have this down here?" She arches a strawberry-blond eyebrow. "A whole entire darkroom?"

"Isn't that convenient?" I smile right back at her. I don't give a damn if she knows.

Elena blushes deeply. "Well…thank you. It's wonderful. And ten times the size of my old darkroom. I can't wait to work in here."

But when I move to close the door behind us, she stiffens.

"What's wrong?"

"Nothing."

It doesn't look like nothing. Her whole body has tightened up, and she's darting glances at the door like she's terrified to be shut in here with me.

"Do you...want me to leave?"

"No." Elena shakes her head with short, jerky motions, her voice tight. "It isn't—it's not you. It's...ugh, *vot chuma*, sorry."

She's pacing now, glancing at the doorway, staring at the floor, running her hands through her hair and tugging at the roots.

I put it together at last: her nervousness to step into the elevator, how she always takes the stairs down from the sixth floor, her reaction when I trapped her by the dumbwaiter, and now her anxiety at being shut up inside the exact workspace she most wants to possess.

"Are you claustrophobic, Elena?"

"I—ah—" Her chest rises and falls with shallow breaths. Her eyes dart between the door and my face, faster and faster. At last, she whispers miserably, "I didn't used to be."

"Come sit down." I put my arm around her shoulders, drawing her over to a pair of mismatched armchairs, one of which used to sit in my father's library, the other from my grandpa's old office.

Elena sinks down into Pop Pop's chair, hands cradling her skull, elbows braced on her knees.

"Deep breaths," I say. "Nice and slow."

I rub circles on her back, my palm like a giant heating pad slowly moving around. I feel her muscles loosening, her breath softening.

How long we sit there, I have no idea. I'm waiting for Elena to feel calm again. For her to know that she's safe.

At last, she raises her head and looks at me. "Thanks, Atlas."

I love how my name sounds on her lips. It's like a whistle, the way it makes all the hairs stand up on my arms. It's a birdcall that only she knows, and I fly right into her cage.

She captured me, and she doesn't even realize it. Because Elena thinks that *she* belongs to someone else.

But I'm the one who will battle her demons. Even the ones in her head.

"What are you afraid of?" I ask. "If I close that door?"

She stares at the doorway, a hole like a missing tooth in the smooth, featureless wall.

"It's not the small space, exactly..." Her voice is slightly strangled. "It's whether I can get out."

Her lips are paler than usual, and when I put my hand on her back once more, her shirt is slightly damp.

"You can unlock the door from the inside. You don't need the key."

"I know," she says, her breath coming faster again. "And I know you wouldn't lock me in here."

"Is it the lack of windows? I could move this to another room...a higher floor..."

"No." She shakes her head. "I trust you. It's not rational, what happens to me, but I can't seem to control it."

She's shaking now, waves of tremors rolling down from her shoulders to her toes. I put my arm around her again and tuck her against my side and hold her there.

"Sorry," Elena says again. "Fuck, I'm sorry."

"Why are you sorry?"

"It's embarrassing." She pulls away from me, sitting upright again, lifting the hem of her shirt to wipe her face. "I'm a mess."

"Elena," I say. "Look at me. *Look at me.*"

Finally, she does. Hesitantly. With fear and shame.

"You're not embarrassing. You've done nothing wrong. I'm sitting here savoring every second I have with you. So please don't waste a moment of it apologizing."

Color returns to her face, blood flowing under the skin. Her eyes go liquid bright, and she blinks rapidly.

I say, "I don't care if you're scared of small spaces, or being stuck in them, or even just how they feel on a Tuesday. I don't care if it's rational or irrational, sane or crazy. I fucking hate snails, I hate 'em. Something about the mucous texture, the little prongy antennae..." I shiver just saying the words. Elena gives a ghost of a smile. "Fear isn't always rational, but it can still hurt us or hold us back."

"Or make us run in the exact wrong direction," Elena says softly.

There's weight in her words. And a sick, sinking feeling in my gut.

She regrets being with Lorne; I know it. But she thinks she's already trapped with him. How can I show her the door's still open?

"It's getting worse and worse," Elena says. "The nightmares..."

"What nightmares?" I cradle her head with my hand, pulling her back against my shoulder. "Tell me everything."

She leans against me, clinging to my arm, her head on my shoulder. Her voice comes out low and distant.

"We were in a car accident...me and my parents. We used to go to the movies every Wednesday. Dad said we needed something to look forward to in the middle of the week. He said, '*Mondays are too bleak; it's too far to the weekend...*' And he was right. It did make the week easy..."

Elena trails off like it's hard to even remember a time when a week felt easy.

All my weeks feel easy when I have the hotel running like a well-oiled machine. But they also feel somewhat empty.

The weeks since Elena arrived have been unprecedently vivid. It all started with that first glimpse of her in the hotel lobby. The light came down from the windows like we were in the cathedral of a church, and she stood by that golden cage as if she'd sprout wings like an angel.

It was a moment of the sublime. Such perfect harmony that I felt at one with the universe.

I didn't know it yet, but in that moment, I became a believer in things I never believed in before. Because some things can't be denied once you've felt them.

There's a connection between Elena and me, invisible but powerful as gravity. I feel it every time we're in the same room.

Her emotions infect me. Her words paint pictures in my head. And every time I come near her, I can see that I have just as much effect on her.

I know how to comfort her. I can feel it when she relaxes under my hands. I know how to rub her back, her shoulders. How to stroke her hair and soothe her with my gentlest voice.

I wrap my arm all the way around her and rest her head against my chest. From the shelter of my arms, Elena whispers, "It was snowing. A truck slipped on the ice and tipped over. All the lumber it was carrying crashed down on our car. I was sleeping in the back seat, lying down. The front windshield smashed in, and the whole car compacted like a tin can. I woke up with this weight and pressure crushing me, squeezing everywhere... I could still breathe, just barely, but I couldn't move, not an inch. And something started dripping down on my face. All these little droplets, like warm rain. It fell in my eyes, and I blinked and it smeared red...and I realized my parents had been...they were...it was their blood running down the boards. Dripping on my face. And I couldn't move. I couldn't stop it. I couldn't wipe it away..."

I feel it all with my arms wrapped around her—the constriction, the panic, the horror, and the terror of a girl all alone, realizing what so much blood must mean. I hold Elena, and I feel it with her, all the awfulness of that night. Forever linked to the sensation of captivity.

"That was when it started," Elena says. "The claustrophobia."

"Understandable."

She lets out a soft snort, almost a laugh. "Yeah, well, my uncle wasn't a fan of how many months it took me to get used to sleeping in a bunk bed. I used to wake up and see the slats overhead and start screaming. But I got used to it eventually. Ukrainians are big believers in exposure therapy."

"There is some neurological evidence that avoidance only strengthens fears."

Elena lifts her head to look at me. "I keep forgetting that you're a doctor."

"Well, you were asleep when I treated you."

"Pardon me, sir?"

"I was completely professional."

"Oh yes…" That strawberry-blond eyebrow is the naughtiest part of her face. "Like how professional you were at dinner last night."

"I take my Hippocratic oath much more seriously than my food-handling license."

Elena snorts. My arm is still around her shoulders. I have no intention of taking it away.

Softly, she says, "It got better for a while. But then there was another…incident…more recently. I was trapped in an elevator at work. And it brought it all back worse than ever. The claustrophobia and…new dreams."

"Like what?"

"Oh, you know, classic stuff…locked in a box, forced down a tiny pipe, drowning in a car as water pours in the windows…"

"All the hits."

Elena sighs. "It got so bad I couldn't even use the darkroom at home."

"The broom cupboard?"

"Yes." She smiles weakly. "The broom cupboard. I stopped taking as many pictures because it started to feel pointless. But that was even worse because I need it. It's my way of looking at things, of understanding them. It's what I love."

I can understand that. I'm not an artist, but I have my own lens through which I examine the world, and that's my hotel. The Monarch is the petri dish where I observe humanity. Most of what I've learned in life was within these walls. The Monarch is where I feel the most myself and the most connected to everything around me.

We all feel the pull of our purpose. To be cut off from what we're compelled to do is just as bad as being cut off from the other necessities of life.

"I want you to have a darkroom," I say to Elena. "One way or another. How can we make it work?"

Her eyes sweep the room, fixing on the doorway nervously. Her shoulders tense, but her voice comes out firm. "I want to work in here. I want to be able to close the door."

"Would it help if I stay with you?"

She lifts her head, studying me, our faces only inches apart.

"Yes. That would help a lot, actually."

"So you don't feel alone?"

She laughs softly. "So I know that at least one of us could break down the door."

"It's the main benefit of being built like a rhinoceros."

"What's the downside?"

"The bad jokes. People can't help themselves. It's the literal elephant in the room."

Elena stands and so do I. She tilts her head, stepping back a little to compare our relative sizes. She's about the height of the average man and only slightly shorter than her fiancé. But still a hell of a lot smaller than me.

To me, she's just the right size—not as disturbingly tiny as some of the women I've dated. There were a couple I was afraid I might crush if I rolled over in the middle of the night.

It would be nice to date someone a little heartier. Someone who wouldn't need a step stool to steal a kiss.

Elena says, "Before I met you, I'd never stood next to anyone who made me feel delicate."

"You are delicate, though." I'm looking at her skin, so smooth and clear it's almost luminescent. Her cheek's more delicate than any silken fabric.

Color flushes through it like watercolor as Elena blushes. It's like watching a painting being made, each expression, each emotion forming and dissolving on her face.

"Atlas," she says in a warning tone.

"That's just a fact. It's not flirting."

Her teeth gleam like pearls in the half-light as she ducks her head, hiding her smile. "Behave yourself."

Never.

"Come on, then, show me how it works," I say. "I've never actually seen film developed."

She hesitates. She knows just as well as I do that every moment we spend together is dangerous. We're all alone in this quiet, dark space. No one can hear us, above or below.

"I'll behave," I promise.

And I will. If that's what she wants.

But I don't think that's what she wants. Not really. Not deep down.

Elena switches on the red bulb and turns off the soft golden light. We're plunged into devilish gloom. Our features sharpen and darken. We're closer than ever, and more alone relative to the rest of the hotel.

We're stripped-down versions of ourselves, red and black, almost two-dimensional. When I look at Elena, it's like I can see all the way beneath her skin to the soul within—naked, bare, without preten-sion. Her fear is clear to me. So is her determination.

"Are you okay?" I ask her, my hand on the door.

She nods.

I close us in the darkroom, deep in the heart of the hotel.

Elena takes several slow breaths. A pulse jumps in the hollow of her throat.

"What do we do first?" I ask to distract her.

For a moment she doesn't answer, still frozen in place with her eyes fixed on the closed door. Then she forces herself into action, preparing the chemicals and the developing tank.

"All fresh and full to the brim," she says of the supplies. "How lucky for me."

"All right, I had Amy set it all up for you," I admit. "It was just a storage room before."

Elena laughs. "I know, Atlas. Nobody has a darkroom anymore."

Her movements are becoming more confident, more assured, as she slips into the routine she knows so well.

"What are you doing now?"

"Checking the temperature. Sixty-eight degrees is best for black-and-white film."

"And then what?"

"I'll show you. Well, I'll sort of show you. This part we have to do in complete darkness."

She switches off even the red safety light, plunging us into solid black. I become all the more aware of her closeness, of the heat coming off her body.

"Here." Elena slips her hands into mine. "We've got to put the film on the reel."

She moves my hands in the darkness, placing the film canister in one, a plastic tool in the other.

"First you pop the lid…"

Elena guides me in opening the canister, unspooling the film, and threading it onto the reel. She moves with calm assurance, having done this blindly many times before.

The darkness is like the deepest mineshaft, not a shred of light leaking into the windowless room. My other senses expand to fill the gap. The little shuffles of our feet on the floor, my heartbeat, and the sound of Elena's breathing become as clear and obvious as someone speaking aloud. The scent of her skin is as distinct as the photography chemicals, honey sweet against the bitter acid.

I've never felt anything so intimate, all alone in the dark, cut off from any other sensation. All I feel are her fingers and mine, our hands moving together.

She takes me through each step of the process, the prewash, the developer, the stop bath, the fixer...eventually we can use the red light again, but the intimacy of complete darkness remains. It's as if we're still in that borderless state where our bodies seem to vanish and there's no barrier between us. Our hands move together, bathing the images, fixing them on paper.

Elena takes the rinsed photographs and hangs them up with clothespins like shirts on a line.

The last photo is the one she snapped of me earlier today next to the fountain. She bathes it in chemicals, and the image darkens, my own features swimming into being.

She took that picture when I was looking at her. And what I feel is written all over my face...

Longing. Hopeless longing.

Elena looks at me, and I look at her. Neither of us speaks; it's unnecessary.

Because there it is, in black and white, captured forever on film...how desperately I want her.

CHAPTER 20
ELENA

I HANG THE PHOTOGRAPH OF ATLAS.

His eyes burn off the page, hungry and dark. Staring into mine.

When I turn around, he's looking at me exactly the same way.

My heart is beating so hard.

I swore, I swore, I swore I wasn't going to kiss him again.

The red light is still on. His eyes are black, his hair is black, and his skin is scarlet. He's every fevered dream I've ever had of him, standing right here…

Dreams of Atlas keep me up at night more than my nightmares. Dreams of what could have been…

Why wasn't he the one I met that day in the café instead of Lorne?

But fate sent Lorne to the Ambassador Hotel. And I was there to meet him. Wishing, praying for that very thing.

And if it's not quite how I imagined it would be…well, I was stupid to believe in fairy-tale endings in the first place.

Real life is difficult and dark. I've always known that.

Sometimes you meet a decent guy, and then you meet the actual *one*. The one who makes your skin burn and your heart race and your spirit soar. The one who looks in your eyes and seems to understand you before you say a word, but he listens anyway. No, he doesn't just listen…he hangs on your every word. And when he answers, it's just the right thing to make you feel safe and at home.

But you're already engaged to someone else.

And that someone else is super fucking pissed at you.

We'll talk about this tomorrow. That's what Lorne texted me last night after two of Atlas's employees carried him up to bed.

I'm not looking forward to it.

I can't kiss Atlas. No matter how badly I'm burning to do it. Lorne will see it all over my face. I'm supposed to be meeting him for dinner in less than an hour. He's already going to wonder why I reek like chemicals. *Blyat*, I need to shower…

Though I'd much rather stay right where I am, I say, "I've got to go, Atlas."

He just stands there watching me. Taking up half the room.

He removed his suit jacket earlier and hung it carefully over the back of the chair, leaving only his black dress shirt, the sleeves now rolled up. I can't see through his shirt at all. But I can absolutely see the shape of his body, the thick muscle on his chest, back, and arms.

Atlas is strong like an animal. You can see it every time he moves. And it brings out something animal in me.

He's only touched me in the gentlest ways. Somehow…that makes me rabid.

I want to feel what he's holding back so carefully. It's all I can seem to think about. All day long, and especially all night…

Atlas says, "Go, then." But his face says the opposite. And he hasn't moved an inch.

I know exactly what will happen if I take a step in his direction.

So I don't even try to slip past him. Instead, I run straight toward him.

I leap into Atlas's arms, wrap my legs around his waist, take his face in my hands, and kiss him. I kiss him long and deep with all my heart. Then I look into his eyes and say, "Thank you."

Nobody has ever given me a gift as thoughtful as a whole entire darkroom.

Atlas sets me down slowly, his eyes locked on mine, his hands lingering and dragging across my skin.

"You have to know, Elena…I'd do anything for you."

I'm getting ready to meet Lorne, but all I can think about is Atlas.

Lorne is fine; he's great, even. Some other woman would probably be really happy with him—Olivia, for instance. But I don't think that group includes me.

I shouldn't have rushed into this, okay, that's obvious. But how fucked am I, really?

I bite the edge of my thumbnail, considering.

Well, if I don't marry Lorne, then I have to go home to Lviv. And then I won't be with Atlas or anybody else because I'll be locked in a prison cell for the rest of my days.

That's…pretty fucked.

But if I want to stay here, I have to marry Lorne. And that might be worse.

Worse than prison?

I guess that depends. Like, for starters, it depends on how angry my fiancé is with me at this current moment. And what he intends to do about it tonight.

I rush through my preparations, twisting my hair up in a knot, slipping on some earrings. I want to see Ivy before dinner, to hear how her dentist appointment went. I know she was nervous.

When I arrive, she's sitting by the window like usual, but she looks like she should be lying in bed. She's wrapped up in her quilt, eyes glazed, face swollen.

"She had three cavities," Mrs. Cross says with way too much satisfaction. "Probably because half her diet is maple syrup."

"How are you doing, Ivy?" I ask, kneeling by her chair, ignoring Mrs. Cross.

She opens her eyes partway, struggling to focus. She raises a slow, wobbling hand to her cheek and winces.

"Have you given her any painkillers?" I demand of Mrs. Cross.

Lorne comes in from the adjoining room, looking mostly recovered. He's freshly showered, wearing a nicely pressed shirt, hair combed back, no glasses today. But his eyes are still bloodshot, and his face is ever so slightly puffy from last night's binge.

He's clearly surprised to see me. "What are you doing down here? I was coming to get you."

"I wanted to check on Ivy. She's not looking well—"

"Of course not; she had three fillings. She eats too much sugar."

Lorne's tone is already clipped and simmering, but I ignore that, too.

"I'm worried about her. I don't think we should go for dinner. Can we order in to the room instead?"

"We're going to dinner," Lorne snaps. "Ivy will be fine. Mrs. Cross is here."

Mrs. Cross gives me a furious nod. But I don't give much of a fuck because Ivy made a whimpering sound when her dad said that.

I stand and look Lorne right in the eye. "I want to stay with her."

Lorne stares right back at me, an awful stillness falling over his face. His voice is stripped bare as steel. "My daughter is going to bed, and you're coming with me to dinner."

The emphasis on "*my*" daughter is slight. But it's definitely there.

Ivy is not my daughter. I have no right to dictate anything to Lorne or even Mrs. Cross. But damn, does it feel like I need to.

The little girl is sickly pale and absolutely miserable. She can barely sit up in the armchair. But I have no leverage, no power here.

"We at least need to give her some Tylenol," I insist. "And a glass of water."

Lorne taps his foot impatiently while I check Ivy's forehead with my wrist, give her the Children's Tylenol, and fetch her already-battered copy of *Firestarter*.

"In case you feel up to reading later," I tell her.

I set the book where Ivy can easily reach it.

"Let's go!" Lorne snaps.

His voice jolts Ivy, who grabs my wrist. She looks into my eyes, one of the longest, most direct stares she's ever given me, somehow all the more clear and direct because of the slight delirium of her fever. It's like it's burned away the veil that sometimes separates Ivy and the rest of the world. Her eyes stare into mine, and she clings to my wrist with both hands.

Her mouth works, and she grimaces. "Ap," she croaks.

"*Ap*?" I repeat. "What's *ap*?"

But Ivy slumps back, letting go of my wrist, her eyes glossing over.

"What's *ap*?" I repeat, half turning as if Lorne will help me. Ivy's never tried to talk to me before. Not out loud.

"She's just making noise," Lorne says.

But that wasn't just noise. She was trying to tell me something.

"What is it, sweetie?" I ask Ivy one more time, bending down, trying to look into her face. "What's *ap*?"

She won't look at me. No matter how I reposition my face to catch her eye, her gaze slides relentlessly away, down my arm to my hand and the ring. She seems to be staring at the diamond, transfixed.

When I told Ivy I was marrying her dad, she didn't seem very happy. She didn't want to look at the ring. But now she can't take her eyes off it.

"All right," I murmur, touching her shoulder gently in the way she doesn't mind. "You can tell me tomorrow." As I stand, I say at a normal volume, "I'll come see you in the morning. We'll make your owl suit."

Ivy has been counting the days until Halloween. Crossing them off in her notebook.

"Let's *go*," Lorne says one final time from the doorway, quietly furious.

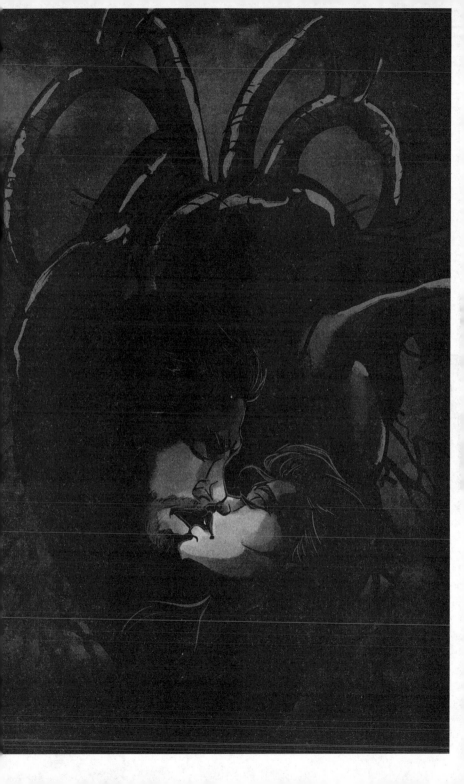

CHAPTER 21
ELENA

THE TENSION IS THICK AS LORNE MARCHES ME DOWN TO THE restaurant. I'm wearing flat shoes and my dowdiest dress. Atlas will have no temptation to look at me, and neither will my fiancé. I'd like to shrink down and disappear, actually.

Lorne hasn't said anything yet other than that one text message. But I know he's pissed about what happened at dinner last night. A reckoning is coming. Probably in about two and a half minutes when we're alone with a pair of dinner menus.

What was Ivy trying to say to me? It must have been important. She seemed upset.

As we enter the restaurant, I keep my eyes carefully fixed on the carpet. I still know Atlas is there because Lorne hisses, "*Is he ever not lurking around?*" and steers me ruthlessly toward the closest table, his fingers biting into my upper arm.

Lorne is furious, but my heart thrills. I'm happy that Atlas is here. Even if it makes everything worse.

As soon as we're sitting down, Lorne demands, "Where were you all day?" He hasn't even spared a glance for poor Olivia pouting over by the bar. All his aggressive, suspicious attention is focused on lucky ol' me. "I came looking for you earlier. You weren't in your room."

Carefully, I say, "I was taking photographs."

"In the garden?"

"I walked down to the town square."

"What do you take pictures of?"

"Things that interest me. Things that don't make sense."

"Things that don't make sense?" Lorne frowns but doesn't wait for clarification. "Show me. I want to see your pictures."

He snaps his fingers like he expects me to have some on hand right now.

"I'd have to develop the film."

Each of my heartbeats throbs like a warning: *keep your mouth shut, keep your mouth shut...*

Lorne can't know about the darkroom. He won't like it. He won't let me go down there.

I *need* to go down there. I need to develop my pictures. It was such a relief to see all the snaps I've taken of the garden, of Grimstone, of Ivy, of the hotel, all fixed in ink at last, the memories resolved like the last few bars of harmony.

And of course...that photograph of Atlas.

I already want to sneak downstairs to look at it again. To relive how it felt to turn and see him there, wind blowing his hair and the tails of his long black coat, dark eyes glittering in his broken boxer's face, huge hands hanging by his sides...

Those hands were my first introduction to Atlas: one wrapping around my entire forearm, the other encircling my waist.

That's what I dream about, over and over, alone in my hotel room in the dead of night. I dream of a pair of huge and powerful hands slipping under the covers, finding me and touching me in the dark. I lie in my hotel bed, thighs squeezing together, a burning feeling building low in my belly, a mounting sensation of heat and panic that builds and builds but never quite tips over the edge...

It's driving me mad.

But I can't kiss Atlas again.

That last kiss was a thank-you. A goodbye. Atlas knows that. We both know that.

"I'll get you a proper camera," Lorne says. "You can download the pictures on your laptop."

I don't want that at all. I like what I've got. But Lorne's gifts are not a suggestion.

"Thank you," I say as sincerely as possible. "But I prefer film."

"That's stupid. Nobody uses film anymore."

My eyes flash up at Lorne. "I like it."

I didn't mean to snap at him. But it's starting to piss me off how he shits on the things I like.

I told him what that camera means to me. That it belonged to my dad.

Atlas understands how important it is to me. He even seemed to intuit the most crucial part of all that I can never explain to anyone… that taking the photographs is only the first step. The memory isn't made real, isn't fixed as a single image in my mind, until I see it there on the page in all its moody light and shadow.

Lorne catches the heat in my look, the annoyance I let slip.

When I'm with Atlas, moods pass between us as easily as smiles. We're like two skiers carving the same mountain, swooping together and apart, symmetry in our lines.

Lorne is like a chemistry set of unknown ingredients. I never know what my reaction will cause in him.

Tonight, my irritation snaps him to attention. It makes him sit up a little straighter in his chair, his bloodshot eyes narrowing as he takes a closer look at me.

"You're flushed," he observes.

I sit still in my chair, trying to breathe at a normal pace, feeling like all my sins are written in ink across my face.

He doesn't know anything. He's just trying to make you nervous.

Lorne scoots his chair closer.

Across the restaurant, Atlas prowls the far wall. He's watching me and watching Lorne. When our eyes meet, I shake my head a tiny fraction. I do *not* want a repeat of last night.

Lorne lifts my hair away from the side of my neck. My throat, my bare shoulder, that whole side of my body closest to him feel horribly exposed.

He tilts his head, leans in, and inhales, his nose and lips millimeters from my neck. I feel the air sucking away, the heat lifting off my skin. And I'm cold, cold, cold.

But I hold still and pretend nothing is happening, while my heart beats so hard, I'm afraid it will explode.

Lorne hisses in my ear, "*Did you have an orgasm today?*"

"No," I whisper.

Just the best kiss of my life…

I close my eyes so I won't look at Atlas. And so I don't have to look at Lorne.

Lorne inhales again, this time with his nose pressed against the side of my neck, holding me steady by a handful of my hair.

"You smell like you did."

My scalp is burning. I can't look at Atlas, but I know he's a ticking time bomb over there.

Beneath the table, Lorne's hand fastens on my thigh like a clamp. He types all day long—eight thousand words a day sometimes, he told me. His fingers are strong and vicious, biting into my flesh in the most tender places, making me want to beg, to submit.

Can Atlas see what Lorne is doing under the table? He's going to figure it out. I'm dreading another conflict, terrified of how it might escalate, but some desperate part of me wants Atlas to see, wants him to know. Wants him to save me.

But Atlas can't save me. No one can.

Because I already bound myself to someone else. His ring is on my finger. His name is on my visa. And his cold, cruel hand is climbing higher on my thigh like an intrusive spider, pinching as it goes, leaving a trail of bruises…

Lorne knows I'm trapped.

Atlas is watching us. He's not even pretending to work anymore. Lorne can see him watching. But his hand moves higher anyway, beneath the table, concealed by the gloom of the candlelight, pinching, biting…

Lorne is testing me and testing Atlas. Seeing if I'll beg for help, verbally or silently. Goading Atlas to further violence.

Atlas has the barely restrained look of someone whose patience is wearing thin. There's something strangely frozen in our three positions—Atlas seeming half-stuck to the wall as if he'll tear away at any moment, me barely breathing, Lorne with his hands on my body…

Lorne dances a maddening line, dragging his fingers tauntingly across my collarbone while his other hand pinches beneath the table so hard that tears fill my eyes.

But I don't move. I don't cry out. I really have become frozen, trapped in some kind of waking sleep paralysis, eyes open but completely unable to move.

Lorne's fingers fumble at the edge of my underwear. "I can check, you know," he hisses in my ear. "I'll know the truth soon enough."

I flush from my scalp to my toes, an instant guilty red.

I haven't had sex with Atlas.

But I did kiss him an hour ago. And I'm pretty sure if Lorne touches me, he's going to find me ten times wetter than I've ever been when he's touched me before.

Low and quiet, I mutter, "You're going to get us thrown out of the hotel."

That's the right way to phrase it…like the two of us are a team. Like I'm also the one pulling my hair out by the roots right now and putting my hand in someone's underwear beneath the table.

Lorne relaxes his grip. His hand leaves my lap, and he sits back in his chair.

The candlelight in the Reinstoff is gentle. Lorne looks young and handsome in his white dress shirt. You can't see the lines on his face, which are also hidden when his hair is messy or he wears those black frame glasses. Sometimes, Lorne can almost look like a kid. I might have thought he was a college student back in Lviv. But when we filled out the immigration paperwork, I learned that he's actually forty-four.

In this moment, he could be the moody, artistic member of a boy band. That's how he's dressed, lean and chiseled in the loose white shirt, his hair growing long and shaggy, a crucifix necklace dangling from a silver chain around his neck. Though Lorne told me he's not religious.

When he smiles at me, it's a charming smile. Perfectly symmetrical with lovely white teeth. But when I look at his face, really look at it, the whole face, not just that dazzling white smile…it doesn't look so nice around the eyes. There…it's just a little bit strange.

My heart goes cold, and I begin to wonder…is everything a costume to Lorne? A role he plays?

I've noticed his exaggerations, the things that don't quite line up. But as I search for what's real, for the genuine core of his identity, all I seem to find is a deep black hole.

Lorne has always been hard to fix in my mind. I can never quite seem to visualize his face. It's always flickering, changing.

When I picture Atlas, he's scowling. Because Atlas is consistent. He's intense and suspicious, aggressive and protective—with me, his employees, his brother, and the guests at his hotel. You know what you're going to get.

As I look at Lorne's face, at the smile I don't quite trust, I realize…I have no idea what's about to happen. My fiancé is a stranger to me. I have no clue what to expect.

And I'm beginning to believe that is highly intentional.

"I'm concerned, Elena." Lorne is still smiling. He doesn't look worried. But he doesn't look friendly, either.

"Why are you concerned?" Playing dumb sounds easy, but it isn't. Not if you actually need to be convincing.

Lorne is not convinced. He's not smiling anymore, either. He stares me down coldly, his blue eyes flat as glass.

We're in a crowded restaurant. Atlas is twenty feet away. But dread spreads like frost across my skin.

"I'm not sure you're properly committed," Lorne says softly, "to making yourself a good wife for me."

"Is there…something I'm not doing?"

Never mind what I am doing…sneaking away to kiss Atlas.

But Lorne doesn't mention Atlas. His eyes narrow, and his upper lip thins and curls, exposing those perfect white teeth. "How about the fact that you haven't learned how to have a *fucking orgasm* yet?" he hisses. "What's wrong, Elena…aren't you attracted to me?"

"Of course I am." *Or at least, I was…*

"Then it should be easy."

But it isn't. Not even close.

"I'm sorry." My face is burning, my eyes smarting. "I'm trying."

Lorne's lips lose all their color when they're pursed or twisted, going pale as drowned worms. The thought of kissing those lips, of letting them touch my body, makes me feel sweaty and sick.

Lorne can feel it. He can feel me pulling back, drawing into myself, and he leans closer, hand on my wrist, demanding that warmth, that adoration, that energy he feeds on when Olivia simpers over him.

"What is it, then, Elena?" he hisses, fingers digging into my wrist. "What's the problem?"

"I've never had one. I told you. I don't know what I'm doing."

"Do you need me to teach you?"

"No!" The horror that shoots through me cannot be examined. "I'm practicing. I'm close."

"Good," Lorne says coldly, letting go of my wrist. "Why don't you go practice right now?"

I stare at him.

"But…our dinner hasn't come yet."

We haven't even ordered. The waitress is still getting our drinks.

And I'm really hungry. I have to wait until Lorne is done working to eat dinner. Sometimes he doesn't finish until nine thirty at night when he's "on a roll." He doesn't apologize, either. It's a "good thing for the book," so I'm supposed to act excited while my stomach is growling.

Lorne got mad the time he saw that I'd opened a bag of chips from the hotel minibar. He pouted and said, "I want you to eat with me."

So I'm basically starving at the moment. I haven't eaten since noon, and I do not want to go back up to my room to *practice*. I want to order a fourteen-ounce steak.

Lorne waits like he expects me to get up from the table this instant.

I slowly stand, staring at him, almost hoping he'll say, "*don't be silly, sit back down.*"

But all Lorne says is, "Don't leave your room until you're successful."

His eyes are two ice chips in an otherwise handsome face.

Or at least, I used to think it was handsome.

Now, I can hardly remember when I thought this man was good-looking. This man who is very clearly threatening me.

I lick my lips. "What happens if I can't?"

Coldly, flatly, without a hint of a smile, Lorne says, "Do you want to find out?"

I don't even try to swallow the lump in my throat. I let my voice come out in a scared little squeak.

"No, Lorne. I don't."

CHAPTER 22
ELENA

So now I'm locked in my hotel room. And I have never felt less like masturbating.

I've been in here for six hours. About four hours in, I inhaled all the snacks in the minibar. I know Lorne will see the charges, but I don't give a damn anymore.

I could have ordered a proper dinner from the restaurant, but I was worried that Atlas would bring it up. Then I'd have to explain to him why my fiancé sent me to bed without any supper like a naughty child.

Well, I could tell you why, but then I'd have to die of embarrassment.

It's bad enough that one man in America knows I'm a twenty-seven-year-old virgin. It doesn't need to be two—and especially not if one of them is Atlas.

He wouldn't be quite so attracted to me if he knew that little piece of trivia. He probably thinks I'm experienced like Mina, that I know all kinds of sexy tricks. He's probably constructed some fantasy image of me in his head, like everybody else seems to do. Isn't that what all humans are up to?

I imagined a whole future life around Lorne. And now I don't like who he is quite as much as the fantasy I built in my head. That's my fault, not his.

That's what I tell myself.

But that's not what I felt, alone in the restaurant with him.

Then, I felt scared out of my skin. Even with Atlas twenty feet away.

Because it felt like twenty feet might not be close enough. Not the way Lorne was looking at me.

Escape from goblins to be eaten by wolves, as the old saying goes.

I was looking into the eyes of a wolf.

So I went upstairs, deeply concerned that I may have gotten myself into a very bad spot.

An orgasm has never seemed more distant. My skin crawls at the thought of my handsome, devoted fiancé.

How could I be so fucking stupid? I don't even know what happened to his last wife. Where is Ivy's mother? Why is that little girl so sad?

I don't know.

But I know what I saw when I looked into Lorne's eyes... fucking nothing.

I don't know how I missed it before.

I guess I was just a little too desperate, hurrying along, grasping at a fairy-tale hope. Even though I'm way too old to still believe in fairy tales.

Some people tell a really good story. For a while, at least. But then the cracks begin to show. The wolf leaks through the walls.

I'm afraid to go downstairs.

Lorne has texted me twice:

How's it going?
Making progress?

I haven't responded to either message, and I don't believe he's waiting in his room. He could be right down the hall, watching to see if I leave.

Atlas wouldn't let him do that.

Let him do what? Visit his own fiancé? Stand outside her room?

A hysterical laugh bubbles up in my throat. The pattern on the wallpaper seems to subtly shift.

Maybe I am in a fairy tale after all. I'm the foolish maiden bewitched and betrothed to a monster.

Calm down, you're overreacting.

The "voice of reason" rings hollow and false. Everything inside me screams that I'm not overreacting. I'm not safe, not in my room and not in Grimstone.

But where else is there to go?

Nowhere. Not for me.

I lie down on the bed in the dark, though I've never felt less like sleeping. I put my hand on my breast under my clothes, mostly for comfort. But that reminds me of what I'm "supposed to be" doing up here, and suddenly, I'm furious.

Am I actually going to practice masturbating? Report to Lorne? Show him my progress?

The thought repulses me.

As does his porn on the laptop—videos of women begging and crawling, slavishly serving the men who handle them so roughly. The thought of Lorne standing over me, looking down at me with that cold, dead stare of his…

Fucking never.

Anger flares again, anger with a delicious, glowing edge that won't die away but instead only spreads, slowly consuming the fear that's been paralyzing me.

I'm never going to come thinking about Lorne.

If I were going to think about anyone while I touched myself… it would be Atlas.

With that one single thought, heat flushes through my body. My hands slide across my breasts under my shirt. My nipples tighten.

Atlas…

That thought spawns countless more, a rush of color and images flooding my brain. His well-shaped hands, his growling voice, his sandpaper laugh swiping down my spine...his intelligence, his self-possession, his kindness to Ivy, to Amy, to me...every stolen fragment of touch, of sight, of sound, all build an image of Atlas that fills my mind, as solid and immovable as the man himself. It's like I can feel him here with me. It's like my hands *are* his hands on my body, bigger, warmer, stronger than mine could ever be.

Heat and pleasure flush down my legs. My skin buzzes, my feet sliding back and forth beneath the sheets. I'm tangled up in the bedding, lost in the rush that comes over me when I think about who I want to think about, when I feel what I want to feel.

I haven't let myself picture this. Not yet, not in detail. The ways I wish he would touch me...how I think it would feel...

I've been holding back out of guilt, out of fear.

But now I've tasted how good it feels to give in, to let Atlas fill my mind, and it's like sliding one leg into a warm bath. I'm dying to sink all the way in.

I slip my hand down the front of my shorts, shocked at the wetness. If Lorne could feel this, he'd know everything.

Fuck Lorne.

I squeeze my thighs together around my hand, applying the pressure that seems so desperately needed in just the right spot. I close my eyes and think of Atlas again. The warmth of his hands... the sternness of his voice...the way it turns smooth as melted butter when he looks at me...the way his eyes cut through me but his words never do...the way I know when he's watching, and it makes me feel safe...

My back arches. Little bolts of pleasure zip across my skin. My hands caress my body, not only between my legs but everywhere, rubbing all over under my clothes the way Atlas would do if he were here right now.

That elusive feeling builds and spreads, not only in a tiny, concentrated point in my belly, but all through my pelvis. It's warm and liquid and melting, and it seems to spread down my legs.

It builds and it builds, and I start to build a rhythm, too, rubbing on my clit softly with two fingers, with so much wetness that there's hardly any friction at all, just a smooth slipperiness that's thin and warm like massage oil, spreading like it's made of pleasure itself.

It's like he's here, right here beside me in the bed. Like I can smell his scent and feel his breath on my skin.

Warm air shivers across my skin…the blankets seem to float and lift…

This room belongs to Atlas. The entire hotel belongs to him. It smells like him subtly, expensive like his cologne, old-world like his suits. He is the Monarch, the Monarch is him, and it's never felt more like he's here and all around me, holding me in his arms…

I'm the closest I've ever been to that thing, that elusive thing, my heart pumping, my hand moving faster and faster but never too much. I close my eyes and imagine I'm down in the darkroom, no lights on at all and definitely no clothes, just Atlas's hands on my body in the darkness.

There's some hollow, scrabbling sound in the adjoining room, odd and sudden. I startle upright in the dark, heart racing, ears straining.

I hear nothing now, but just a moment ago, the noise was real and close. Too heavy to be just a mouse in the walls.

When the sound doesn't reoccur, I spend another four or five minutes stoking my courage. Then I slip out from under the sheets, crack the door, and pass into the main room.

Moonlight streams in through the picture window, gilding the furniture silver. I tidied up hours earlier. The room is so still and silent, so obviously the same as before, that I know I'm alone.

I stand there anyway, waiting. I know I heard something.

But as I wait and listen, I slowly realize…I'm not frightened anymore.

My skin is still flushed, my heart still pounding. But my blood is saturated with all the good chemicals from before, and not even adrenaline can wipe that away.

Instead, I feel a quiet kind of clarity. And with a strange and certain impulse, I walk over to the window and look down.

The rose garden below is bathed in silver, the bare vines spiky and sculptural. The figure that stands in the garden looks like a statue, too, dark and motionless. Taller than any man has a right to be, with that rough, brutal face made achingly beautiful in the moonlight, gazing up at my window.

I raise my hand to Atlas, pressing my palm flat against the glass.

He lifts his hand in return. Then tilts his head sideways, inviting me down.

Flushed with lust and adrenaline, I practically run.

CHAPTER 23
ELENA

I RACE DOWN THE CARPETED STAIRS, NO LONGER WORRIED ABOUT Lorne. If it weren't safe for me to come down, Atlas wouldn't have beckoned.

I make a sharp left at the base of the stairs, not even straining for a glance at the front desk or the lobby, knowing that Atlas is already outside.

I've completely forgotten to put on a coat or shoes. The cold shocks me as I run out into the midnight rose garden, damp leaking through my socks. All I've got on is an old T-shirt and shorts worn thin and pale from years of sleeping.

Then I see Atlas and heat blasts through my blood. I get a rush like no other, and I'm not cold at all anymore, not even a little bit. In fact, I'm warm and throbbing even as my breath makes silver clouds in the air.

I don't stop running when I see him. I don't slow down or play it cool. I sprint down the rows of roses and leap into his arms.

Never in a million years would I chance that maneuver with someone smaller. Atlas scoops me up easily, huge hands around my waist. He lifts me in the air, swooping me up way higher than I expected, terrifying and exhilarating, whirling me around in a sudden vista of stars and only then slowly lowering me to the level of his mouth. I kiss him with my head still spinning.

"I couldn't sleep," he says. "I was worried about you."

"Do you ever sleep?"

"Not much." He smiles slightly. "Not since you've been here."

No smile has ever softened a harder face than his. He looks impossibly stern until, somehow, the parts of him that seemed carved from granite become warm and interested in the subtlest of ways, and my whole body melts.

My skin's burning, my blood's rushing, my heart's pounding, and something deep in my belly is begging *more, more, more...*

"I couldn't sleep either. I was thinking about you." It feels so good to confess it. To say it out loud.

The look on Atlas's face is even better. He hooks his arm around my waist and drags me closer.

"Tell me more..."

I shiver with pleasure.

As I look into Atlas's eyes, I notice something for the very first time. There are bits of green in all that blackness. Flecks of color and light.

I find myself saying something I had no intention of saying. "I was trying to make myself come."

Atlas makes a low, growling sound that thrills me to my toes. "Thinking about me?"

I nod, cheeks flaming.

"But you were *trying,* not succeeding." A smile tugs at his lips. "I wasn't quite enough to get you there."

I almost lose heart. The fact that I can't even make *myself* come is deeply embarrassing to me. The older I get, the worse it is, and the more certain I become that I'm somehow defective. Before I told Lorne, the only person I'd ever confessed it to was Mina. Even with her, I played it off like I didn't care, like it was only a matter of time. But inside I began to worry more and more that there really was something wrong with me.

I thought I'd die of shame if Atlas knew. I thought he'd be less interested.

But in this moment, looking into his eyes, I don't see ridicule and judgment. His tone is teasing, while his eyes radiate warmth and acceptance.

And I realize...

Atlas likes me. He *is* interested. He doesn't know that I'm a virgin, but he knows what I'm like, how I am, how I kiss him, how I touch him...

I've never pretended to be anything I'm not with him, and he liked me the whole time.

So why am I hiding? What am I so afraid of?

"I've never had an orgasm," I tell him. "Never once, in my whole life."

I hold my breath. Watching his face.

Atlas simply nods. "That's completely normal. Of course you never did with Lorne—it's almost impossible for a woman to come if she doesn't feel safe."

Relief rushes through me. My knees go loose, and I almost want to cry. I love this casualness Atlas has with the human body, like nothing can faze him. I guess not much is shocking after med school.

Emboldened, I say, "I haven't slept with Lorne. I haven't slept with anyone."

"Oh." Atlas is mildly surprised now but works to hide it. "Does Lorne know you're a virgin?"

"He loves it," I say, failing to conceal my bitterness.

"I bet he does."

"What about you?" I bite my lip, sneaking a glance at Atlas. "Do you...hate it?"

Atlas laughs in a low, rough way and seizes me in his huge hands. "I don't hate anything about you."

He kisses me, cupping my face, his tongue warm, his stubble deliciously rough. His hands move down my body slowly, deliberately. His huge palms cover entire parts of me: my back, my belly, my breasts, my upper arms. To be touched by him is to be possessed by him, moved, warmed, manipulated in his hands.

He slips a hand beneath my loose T-shirt, caressing my bare breast. His skin against my skin isn't just twice as good; it's a next-level exponent. I groan and kiss him, gripping handfuls of his hair, the taste of his mouth driving me wild.

The heat low in my belly is throbbing and insistent, an urge like hunger, like thirst, to rub, to squeeze, to do something, anything, to find relief.

I press against Atlas, kissing him deeper, wilder, my hands roaming the thick muscle of his arms, feeling how it flexes under my hands, harder and denser than any part of my body but bone. He's not wearing a coat either, only a dress shirt. I fumble with the buttons, then tear his shirt open, greedy for my hands on his bare skin.

I can barely reach all the way around him. The skin on his back is thick and soft like worn-in leather, and his chest radiates heat. I press my lips against it, and it's like the steady heat of a stove, not feverish or sweaty but deeply, endlessly warm.

He tilts my face up in his huge hands, looking down at me. He slides his hands up under my hair and kisses me until my legs seem to disappear.

I press my body against him, his thick thigh sliding between mine. The pressure and heat makes me moan, and my mouth feels especially wet. I press against him instinctively, convulsively.

"Put your hand in your shorts," Atlas growls in my ear. "Touch yourself."

I make just enough space between us to slide my hand down the waistband of my shorts. When I touch my pussy, it's soaked and slippery.

"Feed it to me…"

I lift my hand to his lips. His mouth closes around my fingers, sudden, shocking, and hot. His tongue rasps; his stubble scratches me.

"Mmm…give me more."

I touch myself again, and now I'm soft and aching and so wet that my fingers glisten as I raise them to Atlas's lips.

He closes them in his mouth, licking them clean, sucking my wetness off my fingertips. Then he lifts my shirt, ducks his head, and takes my nipple into his mouth. He sucks it into a point, then pinches it between his fingers, using the wetness to pull and squeeze.

I cry out too loudly. Atlas puts a hand over my mouth, dragging me back against the vine-covered stone wall, out of sight of the hotel windows. Then he covers my lips with his instead, kissing me deeply. He takes both my breasts in his hands, dragging his thumbs across my nipples, catching them, playing, teasing, driving me to a frenzy, smothering my cries with his tongue in my mouth.

I grind against Atlas, touching myself, hand sliding frantically between my thighs. That feeling is building; it's the closest it's ever been…a fever, a frenzy that surely has to break…

"Please," I groan in frustration, touching, rubbing myself.

Atlas slips his hand down my shorts, completely covering mine. His hand is paw-like and heavy. My body is butter, and his heat makes me melt. My hand slides away, and his takes its place. His big, thick fingers sink into my flesh in the most delicious of ways as he begins to rub slow circles around and around…

I start to come. There's no tipping over, no slide down a hill like a sled. It's more like a bomb that explodes not once but three, then four, then five separate times, the blasts rocketing outward in concentric rings.

Pleasure flows from my belly down my limbs, all the way up my spine to the base of my brain. I close my eyes and press my face against Atlas's arm, clinging to him, breathing in the scent of his skin. I think of his face, and the way his scowl softens, and those green flecks in his eyes, and the delicious friction of his fingers…and my mind explodes into ten thousand stars.

And when it's all over and I'm taking deep breaths, still drunk and swaying on the chemicals flushing my body, Atlas keeps his hand cupped on my pussy, warm and dissolving, his other hand stroking my back.

"See?" he says, in that deep, soothing voice. "You can do it if you just relax."

I cling to his arm, swaying like a drunken sailor. Whatever I thought I would say turns to helpless giggles instead. I'm half-hysterical on the glee of what I just felt. And the relief that I finally know what it's like.

I snort, "You should add that onto your spa services."

Atlas's hands tighten on my body. With a wicked chuckle, he says in my ear, "I'll put it on your tab."

CHAPTER 24
ATLAS

ELENA'S SHIVERING.

"Come inside," I say, wrapping my arm around her and drawing her toward the door.

But she hesitates, looking nervously up toward the bank of dark windows.

"His room is on the other side," I remind her.

"I know," Elena says, but her voice is tight and nervous anyway.

I hate that she's afraid to be seen with me. I hate that she's afraid at all.

She shouldn't belong to him. It's wrong. *He's* wrong for her.

As we enter the hotel, Elena grows stiffer and tighter, her shoulders hunching, her eyes widening as she startles at every creak and groan of the ancient walls.

"Lorne's up in his room," I tell her. "He went up after dinner."

"What if he came down, though?" Elena whispers. "While we were in the garden?"

It's one o'clock in the morning. The hotel is silent, the lights dimmed. There's no one around. But Elena's only growing more frightened.

"I should go to bed," she says. "It's late."

"Stay with me."

"I can't."

"Tomorrow, then." I won't let go of her hand until I know when I can see her again. Not in passing, in the lobby, at the restaurant…I need to know when we'll be alone together. When I can touch her again.

Elena hesitates at the foot of the stairs, biting at her lips. She's tense with anxiety, but she clings to my hand just as much as I'm holding on to her.

"All right then," she says, color rushing into her cheeks. "Tomorrow night. In the darkroom."

She throws her arms around my neck and kisses me again, there in the open where anyone could see, if anyone else were awake. But the only witness is the slowly ticking grandfather clock.

When she lets go of me, she gazes up at me with those wild blue eyes, clear as a winter's sky.

"Thank you, Atlas," she murmurs and kisses me once more, softly. "For…you know."

"Anytime," I say.

And I absolutely mean it.

———————

Once Elena is back up in her room, I still can't sleep.

The fear on her face concerned me more than the ugliest expressions I've caught from Lorne. I suspected that the author had a dark side. But Elena is the one engaged to him. She's experienced that dark side leaking out. And whether she'll admit it to herself or not, Elena knows even better than I do what kind of person her fiancé really is.

She looks like a hunted creature.

The problem is…she's already fallen into his trap. She's already captured.

It's up to me to set her free.

Which means I've got to figure out exactly what kind of trap this is. And what breed of hunter I'm dealing with.

I've started reading Lorne's books, picked up this morning at the Books 'n' Brews six doors down. An entire table was covered in tall, shiny stacks, probably five times more books than any other author in the store.

Which seemed impressive, at first.

But then I thought, *No, that's strange. That's a huge pile of books.*

I asked the clerk, "Do you sell many of these?"

"Not really." He made a snorting sound. "I mean, some. But not as many as he brings in every week."

Interesting.

I scooped up all seven titles. "I'll help you out."

It seemed to confirm something I'd heard before. Only a rumor, but from a friend with no reason to lie. No reason I knew about, anyway. You can never be entirely certain what hides inside a human heart…or their history.

Take Lorne, for instance. He's lived in Grimstone almost all his life. But he did leave for eleven years. When he came back, he had a young daughter. And he'd become a wildly successful author, apparently, with enough money to immediately start construction on the most grandiose private property Grimstone has ever known.

Grimstone has its share of hidden jewels, tucked away deep in its hills. Places few people have seen besides their owners. My parents' house used to be exactly that sort of place.

But Lorne's property would outshine them all. Or so it seemed at first.

He kept changing contractors and firing architects. My brother's friend Tom Turner was one of those contractors. He told me the plans made no sense and the orders were bizarre.

I find that interesting, too.

Three pieces of information that all seem to indicate the same thing.

One means nothing. Two could be coincidence. But three… three is a pattern.

And then there are Lorne's books. I've already skimmed the first two. They're simple, easy to read, with a clever twist at the end. But I've noticed another pattern.

I know it's fiction. And in fiction, it's foolish to assume that an author is promoting their own views or inserting their own personality. But I can't help hearing Lorne Ronson's voice on every page, oozing out of his characters. The good ones, the bad ones, and especially the very, very bad ones.

And maybe that wouldn't be so terrible…except for the fact that Lorne Ronson writes very dark books. And very dark things happen to his heroines. Sometimes they don't survive.

So far, the odds seem to be about fifty-fifty. Whether the heroine lives or dies doesn't seem to matter much to the author—the tone of the ending is much the same either way. All that matters is what happens to his hero.

I keep trying to figure out what happened to Lorne's wife. There's not a lot of information online. But what I found is suspicious.

Carbon Monoxide Leak in Clark County Kills Wife of Local Author. 8-Year-Old Daughter Spared.

I don't want to jump to conclusions. After all, I've got a brother whose first wife died in a suspicious way, and I'm ninety-eight percent sure he didn't kill her even though ninety-eight percent of people around here think he did.

So I'd like to give Lorne the benefit of the doubt.

But Ivy's nine years old right now. And that article is from December of last year. Which means that Lorne's wife has been dead less than a year, and he's already got a ring on Elena's finger. And a wedding date that he's rushing as fast as he can.

What's the hurry, exactly?

I don't think the reason is the same for Lorne as it is for Elena.

I toss and turn on the huge bed in my cave of a room, the heavy fur blankets already kicked onto the floor. It's usually as cold as a refrigerator in here, in this suspended stone slab that hangs out over the ocean, which is exactly how I like it. But tonight, it's stuffy even in here.

Amy took over an hour ago. I'm supposed to be sleeping. But I can't.

Something's wrong. I can feel it.

Something's wrong with Lorne. And his fucked-up castle. I need to drive out there again to see it.

My phone buzzes next to the bed. I snatch it up, heart leaping when I see an unfamiliar number.

Elena's voice comes through the line, tight and terrified.

"Atlas…there's someone in my room!"

CHAPTER 25
ATLAS

I've never made it up to the sixth floor faster. I unlock Elena's door and barrel inside, into the chaos of a sitting room that's been completely destroyed, books thrown around, cushions slashed, feathers everywhere. And written on the wall in streaky red letters, the words *GET OUT! GET OUT! GET OUT! GET OUT! GET OUT!*

"Atlas, is that you?" Elena calls from the bedroom.

"Come unlock the door."

She scrabbles with the lock, then hurries out of the bedroom, wide-eyed and pale. "I heard them in the other room! At first, they were quiet, but I wasn't asleep. I could hear rustling. I could have unlocked the door, maybe seen who it was, but then they started smashing things, and I—"

"You did the right thing calling me."

"How did they break in?"

"I don't know. The door was still locked."

"But I thought no one else had a key!" Her voice rises hysterically.

I put my arms around Elena and pull her against my chest, stroking my palm slowly down her hair, down her back, down her hair, down her back, until she calms.

That's what concerns me, too…the curious case of the locked door. Because I'm the only other person who has the new key. Even the maids have to borrow it from me, then bring it back again.

"Oh god!" Elena stiffens in my arms. "My camera!"

She rushes over to the table, feathers whirling from the slashed cushions. My stomach churns. The lamps are tipped over, paintings pulled off the walls, pages torn out of the books. If someone were here to fuck with Elena, the very first thing they'd do is smash her beloved camera.

But when she lifts it off the table and turns it over in her hands, her voice loosens with relief. "I think…it's okay."

That's…unexpected.

In fact, it might just change my mind about what's going on here…but I'm not sure yet.

"I don't understand." Elena stares miserably at the new mess on her walls, the words wilder and messier than ever, jumbled, streaky, almost delirious. "Who's doing this?"

It almost looks like—

"You won't leave me, will you, Atlas?" she begs, turning tear-filled eyes up to me.

Not a fucking chance.

"You couldn't get me out of here with a wrecking ball."

Elena throws her arms around my waist and buries her face in my chest. "Thank you. I was freaking out, I'm sorry."

"Understandable."

She laughs a little, looking up at me again. "You always say that."

"Because it is—of course you were afraid when someone broke into your room in the middle of the night. Anyone would be. We're all the same—we get scared, we freak out, we make and break promises. We fuck around, we avoid work, we cheat on our diets. We're humans. And it's a bit better than a chimp but not much."

Now Elena laughs the hardest I've heard, rich and throaty. "Just when I was about to say, 'he's so empathetic.'"

I shrug. "Empathy is understanding even the ugly things. And there are a lot of ugly things."

"But a lot of beautiful things, too." Elena is looking up at me as she says it. Looking right at a face that I don't think anybody's ever called *beautiful* before. But if you looked at *her* face, you'd think she was gazing at a piece of art.

It's dangerous when looking into someone's eyes makes you feel smarter and stronger and more beautiful. When their mirror makes a hero of you.

Because then you might want to live up to it.

You might do all sorts of wild things so that image of you in their eyes never fades, never tarnishes.

But here's the problem…I already looked. I saw myself as she sees me. And now it's burned in my mind.

I sit down on the couch and pull Elena onto my lap. It's nearly three o'clock in the morning, and she's obviously exhausted, swaying on her feet, dark circles under her eyes.

She curls up with her toes tucked under a slashed cushion, her head in my lap.

I stroke her hair gently until her body grows heavy and warm and her breathing slows. All the while I'm staring at the closed, locked door.

CHAPTER 26
ELENA

WHEN I WAKE UP, I'M BACK IN MY BED, TUCKED IN SO NICELY THAT I know Atlas must have done it. My curtains are open, but the light streaming in is watery gray, the sky an uneasy sea of clouds, the ocean beneath dark and churning.

I slip out from under the covers and stand at the window, looking down into the walled garden. It's empty, no Atlas and no Ivy, only the bare, thorny bushes, every last bruised petal now blown away.

I shower and dress quickly, wanting to check in on Ivy. She looked terrible last night. But when I get to her room, Lorne is inside. He's sitting on the couch, almost as if he's waiting for me.

"Where's Ivy?" I say, looking at her empty seat next to the window.

"She's in bed."

I start walking toward her door, but Lorne stands up from the couch and cuts in front of me, blocking the way.

"She's sleeping."

I glance from Lorne's cold, stern face to Mrs. Cross's. Her barely concealed glee gives the whole game away—Lorne is punishing me by not letting me see Ivy.

"When should I come back?" I ask tentatively. "I'm supposed to help make her costume."

"I'm making it," Mrs. Cross says, not bothering to hide her satisfaction in the slightest.

"She wanted to be an owl—"

"She's going to be a princess."

Ivy and I made careful plans earlier in the week. She drew the costume in her notebook, and I promised to help her source the feathers. She's been highly interested in the Halloween decorations going up all along Main Street. I made Lorne promise that she could come with us to the Reaper's Revenge.

But now that's all turned on its head, and there's nothing I can do about it.

Mrs. Cross knows it. It's why she's smiling like that, smug and gloating.

Lorne knows it. That's why he's watching so closely to see what I'll do.

I make one last, pathetic attempt. "What about the work on the house? Shouldn't Mrs. Cross be there?"

"The work is as good as finished." Lorne is still watching my face. "We can move in right after Halloween."

"Amazing." I hope my smile looks more convincing than it feels.

Inside, I'm silently panicking.

Halloween is less than a week away.

Lorne glances at Mrs. Cross. She takes the hint and gives the little bob of her head that's practically a curtsey, saying, "I'll tidy up before you start writing." She slips through the door connecting Lorne's suite to Ivy's, closing it behind her, leaving me alone with Lorne.

My stomach sinks like a stone. I try to edge toward the exit without being too obvious. But it is obvious to Lorne and it makes him smile. He grabs my wrist and pulls me close, taking my chin in his other hand, tilting up my face to look at him.

"What's your rush?"

"I…I don't want to make you late starting work."

"How considerate." His blue eyes search mine, cold and searing, until I feel utterly exposed. "What about last night…were you successful?"

Sensations flood my brain, Atlas's huge hand down the front of my shorts, his dark eyes looking into mine, the warm, wet flush that flooded through my body like a spring melt after a hundred years of winter…

"I, uh…I think I'm getting close."

My cheeks burn and my heart pounds. Lorne's eyes narrow as he studies my face.

Whatever he sees, a slow smile spreads. "I can't wait for you to show me."

He releases my wrist.

I could almost sob with relief.

Especially once I'm out of the room, practically fleeing down the hallway.

I walk down to the restaurant alone, no Ivy with me, wishing I could have checked for myself to make sure she was okay. I don't believe she was sleeping.

How long is Lorne planning to punish me? Until I prove I can have an orgasm?

The thought makes me enraged.

And moving in with him *next week*?

Yeah, I can't think about that at all.

Marrying Lorne and moving into his castle was becoming conveniently hazy in my head—a future problem that future me would have to deal with.

Now it's crushingly close.

It's October 27. Something else my brain had subtly stopped keeping track of. It's so easy to let the gray, gloomy days bleed together in Grimstone. Halloween is on Friday, four days away.

Lorne might expect me to move into his house as soon as Saturday. And get married…right away.

My heart is squeezing, jerking in my chest like a fish out of water. My skin is cold and clammy.

Am I actually going to marry Lorne?

"Table for one?" the hostess says in a slightly sassy way. This is Sienna, who was dumped by her boyfriend my first morning in Grimstone and who likes to stand by the silverware gossiping with Olivia. They're friends with each other but not with Ralph the bartender, who hates his lederhosen.

"Table for one," I confirm, trying to make it sound bold instead of pathetic.

I'm looking for Atlas, and I keep looking way too long after it should be obvious he's not here. I try to hide my disappointment, but Sienna smirks and says, "He hasn't come up yet."

"Who?" I act innocent.

Sienna snorts, tossing my menu down on a table. "You know who."

I sit down, blushing furiously. Only to lock eyes with Ralph, who winks at me.

I cannot imagine what color my face is now.

"Got your cappuccino, Amy!" Ralph cries, swooping a cappuccino from out of nowhere in front of an extremely startled Amy.

"Whoa JESUS!" She has to take it or wear it.

Ralph is always doing favors for Amy, usually unasked. I think this indicates a crush but one that does not seem to be reciprocated.

"Thanks." Amy dumps the cappuccino directly into a plant.

Ralph looks heartbroken.

Amy looks supremely chic. No apron today, she's in a smart black suit.

I ask, "Are you staging a coup?"

She winks at me. "You just keep Atlas distracted."

I pull her down into my booth, hushing her. "*Does the whole goddamned staff here think I have a thing for Atlas?*"

"No," Amy says, smiling and gently extricating my hands before I wrinkle her suit. "They know that *he* has a thing for *you*."

My blood chills. That means Olivia knows, and there's a very good chance she'll tell Lorne—if Atlas lets her have five minutes alone with him.

"Why do they think that?" I'm wondering how much I can backtrack.

Amy gives me a look that says I can backtrack about zero point zero meters. "Because it's completely obvious. He's acting insane. By which I mean he's stopped acting insane in all the ways he used to and has begun acting insane in entirely new ways."

"I have to know what that means."

Amy lists her boss's sins on her fingers: "He used to work twenty-four seven, never sleeping, constantly roaming the halls, popping out where you least expected him, sticking his nose into everything. Running this place…" She raises her hands in a gesture like an orchestra conductor and says, in a remarkably accurate impression of Atlas, "Like a well-oiled machine."

I am very curious to know if Atlas is aware how well his assistant can imitate him.

"And now?" I ask because I'm shameless. If I have the power to knock that boulder one inch off its path, I have to know it.

Amy's eyes glint. She's unashamedly gleeful. "He's a goddamned mess. Still never sleeps, but now he's never working, pays attention to nothing, and follows you around."

I laugh. "You're exaggerating."

"I wish I were. He's been on a rampage about someone break-ing into your room, *again*, despite all his draconian rules about your keys. He told me to send up a new locksmith and put on an extra bolt this time, plus new locks on the windows."

"I don't think anyone came in through the window." I remind her, "I'm on the sixth floor."

Amy shrugs. "I'm just telling you what Atlas said."

"He's lucky to have you."

"Damn straight." Amy lifts her chin proudly. "I'm taking over before he sleepwalks into traffic or his business crumbles. Plus, I've got to get the hell out of the Onyx. You think the guests are weird here, you can't even imagine the types they get there."

"I'm a guest here," I remind her.

She grins at me, unrepentant. "If the shoe fits…"

I realize now that we've truly become friends. Amy can tease me, and I can know that it's said with love.

And finally, I can ask her, "What's the deal with Ralph? You don't like him?"

Ralph is blond and dimpled and has a body under that lederhosen that looks made to hew timber. Also, his cappuccinos are heavenly. I was shocked when Amy dumped hers into the ficus.

But Amy's face darkens until she no longer looks mischievous and laughing and begins to look like a dangerous woman. "Oh, I did like him. A long time ago."

The "not anymore" and the reasons why remain unspoken as Amy takes a moody sip of my cappuccino. I knew she'd regret throwing away hers.

Apparently her thoughts are not on Ralph at all because when she speaks, she says, "You know, I was just a maid last year. I mean, I'm still a maid at the Onyx. But not here."

I smile. "Atlas knows talent when he sees it."

Amy laughs. "He knows a good deal—it's not hard to beat what the Onyx pays me."

"He trusts you. He already told me he's going to hire you on full-time."

"Really?" Her eyes light up.

"Yeah. But don't tell him I told you—he says he wants to see what else you come up with in the filing systems while you're still trying to impress him."

"Oh, don't you fucking worry!" Amy is gleefully profane. "I've got filing systems that'll blast his fucking brain!"

"You've got Atlas right where you want him," I assure her.

"That's right." She lifts my cup again, sipping slowly. Her eyes fix on Ralph across the room, and that fixed fury burns in them again. "And that's why I'm not going to kill Ralph."

I've heard a lot of people joke about killing their ex. This is the first time I felt like that ex got lucky.

"Right," I say carefully.

Amy glances at me sideways, raising an eyebrow. "He'll be fine. We're never dating again, so he can't cheat on me twice."

I snort into laughter, and Amy laughs, too, so wickedly that I really can't decide how safe Ralph might be.

But I've got other things to worry about—somebody who needs me more.

"Amy, what rights does a fiancée have?"

Amy tilts her head, eyes as bright as a raven's. "What do you mean?"

"I was just wondering…" I pick at my paper napkin, tearing it to shreds. Trying to figure out how to say this. "I'm worried about Ivy. And I wondered if…I have any say in what happens to her. Since I'm engaged to Lorne."

Amy's face fills with sympathy. "You really bonded with her, huh?"

It didn't happen how I imagined it would. I thought it would be me, Lorne, and Ivy as a trio, making popcorn, watching movies together, laughing and joking.

There are not a lot of jokes with Ivy, at least not verbal ones, and not a ton of laughing, though she can be silly and playful when the mood strikes her. And we hardly spend time with Lorne at all.

But Amy's right—the bond I hoped to build with her is there all the same. And it's purer and stronger and more fulfilling than I could have imagined.

What I pictured was shallow and generic because I didn't actually know Ivy yet. I didn't know what was fascinating and charming and heartbreaking about her as her own little person.

And I didn't know how easy it is to get invested in kids, their triumphs and failures, fears and elations. Ivy kept trying to sketch the rabbits in the garden, but they'd always dash away. When she finally crept up on a cottontail and completed her sketch, she ran to show me, her face euphoric. And I felt just as euphoric.

Powerful little emotions can brighten or darken a day in an instant, and Ivy's affect me all the more because they're so overwhelming to her. I feel the need to take care of her because she needs it more than most.

And if I'm honest with myself...I don't like how Lorne treats her. I thought he was this great dad because that's what *he* told me. But when I had the chance to see for myself, it was yet another instance of his words and reality not lining up.

"She's a good kid," I tell Amy. "What they say about her isn't true."

"Who?"

"Lorne and Mrs. Cross. They think she's badly behaved, but she isn't at all. She just gets upset because Mrs. Cross is constantly messing with her. Making her wear these itchy clothes she hates and go to all these places she doesn't want to go, picking at her and criticizing her..."

I trail off because I just realized two things.

First, everything Mrs. Cross does, she does on Lorne's orders.

And second, everything I just listed is exactly what Lorne does to me.

"I...I'm just worried about her," I repeat, confused and uneasy. "So I wondered, legally speaking...do I have any say?"

Now Amy looks both sad and sympathetic, and my heart sinks. "No, honey. I'm sorry. He's her dad."

"And a fiancée...doesn't really mean anything."

"Not really. After you're married, if you adopt her, then she's your daughter. But at this moment…you might as well be a stranger."

"But what if he doesn't take care of her?" I think of Ivy up in her room, banished to her bed, mouth swollen. I don't trust them to get her something she can actually eat. If they bother to order food for her at all.

Amy's face slackens, and her eyes get a slightly hollow look. "It's got to be pretty bad for them to do anything about it."

"How bad?"

Her mouth tightens, the corners turning down. "My mom was a mess for a while. She did some pretty fucked-up things. Bad enough that some people reported it—but never bad enough for anybody to do anything about it." She shrugs in a jerky kind of way. "That was a long time ago, though. I don't know what the new sheriff's like."

"I'm so sorry."

She shrugs again, almost like a reflex, like that's her way of brushing aside the whole thing. "Just trying to be realistic with you. Like I said, a couple of people tried to help me and my brother, Aldous—a teacher at our school, for one. But parents have a lot of rights."

I give up on the napkin and do what I actually want to do, which is bite the edge of my thumbnail. Except, I've been doing that so often lately, there's no thumbnail left and not a lot of cuticle, either.

"What about if they're not actually homeschooling her?" I've never seen Ivy doing schoolwork. Just errands and art and a whole lot of window-gazing.

"Pretty flimsy," Amy says with brutal honesty.

I sigh. I'm glad she told me the truth. It's what I guessed, anyway. I can't do anything if Lorne assigns Mrs. Cross to babysitting duty purely out of spite or even lets her ruin Ivy's Halloween costume. Being an asshole isn't a crime.

CHAPTER 27
ELENA

I STEP OUT INTO THE WINDIEST DAY I'VE SEEN IN GRIMSTONE YET. Wet leaves whip down the street, slapping against my legs like runaway starfish. Sudden gusts whirl my hair around my head in a blinding tornado.

I hold tight to my camera with both hands, glad for the extra security of the strap around my neck. I'm infinitely relieved that my most prized possession escaped unharmed, and I'm sure as hell not going to drop it the very next day.

The clouds overhead are dark, billowing mountains of smoke. I lift my camera and snap an image. But then I consider the better vantage point of the beach, and I know I need to brave the wind and climb down.

The winding wooden staircases set into the rock, the only way down to the beach from Grimstone's Main Street, are a primary reason for tourists to pick the shiny new Onyx resort, which is located directly on the sand on the north end of the bay.

Grimstone, however, tends to attract thrill seekers. Atlas has no problem stuffing his hotel with people happy to make the climb down to the ink-dark sand. Even during what he tells me has been an exceptionally cold and wet October.

I cross Main Street, busier than ever with tourists crowding the town for the Reaper's Revenge. A clutch of college-age girls spill out of Books 'n'Brews, clutching coffee and cocoa and a copy of Lorne's book—the one with the staring eye—tucked under the last girl's arm.

It looks exactly like Lorne's eye peeking at me. My heart gives a sickening squeeze. I feel horribly exposed even though I'm not doing anything wrong. Not doing anything at all at the moment besides walking in the wind. But I'm scared and guilty, staring around.

I can't stand the anxiety. I wasn't made for sneaking around. And I've been sneaking for a while now...since way before I came to Grimstone.

I finger my phone in my pocket. I've been texting Mina, trying to get updates without being too obvious.

What's going on with the bookshop?
Any news?

The pressure's rising. Anytime now, I'll hear something... Will it be Mina who calls me? Will anybody call?

Someone will call...

No, maybe not. I might have gotten away.

I bite the edge of my thumb so hard I taste blood, bright and coppery in my mouth. I feel panicked, hunted, and I think suddenly of Atlas and want to call him on the phone, as if I'm in my room and can summon him to take care of my problem.

But I'm not in my room. And Atlas can't fix this for me.

So I climb down the splintering staircase to the beach. The sand is flat and black as an oil spill, the waves washing the shore slate gray with shocking bursts of white foam.

I'm dressed head to toe in clothes that Atlas bought for me, and that's the only reason I can stand the icy wind. Leather gloves and a leather bomber, a thick scarf, and flat boots, the kind you could walk around in for hours—just the right thing for the wet and insistent cold.

The clothes are as warm as Atlas's arms around me, and I'm thinking about him in a tangible way as I walk down the spongy sand.

Most people walk north along the black sand half-moon that terminates at the Onyx.

I've gone the opposite direction, though it involves climbing over piles of slippery black rock, because I want the cliffs under the town of Grimstone as my backdrop.

The sheer black walls tower overhead, the long strip of Main Street visible only in terms of rooftops. The roof of the Monarch rises highest of all, its Gothic spires and chimneys silhouetted against the sky.

The ocean sucks in and out of hidden holes in the cliffs. The wind makes a whispering sound, crying like a child, moaning like a lover, making the hair raise on the back of my neck.

Nobody has walked out as far as me onto these rocks. I can't help thinking of rogue waves that reach up like hands out of the sea and snatch people. But the boots Atlas bought me have excellent grip, and this photograph is going to look so fucking cool.

I'm directly beneath the Monarch now, gazing up at the brick wall that surrounds the back garden and, above that, the many black stone gargoyles on the cornices, snarling against the cloud-filled sky.

I lift my camera and take photographs until I've exhausted an entire roll of film. Then I slowly lower the lens.

As my eyes drag down the cliffs, I see something that almost seems to be an optical illusion: a completely naked Atlas standing inside a cube of glass.

This cube is embedded in the cliffs about thirty feet over my head. Atlas, nude from head to toe and bathed in silvery light, looks like the statue of Hercules.

He stretches, thick arms lifted overhead, his stomach tightening, the muscles of his thighs bulging. My eyes are drawn to something else, ah, *bulging* in a nearby area. My insides slowly liquify. *Nichoho sobi…*

I think Atlas just woke up. His cock hangs swollen and heavy, his whole body flushed, his hair messy, his stubble on its way to a beard. He yawns and runs a hand down his chest, his eyes moving down from horizon to shore.

And that's when he sees me standing there. Staring at him. Holding a camera.

"Oh shit," I say out loud.

Atlas's hand freezes, and he tilts his head, eyes narrowing slightly.

"It's not what you think!" I shout up, even though there's no way he can hear me over the wind. "I wasn't taking pictures! I mean, I was taking pictures, but…"

A distant elderly couple struggling up the beach lift their heads to stare at me. *They* heard me. But I don't think Atlas can. Not behind that glass.

Atlas holds up one finger and steps out of frame. It's only now that I'm realizing I'm looking up at what must be his bedroom, built in an underground part of the hotel, directly in the cliffside.

Atlas returns, a towel wrapped around his waist and his phone in his hand. My phone buzzes in my pocket.

You little pervert.

I look up at him, shrug, wheel around, and pretend to walk into the sea.

When I turn back again, I can see Atlas silently laughing. I mean, it's silent to me. I'm assuming he's making noise up there in his glass box.

My phone buzzes with:

Are you coming up here or am I coming down there?

I check the time—six whole hours until dinner. Assuming Lorne is even on time.

And after all…why put off until tonight what you can do right this moment?

I send:

Meet me in the darkroom.

CHAPTER 28
ATLAS

I COULDN'T BELIEVE MY EYES WHEN I SAW ELENA STANDING BELOW my window, the exact mirror of our positions last night when I stood beneath *her* window. Only, I have no idea how she found mine. Not even Amy's seen my bedroom.

Elena's hair looked redder than ever against the black sand and her leather coat, color whipped into her cheeks. That's how I knew she wasn't a ghost, because she'd never looked more alive—no matter how impossible it seemed for her to be standing there.

I shower quickly and still beat her to the darkroom. When she comes in, her skin is cold and salty and smells fresh as rain. Dew droplets soak her hair. She's damper than I am until she strips off her coat. Then she slips into my arms in a thin jersey top, warm and completely dry on her torso.

"How did you know where my room was?" I demand because the mystery's driving me crazy.

Elena laughs, equally delighted. "I just looked up, and there you were! I climbed over the rocks to take a picture of the back of the hotel. Do you always just stand naked at the window? Doesn't anybody walk there?"

"Barely ever. And they never look up."

"I did," she says with a delicious thrill, standing up on tiptoe to kiss me with her arms around my neck. Her mouth is hungry, warmer even than her body. She tastes of coffee and sea salt and her own sweetness.

I run my hands all over her body beneath her shirt, lifting and caressing her full, warm breasts. She's not wearing a bra, and I love the way my hands glide across her skin.

"Close the door," Elena murmurs.

I lean over to pull the door tightly shut, sealing us in the window-less chamber deep beneath the hotel. We can be as loud as we want, and no one will hear us.

Elena's body tightens and her breathing quickens when I close the door, but the surge of adrenaline only seems to fuel her. She throws herself into my arms, kissing me wildly. I kiss her and kiss her in the dim red light, my heartbeat pounding in my ears.

Each thud of my heart is a clock ticking down the seconds I have left with her. Every hour is stolen—she always meets the author for dinner.

How do I get her away from him?

I touch the body that should only be touched by me, that should *never* be touched by him. I hate that he found her first. I hate that he put his ring on her finger.

"Take that off," I say to Elena, eyes fixed on that hideous, glittering rock.

She touches the ring with her right hand but hesitates. It means something to take it off. We both know this.

She looks into my eyes and slips the ring from her finger, setting it down on a nearby shelf.

There's no speaking after that—just my lips on hers and my hands drawing gasps and moans out of her body.

I lift Elena onto the worktable, her thighs parted so I can stand between them, my hands cupping her face. She lifts her lips, her tongue slipping out to meet mine. She tastes like honeysuckle, like dew, like fresh morning air. In the underground darkroom, Elena blooms like a flower, fresh and alive.

"My whole body's been throbbing all day," she murmurs, her hands stroking through my hair. "What we did last night…it's like a flood that's still washing through me."

"It's good for you. Orgasms are healthy. They help with blood flow, heart health, reduce depression…"

Elena laughs softly, bringing kisses light as butterflies to my forehead, cheeks, chin, and mouth. "I was *way* less depressed afterward."

I cup the side of her face with my palm, looking into her eyes. "Are you depressed?"

She looks right back at me, her eyes clear and unblinking. "No. But I'm stressed. Can you help me, Atlas?"

She scratches her nails against my scalp, gazing up at me. Asking me for exactly what she wants with those arctic-fox eyes.

"You know I'll always take care of you." I take her left boot in my hand and begin to unlace it. Elena watches me closely, her eyes on my face. "Do you know that's true, Elena?"

"You will?" she says softly.

"Yes. I will." I pull off the boot and strip off her sock, taking her bare foot in my hand. It's warm and clean and soft. I press my thumb into the arch of her foot, making her groan. "You can trust me, Elena. I won't hurt you. And I won't let anyone else hurt you."

I massage the arch of her foot with both thumbs, then the ball of her foot, and even her toes. Elena slumps back onto her elbows on the worktable as the deep pressure in her foot unlocks the tension in the rest of her body. I set her left foot gently down and pick up the right, slowly unlacing her boot.

"I like taking care of you," I admit to her. "I like seeing you safe and happy." I take off her sock and massage her right foot. I can fit her whole foot easily between my hands. I can rub long, slow strokes that make her eyes roll back.

"*O bozhe…*" Elena groans, her eyes glazed with pleasure. "*Do* you work at the spa? I'm starting to wonder…"

"You're going to have quite the bill at the end of the week." I scoop her up, setting her on her bare feet only long enough to unbutton her jeans and slip them down. Then I lift her back onto the table, pulling away her jeans and her underwear.

It's impossible to tell if Elena's blushing in the scarlet light, but she goes still and quiet, her thighs pressing against the outsides of my hips. I drop to my knees in front of her, hands on her inner thighs, her exquisite pussy spread open in front of my face.

But then I stop. Because even in the red light, I can see marks on her inner thigh. Clusters of bruises, dark and shaped like fingerprints.

The rage I feel is a flaming furnace, turned instantly from zero to inferno.

"Did he do this?"

Elena stiffens. She's staring at my face, shrinking away, and that's what makes me realize how awful I must look. And how awful I sound.

When I'm with her, I forget that I'm scary to everyone else— even Amy sometimes. But never, I hope, to Elena.

"I'm sorry," I say in my gentlest voice, massaging her thighs with my palms, loosening the tension. "I'm not angry at you." But then I lift my head and look into her eyes. "But if he does that to you again, I'll fucking kill him."

"Don't say that," Elena whispers.

"Why not?"

"Because I don't want anyone to get hurt."

"I'm afraid that's exactly where we're headed. Because I'm telling you, Elena, I won't let him hurt *you*."

She can't even pretend that he won't. Because there it is on her thigh, the evidence that he already did.

"Leave him." I should have said it before, a hundred times.

Elena shakes her head, biting her lip, looking away. "It's not that simple."

That's what *she* said before, many times, in many ways. She's trying to tell me there's another piece, something I don't understand. But she won't come out and say it.

Fear makes us want to run and hide.

I see it in her dilated pupils, the tension in her muscles, the pallor of her skin. Elena's running on a level of anxiety that won't let her think straight.

In the Victorian era, doctors invented vibrators to help their female patients unwind. It was a popular therapy because it does actually work.

I look up at Elena, leaning my head against her inner thigh.

"Fine. You're right, it's impossible; it could never ever work."

Her mouth quirks slightly as she shakes her head. "Don't make fun of me."

"Oh, I'm not." I spread my fingers, palms covering her inner thighs. I gently press her knees outward, breathing in the warmth of her skin. "I just can't fight with you. Not when you're not wearing any pants."

I lean forward and press my face into her cunt and inhale her sweet, sweet scent. Elena gasps, thighs tightening around my ears, hands thrusting into my hair.

"You smell incredible," I tell her. "So I give up. Just tell me what I have to do to taste you."

Elena bites her lip. Her smile slips out anyway, wicked and white. She seizes a handful of my hair and pulls my face toward her.

I nuzzle my nose against pussy lips, softer than rose petals, and slip my tongue up her soaking-wet slit. Her taste is like her mouth, like her breath, like her sweat, like her skin, a chemical combination that only becomes more intoxicating as it slowly sinks in.

Elena gasps and shivers as my tongue glides across her skin, crying out when I find the nub of her clit. I lap it with my tongue, slow strokes, then circles, and then back to strokes. I read the shudders of her body with my hands, the way she bucks her hips and clenches her thighs around my ears, finding what she likes best, teasing her with it, pulling back, and building up all over again…

I draw it out much longer than the night before, building the waves in sets, taking her all the way to the edge again and again. Her scent is feral, her thighs sweating, her pussy swollen and sensitive in all the right ways. When I slide one single finger inside her, her puffy, warm flesh grips me and she lets out a long, dragging groan. Her back arches, and her nails dig into my scalp.

Latching my mouth gently on her clit, I hold her by the waist, sucking and flicking lightly with my tongue. Elena gasps and squirms, the stimulation almost too much to bear. I slide my hands from her waist down to her hips, cupping her ass, pulling her body toward me. Elena rocks her hips, holding my head with both hands, my face pressed between her thighs.

Her cries grow higher and louder. She rocks her hips against my face, sliding her clit over my tongue. Her pussy is so soaked, I'm drowning in it, to the point where I'm not getting air. Black sparks snap across my eyes, but I already decided I'll pass out on the floor before I'll interrupt her orgasm.

She's right there, no going back now. She holds my head between her legs, back arched, face tilted up to the ceiling, crying out long and loud. And then she collapses all the way forward, sliding off the table to join me on the floor, curled up in my lap, her face against my neck.

She's still breathing hard. I can feel her pulse throbbing through her body, even down her arms and legs.

"Holy Jesus," she gasps. "That was…even better."

CHAPTER 29
ELENA

AFTER ATLAS DOUBLES THE NUMBER OF WAYS I'VE SUCCESSFULLY managed to orgasm, we spend the next several hours developing film. Atlas is a quick study—he's almost able to spool the film all on his own by his third attempt.

"I can see why you like this," he says, pulling a dripping photograph of the Monarch out of the bath. "It's not quick washing these damn things fourteen times, but it is sort of soothing."

"What do you do to relax?"

"Read," he says. Then he opens his mouth partway and immediately closes it again, like there was another item on the list but he decided not to tell me.

I'm way too curious to let that pass. "What was that? You were going to say something else..."

Atlas looks mildly surprised that I caught him—and mildly annoyed. "I don't want to tell you the other thing."

"But I have to know."

He heaves a pained sigh. "I write sometimes. Just for fun. Not like your fiancé." The ring on the shelf gets a malevolent glare.

The ring receives nothing from me because I'm too interested in what Atlas just said. "You like to write? Why didn't you want to tell me that?"

Atlas scowls, hands jammed in his pockets. "I don't tell anybody.

Dane would be thrilled to know he could have been giving me shit about it this whole time and not stopped with that poem I published in the fourth grade."

"You write *poetry?*" I squeal.

I should have reined that in. Now Atlas is truly embarrassed, and he's not going to tell me anything else. Or show me this goddamned adorable Baby Atlas poem.

"Not much anymore," he says with his last shreds of dignity. "Now I mostly write character sketches. That's what I like about the hotel—every kind of person passes through here, every shade of human nature. I see things happen every day that are stranger than fiction. It's endless inspiration."

"I want to read them."

"I don't know about that." Atlas is already looking regretful, and I can't let that happen. Not when I have an irresistible chance to look inside the locked vault of his head.

"Please show me," I beg. "It's only fair. You've seen my photographs."

Fairness is an effective lever with Atlas. His sense of honor is unconventional but ironclad. He'll pay what he thinks is owed.

And he expects the same in return.

"I'll make you a deal," he says, in that dangerous low voice, gently brushing back a strand of hair from my forehead. "I'll show you my writing...but only if you take a photograph for me."

"I already took two!"

"Not a photograph *of* me," Atlas says patiently. "A photograph *for* me. Of you."

My heartbeat quickens. "What sort?"

Lorne's pornography flashes through my head, all the extreme and degrading poses.

But Atlas looks in my eyes and says, "Whatever you want. As long as it's you."

I go warm and soft and mushy inside. But not weak. No, actually, the opposite happens…something deep inside of me becomes firm and resolved.

I don't want my first time to be with Lorne.

I want it to be with Atlas.

And I can't stand for it to be anything different.

But in the same moment I realize that one burning desire, I also understand its opposite:

That's the thing that Lorne would hate most. The thing that would make him angriest.

———————

"Come see me after dinner," Atlas says when I really do have to leave, when I'll barely have time to change clothes.

"It'll be late," I warn him.

Lorne's been keeping me at dinner until I'm yawning and practically falling asleep at the table. I'm sure he's doing it on purpose, and I'm sure it makes the waitstaff hate us.

"I don't care how late it is," Atlas says. "But meet me in the library—I don't want you to come all the way down here alone."

I hesitate. "Lorne writes in there sometimes at night."

Atlas shakes his head. "Not my father's library—my mother's. On the sixth floor."

"I didn't know there were two."

He smiles. "You've never turned left?"

"I didn't know you were hiding extra libraries up there. Why are there two?"

"Oh, because my parents hated each other. Yeah, it's true." Atlas nods in the face of my disbelief. "They really did sometimes. Couldn't stand to be in the same room. But other nights…they would have set the hotel on fire for each other."

"Why did they fight?"

Atlas tilts his head, considering, his eyes completely black in this light, no green at all in them and no differentiation between iris and pupil. At last, he says, "There are two hearts in every soul; that's what my mother used to say. And both of those hearts want things very, very badly. But only one of them will admit it."

I think about that for a moment. "You mean…people want things that conflict?"

"What it means," Atlas says, "is that we're driven by impulses all the time, some very powerful. And some disguise themselves, pretending to be other things. So all of us are acting all the time, thinking we're in charge. But none of us know what our secret heart wants or how it's subtly influencing us."

"What did your mother want?"

"She thought she wanted love, marriage, kids, this hotel…"

"But what did she actually want?"

Atlas sighs. "Freedom."

He looks so unhappy that I ask him, "Did she leave?"

But Atlas shakes his head. "No. Because it's not an off-on switch, one or the other. She wanted freedom. But she also wanted us. And so she stayed, but she did contrary and angry things because she was at war with herself. And when that other part of her was winning, it warred with us and, most of all, with my father. Because he had his dark side, too."

I think of the wounds inside of families. The hurt done to one that impacts the others.

When I was hurt, when I lost the people I loved, I closed off and hid in the bookshop for years. I only came out because I had to.

But because I'd sheltered myself, cut myself off from the world, I came out from the dark bleary-eyed and blinking, easily blinded by anything that dazzled. And Lorne knows how to dazzle. He's very, very good at it when he wants to be.

I stumbled right into the wrong man's arms, and now I'm not sure how to get out again. Because I don't think Lorne will easily let me go.

"I'll meet you," I say to Atlas. "In her library, tonight."

He kisses me, his huge hand warm on my jaw. "I'll be waiting."

Before I leave, I have to slip Lorne's ring back onto my finger.

Nothing has ever felt more wrong.

CHAPTER 30
ELENA

I BARELY HAVE TIME TO FINISH CHANGING CLOTHES BEFORE LORNE knocks on my door at ten minutes to seven. I have a sneaking suspicion that he's only early to prevent me from walking down to the fourth floor to check on Ivy.

"Why's there an extra lock on your door?" Lorne says by way of greeting.

"Atlas had them changed again."

Lorne's face darkens, probably from the mention of Atlas's name, not the lock itself.

"Why?" he barks.

"Because someone broke in again."

Lorne's jaw tightens, his pale lips compressing until they turn white. "And you didn't think to mention that to me?"

"It just happened last night. I didn't want to distract you when you're so close to the end of your book."

Also, a not-insignificant part of me thinks you might be the one doing it.

But Lorne doesn't look guilty or secretly satisfied. Actually, he looks pissed.

"Has it occurred to you that it's probably Atlas?"

"Probably Atlas...what?" I say blankly.

"Writing on your wall," Lorne hisses.

He thinks I'm being obtuse, but I really had no idea what he meant. The idea that Atlas would deface the hotel that is his home and his legacy seems laughable. But, of course, Lorne doesn't know Atlas quite as well as I do.

"Why would he do that?" I ask carefully.

"He's running his haunted hotel shtick so you'll ring him in the middle of the night—which is exactly what you did!" Lorne accuses.

I would toss that out as jealous nonsense. But then I remember something that did strike me as odd at the time. Miraculous, almost.

My entire living room was destroyed in a frantic, two-minute frenzy that had me diving off the side of the bed, terrified, scrabbling for the phone. When I crept out, feathers flew in the air like snow, the couch cushions slashed, books tossed around the room, splayed open with their pages torn out. But my camera was just sitting there on the table, completely untouched.

If the person doing this wanted to hurt me, how did they miss my camera?

Unless they didn't miss it at all. Unless…they couldn't bring themself to smash it.

Lorne doesn't give a fuck about my camera. He thinks it's old and useless; he'd probably love to chuck it out a window.

But Atlas wouldn't. He knows what it means to me. I don't think he could bring himself to hurt me like that.

Lorne can see my mind working. Low and gloating, he says, "Yeah, you didn't think about that, did you? While you were letting him comfort you, wrap his arms around you and hold you tight— you didn't realize he's the one fucking with you. Trying to wedge between us."

I can't help shivering. That can't be true. Atlas wouldn't do that.

But on the other hand…the books that were torn the worst were Lorne's. His entire series that I bought at Books 'n' Brews was shredded, even the covers ripped to bits. Lorne is so proud of those books and his status as a famous author, I have a hard time imagining him destroying them. Even to scare me. Even to blame it on Atlas.

"He's been preying on you since you got here," Lorne says, his fingers digging into my upper arm. He always holds my arm when we walk, steering me. He doesn't hold my hand or let me tuck my arm in his. "He probably does this all the time, whenever he sees a guest he likes."

The idea of Atlas flirting with a parade of guests before me, like Lorne's parade of porn girlfriends, makes me sick.

But he does have all that replacement wallpaper handy. He could have done this a hundred times with a hundred different women.

Heart pounding painfully, I rip my arm out of Lorne's grip. "You don't know anything about Atlas."

"You think you do?" Lorne laughs. "He's playing with you. *I* put a ring on your finger, not him. I'm marrying you. I'm taking you away from whatever shit you were in back home—that's right, I'm not fucking stupid, Elena. You'd never even been to a wife swap before that day. You stuck out like a sore thumb."

Slowly, I say, "You saw me upstairs?"

"Of course I did! I saw you the second you walked into the room. You were a giraffe in a herd of gazelles."

He says it coldly, deliberately, looking into my face, his words chosen to hurt me.

"And you came and sat down at the same table as me on purpose…"

"You're missing a part." Lorne smiles. "First, I waited in line behind you and bought the same tart. You're not very observant."

My face burns. I know he's telling the truth. Because nobody buys rhubarb tarts besides me. That's why I thought it was so funny and sweet.

I'm such a fool. Seeing exactly what I hoped to see.

Show up looking for a miracle, and how easy it is to convince you that's exactly what you found.

We've reached the restaurant. Lorne lets go of my arm and puts a possessive hand in the middle of my back instead.

"Table for two," he says to Sienna with his most charming smile.

It is so fucking creepy how different his voice sounds speaking to her compared to just a minute ago talking to me. He sounds relaxed and mellow, like nothing could possibly make him mad.

But he's not mellow at all, steering me through the restaurant. He's glued to my side, hand on my spine, watching everywhere for Atlas.

I'm sure Lorne notices that, for the very first time, Atlas is absent from the Reinstoff while we're eating. He must be hanging back, giving me space so he doesn't agitate Lorne. But that doesn't seem to please Lorne. His eyes narrow, and he only becomes more tense.

Sienna takes us to what I would call *our table* if I enjoyed thinking about it that way. It's the coziest table in the restaurant, tucked under the low, thatched roof, close to the fireplace. When Sienna's only seating me, she puts me in the booth by the bathrooms that has a rip in the seat.

"Here you go." She smiles at Lorne.

You can have him.

No. I wouldn't wish that on Sienna.

I sit across from my fiancé, feeling slightly sick. There wasn't much affection left to destroy, but knowing that Lorne has been manipulating me from the beginning sure as hell kills any remaining guilt. Is anything he told me true?

What has he even told you?

Not much. He distracted and pressured and scared me away from pushing for details. And I made it all so easy.

But not anymore.

Before the waitress has even arrived to take our drinks, I demand of Lorne, "What happened to Ivy's mom?"

He stares at me, blank faced, unblinking. "Why are you asking that?"

"I want to know."

"She died."

"How?"

"Why?" Lorne says softly. "Are you worried?"

My mouth goes dry. There's no water on the table. My tongue, when it touches my lips, is about as moistening as a finger. "Should I be worried?"

"No," Lorne says, reaching across the table to take my hand. But as he gazes at me, the pupils of his eyes seem to spread and darken like oil, and his voice flattens and drops. "You don't have to worry about anything, Elena. Because I'm going to take care of you. That's what you want, isn't it?"

I want to pull my hand away. Lorne's grip is too strong. Painful, almost. He waits until I nod one tiny millimeter. Then he begins stroking his thumb back and forth across my hand. The longer he touches it, the less it feels like it's attached to my arm.

Softly, he says, "It's Atlas who should worry."

I go cold, so cold I'm sure that Lorne can feel it. But his thumb swipes back and forth over my hand like a ticking clock.

"You don't have to worry about anything, Elena, because you're a good girl, loyal, faithful. But if Atlas tries to take what's mine... his size won't save him." He holds my gaze, his eyes cold, clear, and completely serious. "Do you understand?"

"Yes," I whisper.

Olivia saunters up to our table, a bottle of wine in one hand and two glasses in the other, crossed at their stems. "Looking for this?"

Lorne turns, his face coming to life like an animatronic. "Olivia! You changed your hair."

"Just a trim." She touches the ends modestly. Her hair looks like a shampoo commercial, like somebody must be shining a floodlight on it to get that kind of glow.

And I do not give one single solitary fuck. I hope Lorne spends the rest of the night flirting with her and doesn't look at me once. The last thing I want is more of his attention.

Glad to have my clammy hand back in my lap, I sneak a glance around for Atlas—but not for eye candy. I'm scared. Of what Lorne might do to him. Atlas is way bigger, but that won't matter if Lorne has a weapon or if he ambushes him, sneaks up in the middle of the night...

Do you really think Lorne would do that?

I think of his face when he's not smiling, when he's not putting on the charm. When he's looking me in the eye and threatening me.

I think he'd do much worse.

As I suspected, Lorne makes dinner drag on and on. He keeps pressuring me to drink more wine. I refused to drink any until he did first, even though this bottle came sealed, Olivia popping the cork tableside.

Lorne seemed to find that amusing and made a big production of taking his first sip. I still waited for him to finish half a glass before I drank any.

Now I'm on my third glass, trying to quiet the anxiety building in my chest.

Half of me is glad that Atlas isn't around. What Lorne said scared me. And the longer Atlas stays away, the more Lorne relaxes. But the other half can't feel comfortable without my own personal bodyguard on the other side of the room.

I don't care what Lorne said about Atlas and the writing on my wall. I feel safer when he's near, and I trust him to protect me. It's Lorne who scares me.

Amy's still here, watching us with so much intensity that I'm sure she's doing it on her boss's orders. But tiny Amy is not as reassuring as Atlas. Especially as Lorne drinks more and more.

She is, however, devious. She's unleashed both Sienna and Olivia on our table for maximum flirting. Barely two minutes can pass without one of them popping by to "see how we're doing," which means Lorne can only make so many cutting comments, and he definitely can't pinch me under the table.

I try to resist the many times he refills my glass, wanting to keep my wits about me, but Lorne is still being enough of an asshole that the alcohol helps take off the edge. It makes me a little less afraid and a lot more bold.

Flushed with liquid courage, I demand, "Are you going to let me see Ivy tomorrow?"

Lorne's face is also flushed, his eyes slightly dull, cloudy marbles instead of clear, cold sky. "That depends."

"On what?"

"On how nicely you beg."

I really don't know how I ever thought this man was attractive. His eyes are bloodshot, his lips puffy in a face becoming increasingly bloated with alcohol. But that's not what makes him ugly. It's his expression, flat and uncaring, interested only in what stimulates him.

He doesn't give a fuck about Ivy. Or about me. He only cares about what he can make me do.

But *I* care about Ivy.

Enough to do this:

I take a heavy swig of wine and set down my glass.

Clasping my hands in front of me in a praying position, I say, "Lorne, please, please can I see Ivy tomorrow? I promised to help her make her costume. It's important to her. I really don't want to disappoint her."

Lorne takes a sip of his wine, too. "That's pretty good. But I'm not totally convinced."

His expression makes my stomach turn. He's looking at me like you'd look at a worm on the sidewalk, squirming, baking in the sun.

Assuming you had a grudge against that particular worm. And you got a visceral enjoyment from watching it burn.

But Ivy does not want to be a princess. She probably drew fifty owls in her notebook. So I humble myself again.

"Please, Lorne. I'm begging."

"That's not begging." Lorne jerks his chin toward the floor. "You know how to beg."

I stare at him. The restaurant is completely packed. Every table is full. And Sienna and Olivia are already watching us.

Lorne is not joking. He gazes calmly back at me, waiting.

He has all the power here. I know damn well that he has no problem at all making Ivy wear some princess bullshit, which Mrs. Cross will make as itchy and ugly as possible because that's her joy as well as her personal taste.

I'm not letting that happen. Even if I have to make a complete fool of myself.

I slide out of my seat in my dress and high heels and get down on my knees on the floor of the restaurant with at least a hundred people watching. Heads immediately turn, everyone thinking a proposal is about to happen, all the more interested when they see it's a woman down on her knees.

But I'm not proposing. I'm begging my fiancé not to be a spiteful piece of shit to his own daughter.

As I lift my clasped hands and plead with his smug, smirking face, I realize how much I'm truly beginning to hate him.

"Please, Lorne. I'm very, very sorry for upsetting you. I was so stupid and ungrateful after everything you've done for me. Please forgive me."

The smile on his face is disturbing. Because I think it's genuine. This is Lorne happy and satisfied. When I'm humiliated, down on my knees.

"That's better," he says.

I stand up, stiff and nauseated. A strange silence has fallen in the restaurant, half the diners looking away, half still staring uncomfortably at what is very clearly *not* a proposal. Even Sienna and Olivia seem slightly disturbed, Olivia standing still with furrowed brows and Sienna whispering to Amy, who responds with a tense shake of her head.

Now that I'm on my feet, I'm realizing how drunk I've become. And how little self-control I have remaining.

Holding the edge of the table so I don't sway, I tell Lorne, "I'll come at ten tomorrow morning."

He smiles at me, the smile I'm beginning to think is the only one that's genuine. The one that shows no teeth, no crinkling of the eyes, and no kindness at all.

"Where's my kiss?"

My stomach churns. I would rather get down on my knees again and kiss the floor.

But I bend at the waist and press my dry, cold lips to his, promising myself, *that's the last time we'll ever kiss.*

CHAPTER 31
ATLAS

I HATE LEAVING ELENA ALONE OVER DINNER. I ONLY DO IT BECAUSE I know she'll be in the dining room the whole time, surrounded by people, Amy watching and reporting back to me. But every mile I drive away from the Monarch makes me more nervous—because it's a mile I'll have to drive to get back to her again.

I know she wants to leave Lorne, but I really don't think she understands how dangerous he is. She underestimates him.

And maybe…so have I.

So I drive back up to his castle, alone this time. When I know he'll be busy. When I know his work crews will be away.

But when I see the uneven spires rising over the pine tops and then the high, barred gates and the empty, muddy yard, I realize there's no need for work crews anymore. The castle is finished.

It looks monstrous. Maybe it's the rain slicing down, or the purple clouds, or the hunched, humped look of the uneven spires… or maybe it's the black soul of the thing, built by a man with no soul at all.

No architect made that. That castle came out of Lorne Ronson's head, stitched together from the plans like Frankenstein's monster.

I'd planned to scale the gates and search the place, but I can already see the cameras mounted and the heavy iron lock on the bastille-style door.

I don't need to see inside to see the truth.

This isn't a castle.

It's a prison.

Built for Lorne's bride.

———————

By the time Elena stumbles up to the library, rain pounds against the windows and wind moans down the chimney. She's obviously come directly up from the Reinstoff, her hair smelling smoky and sweet from the straw thatch and the carefully enclosed fireplace. And she obviously had a few, her ankles wobbly in her high-heeled shoes, her cheeks deeply pink.

"Atlas…" She puts her arms around my neck and leans against me, warm and heavy, kissing me in that immediate, hungry, wet way that makes me suspect I might have a drunk little slut on my hands. Which happens to be my favorite thing.

"You drunk little slut," I growl aloud in her ear. "You better not have kissed him like that."

"Never." She grabs the front of my shirt, yanks me forward, and puts her tongue in my mouth. She tastes fucking fantastic, and her wild tongue is lighting me on fire. I have to talk to her, but also, I have to put my hands on every inch of her body right now.

I shut the library door and lock it. It locks from the inside—that probably should have been a clue that Mom had a lover. I'm realizing that now that I'm using this library for similar purposes. I found out about the lover when Dad shot him at a party. So I'm no stranger to the passions you can inflame when you steal someone else's partner.

But Elena is supposed to be mine. I know it every time I touch her. I know it when she looks at me and says my name. I can smell it on her skin and taste it on her lips. I hear it in her laugh, and I read it on her face.

That's why it feels so good when I take her in my arms like this.

Not good like a massage—good like I'll burn down my life to have it. To have her. To have this moment, and then this one, and then the next…her hand sliding inside my shirt, her mouth trailing down my chest. Elena on her knees, surprising me with her hands unbuttoning my pants…

"You're too drunk." I put my hands over hers though it's the last thing in the world I want to do.

"Three drinks over four hours," Elena scoffs, batting away my hands.

"How full were those drinks?" I've seen Lorne pour half a bottle into his glass.

"Don't complain unless you don't like it," Elena says, which doesn't exactly answer my question.

Then she puts her mouth on me, and I think, *I'll give my whole fucking life for this moment,* and then I can't think anything at all, because it's a kind of pleasure without words or even images.

It's pure sensation, almost unbearable, and so good that it becomes a new standard. Anything that feels good in the future will forever be compared to this.

The rain thrashes outside, furiously wet, but the heat of her mouth is softly unwinding…

I close my eyes and put my hand in her hair. It's so pleasurable, I could never ask her to stop. The rain washes against the windows and washes out the inside of my brain. I almost lose it right there in her mouth.

Elena lifts her head, giving me a wicked look. "That's what I'd do if I were actually sorry about something."

"*Please* do something horrible to me. I need another apology."

Elena laughs and puts her lips on my cock. *Almost* losing it turns into exploding.

I warn her. She carries on anyway, using her hand as well as her mouth. The new standard of pleasure gets blasted apart, and the *new* new standard takes its place.

I give her my pocket square to clean up.

"You're still hard," she observes.

"You still look fucking gorgeous."

She laughs. She's sitting on the couch in that black velvet dress, flushed and glowing. There's a kind of hectic energy I haven't seen in her before—nerves with an edge of aggression.

I ask, "What happened?" Amy's updates were slightly enigmatic.

"It doesn't matter." Elena shakes her head.

"Did he hurt you?" I'd be furious if Amy didn't tell me that.

"No," Elena says firmly. "He didn't lay a hand on me."

I believe her, but something is off. She's too keyed up.

I'm dying to touch her again, to somehow try to repay the most pleasurable experience of my life. But I have to talk to her first. So I zip my pants and sit down next to her, putting my arm around the back of the sofa, not quite around her shoulders.

"Are you sure you're okay?"

She nods, eyes bright, cheeks flushed, lips swollen. "I'm fine, Atlas, I promise you."

Hoping that's true, I say, "I need to talk to you."

"I'm listening."

"I want you to leave Lorne. I don't know what your circumstances are, what you might have done back home, and I don't care. I'll help you."

Elena stiffens. I put my arm all the way around her, drawing her close against my side. Looking into her eyes, I say, "Elena, I will help you. I will protect you. I don't care what you've done. You can trust me."

Her breathing is so shallow, it's almost nonexistent, her eyes wide and strained. In a tiny voice, she says, "What if I did something really bad?"

"I see who you are. I don't care what you did."

She presses her lips together, squeezing my hand, eyes lifted, almost believing…

I ask her, "Was it a mistake?"

She nods.

"Then I don't care."

She finally believes me, shoulders dropping with relief. "Really, Atlas?"

"I promise you, I'll help you. But you have to leave Lorne. He's lying to you. He's dangerous."

Elena drops her head, looking at her hands wrapped around mine. "I know."

"You do?"

"He lied to me about how we met. And a lot of other things, too. It seemed like it was little things at first—how long he'd been staying at the hotel, when the move-in date would be…but then I realized he'd misrepresented almost everything. Especially his relationship with Ivy." Elena falls silent, frowning.

"I think it's a lot worse than that. Do you know what happened to Ivy's mom?"

Elena bites her lip. "I read online there was a carbon monoxide leak."

"Ivy almost died, too. Lorne was conveniently out of town."

"You think he did it?"

"Here's what I know: Linda Lovelace was from a wealthy family. From what I hear, they didn't like Lorne. They thought he was a deadbeat and a leech."

"Lorne makes good money," Elena points out.

"I don't think his books sell nearly as well as he wants people to think. That 'award' of his, it doesn't exist. His books were self-published on Linda's dime—or so her sister tells me. And the clerk at Books 'n' Brews says they only sell a couple of copies a week—copies Lorne brings in himself."

"But he has a Wikipedia page!"

"Anybody can make those." I didn't want to tell Elena all this until I knew for certain because it makes me look petty and jealous.

But I don't think there's anything petty about this at all, not when it's a pattern: Lorne is not who he pretends to be.

Which means we have no idea what he really is.

"He's dangerous," I repeat. "You need to leave him."

"I know," Elena says. "I will."

Good.

"But not until after Halloween."

Not fucking good.

"No way," I growl. "It's not safe, Elena. He's escalating."

"I don't care," Elena says, her chin firmly set. "I promised Ivy, and I'm not breaking my promise."

I know I have to tread carefully here. "Elena...she's not your daughter."

"I'm aware of that."

"And you can't marry Lorne because of her."

"I know that, too." Elena looks at me steadily with those clear blue eyes. "I'm not marrying Lorne. But I made plans with Ivy for Halloween, and I can at least keep that promise. It's one more day."

A lot can happen in a day. But I can tell she's already made up her mind, and I don't want to pressure her.

"You'll leave after that?"

Elena sits quietly for a moment, looking unhappy. "As soon as Ivy goes to bed," she says at last. "Before midnight." Her hands tighten on her thighs, and she looks up at me. "But I'm still going to try to help her."

"Fine. I'll help you help her. But not anywhere he can hurt you."

I don't know what Elena can do for Ivy, but she can do it safe and sound with me.

I hate the idea of giving Lorne even one more day.

But he's not the one asking for it...Elena is. And I'd give her anything.

"Stay with me," I tell her, kissing her gently, caressing her face. "Be with me always. Live here. Love me. Let me love you."

"That's crazy," Elena gasps, but she's kissing me back, hands on my face, sliding onto my lap. "We just met."

"It doesn't matter. I love you."

"No, you don't."

"*I love you.*"

She makes a sound that's almost a groan.

I kiss her. "Do you feel that? I love you." I kiss her again and again. "What do you want me to do to show you? Ask me for anything. I'll give it to you. Will that prove it? Ask me to do anything. Try me, Elena."

She looks into my eyes a long time, hands on either side of my face. With a soft sigh, she says, "I already believe you."

She kisses me, and there's a new taste in her mouth, pure and bubbling and bright. I can taste that she's happy. I feel it in her hands in my hair, in the way she kisses me, in the shape of her lips on mine, almost smiling.

She whispers, "Because I love you, too."

I feel a burst of pure sunlight, though the wind and the rain are howling.

I meant to take her down to my room to do this properly. I meant to wait until she was mine, fully and completely. But Elena's looking into my eyes, sliding down her underwear. And I'm unbuttoning my trousers, cock springing free.

She straddles me on the sofa, still wearing her black velvet dress, her hair glowing in the firelight. The long, loose strands dangle around her face, her lips red and swollen. She positions herself over my cock.

"Wait," I say, and I tip her over on her back, her head tilted over the arm of the sofa, her thighs around my face. Even though she's already wet, I lick her until she's swollen and shivering and drenched.

Then I pull her back onto my lap, just as she was. And I let her slide the head of my cock around with her hand, lining it up where it feels right until with tight, exquisite slowness, she lowers her weight and begins to slide down.

Her arms around my neck, she looks into my eyes. "I want to give this to you and only you. Because I trust you, Atlas. I know you'll be gentle and make it feel good. And I won't regret it after."

The pressure and friction increase. Her face turns pink, her eyes widen, her mouth opens, and she gasps.

For me, the squeezing and sliding are like being eaten alive by a boa constrictor if the last living moments were pure pleasure. I hold Elena's waist to help her down slow, but it's hard not to squeeze her back because every inch of me feels like it's compacting, compressing, like she's somehow sliding down my whole entire body.

When my fingers tighten on her waist, her stomach tightens, too, and she moans. She throws her arms all the way around my neck, pressing her body against me, turning her face to my neck. I hold the back of her head and breathe in the scent of her hair. All of a sudden, I'm right on the edge. I thought I was safe since I already came, but here we are again way too soon.

"Jesus, slow down," I groan, cradling her head and the small of her back. Her body feels unreal in my arms, like an idea, a fantasy brought to life. It's too much to have what I wanted so badly. All my control is shredded.

"I'm barely moving," Elena murmurs in my ear, sliding another delicious millimeter down my cock.

It's like a countdown to a rocket launch. Ten seconds, now nine... I have to make this last, but she smells so good, it's outrageous.

And I've never felt a sensation quite like this, the inside of her pussy softer than that velvet dress...

"I'm not going to make it," I moan when I can't take any more. *Eight... Seven... Six...*

"It's okay," Elena whispers into my ear. "I'm right here." And she slides all the way down, letting out a sigh.

Five... Four...

She barely made a sound, but her whole body relaxes, and then comes the groan. So long and so satisfying that I finally understand that she's coming as she rocks her hips an inch up and down.

Three... Two...

On the last rock, I explode. I've never come in so little time or from so little motion, but I've also never come so hard. She curls her body around me, legs wrapped around my waist, arms around my neck, my cock squeezed tightly inside her. I blast and blast upward until I reach the starry skies.

Eventually, I'm back in the library. It's the same books, the same dusty sofa, the same fireplace, and the same rain.

But I'm a new man.

Elena straddles my lap, her hands in my hair. Her hair has come undone and her dress is slipping down her shoulders. She's flushed and rosy all the way to her breasts.

"Marry me," I say, "not him."

She laughs and shakes her head, saying again, "That's *crazy!*"

But when she sees I'm not smiling, she stops laughing. Her hands slide down to my face.

"Do you mean it, Atlas?"

"Kiss me and see if I mean it."

CHAPTER 32
ELENA

I WAKE UP ON HALLOWEEN CERTAIN THAT TODAY WILL BE MY LAST day with Lorne. The rain has finally stopped, and sunshine is pouring in the windows…the first truly sunny day I've seen in Grimstone.

I shower and dress quickly, excited to see Ivy. When I knock on her door, Mrs. Cross pulls it open, and I hustle right past her, not waiting for any more bullshit.

Ivy is sitting up by the window, but she looks terrible. Dark circles line her eyes, her hair limp and greasy. She's slumping in her chair, head leaning listlessly against the glass.

When she sees me, she lifts her head, surprised and almost stricken. She obviously didn't think I was coming—she's still in her pajamas.

"Hey, sleepyhead!" I say, trying for cheerfulness, though my heart squeezes when I see how thin and pale she looks. Guilt comes rushing back at the thought of leaving her like this. "How are you feeling? You don't look swollen anymore."

Ivy gives one small nod, but she's not smiling.

"Come on," I say, holding out my hand. Only then does she slowly slide off the chair and take my hand.

I wait in her bedroom while she showers and dresses. Her bedroom is spotlessly neat, the bed made, but I'm irritated to see that the books I bought her are missing. Assuming Mrs. Cross took them away, I plot to get them back again. But then I realize Mrs.

Cross can just take them away again tomorrow—and I won't be able to do anything about it.

Ivy comes out wearing one of the outfits we bought together, a black tunic with a gold cat knitted on the front and black-and-gold-striped leggings. It makes her look like a tiny witch, especially with her dandelion-floss hair all tangled and weedy wet. I brush her hair, careful not to yank the snarls, and help her fasten the clasp on her birthstone necklace.

Ivy examines herself in the mirror. I stand beside her, smiling. I'm all in black, too—dark jeans and the leather bomber Atlas bought me. As usual, Ivy has dressed to match me. She looks up at me and steps closer. Automatically, I put my arm around her. Ivy gazes at us both in the mirror. And finally smiles.

I feel so horribly, awfully guilty, I can't stand it. I have to turn away, blinking tears.

"Come on, sweetie. Let's get going."

I take her down to Main Street once more, just the two of us. We walk through the drifts of crunching leaves, dead and brown now and blown around by the wind. The streets are freshly washed, and the air smells clean and salty. But already, thick rafts of clouds are blowing in again. The sunshine was rare and temporary.

The streets are packed with excited tourists clutching coffee and cider. The burned-sugar scent of kettle corn and roasting nuts drifts out of the candy shop.

Stacks of hay bales form makeshift benches all along the street, with carved jack-o'-lanterns already flickering from every window-sill. A swarm of black bats dangles from the branches of a massive grandfather oak, and ghostly wraiths swing from the lampposts. But all the decorations are dwarfed by the twenty-foot-tall specter of Mr. Bones at the end of the street.

His long, bony arms reach outward, his eyes huge, dark pits in his skeletal face. He wears a burgundy suit too short for his straggly legs.

I feel a deep chill looking at him. At his hungry, gaping mouth…

I take Ivy to one of the first booths to be set up, a cotton candy stand where they shape colored candy floss into gravity-defying sculptures skewered on paper cones. Ivy requests a pink and purple panda bear. She watches its creation and smiles when the lady hands it to her, but she only takes one bite before sinking back into sadness.

We visit the craft shop next to purchase several bags of turkey feathers, a short piece of rope, and a needle and thread. I ask Ivy if she wants to visit the toy shop next door, but she shakes her head.

"Well, come on, then. Let's go back to the hotel. Who knows how long it will take me to sew on all these feathers!"

Ivy owns a lumpy brown sweater that will form an excellent base for her owl suit. The turkey feathers are long enough that they should look like wings hanging down from her arms.

Ivy follows me at first, but her feet seem to drag the closer we get to the Monarch. I stop and crouch down to look at her face. "Honey, what's wrong?"

At first she won't look at me, but when at last she lifts her head, I see her eyes are full of tears.

"Ivy, please," I beg. "Tell me what's wrong—is it Mrs. Cross? Is it your dad? Did something happen?"

She looks down at the pavement, shaking her head.

I don't know what to do. Some part of me wonders if Ivy senses I'm leaving—if that's why she's upset. I'm sick with guilt and a horrible sense of powerlessness.

"Is it something about tonight?" I ask helplessly, but Ivy still shakes her head. "Okay," I say, putting my hand gently on her shoulder, "let's get back to the hotel."

Feet still dragging, she follows.

Things go better while we're making the costume. I put on a playlist of spooky Halloween music, not too loud, which Ivy seems to enjoy, and she takes pleasure in laying out the feathers for me in neat rows, ready to be attached.

Ivy's costume takes several hours to assemble, but it's well worth it when she tries it on in front of the mirror, pulling up the hood of her sweater, which I also feathered, creating a little mask that hangs down over her eyes. She peers at herself in wonder, then slowly turns around, arms spread, head turning at the last minute as if she can't tear her gaze away from the magnificence of her wings.

"You like it?"

She throws her arms around my waist and hugs me.

Inside, I break a little.

My own costume is easy to make—it's basically a bedsheet, artfully arranged with the little bit of rope tied around my waist.

But Ivy gets it at once when she sees it. She turns to the correct page in our Greek mythology book, grinning at me, pointing at the goddess Athena with her owl on her arm.

"That's exactly right." I laugh. "God, you're clever."

I hear Lorne's voice in my head saying, "*Sometimes I think she's just not that smart,*" and I feel sicker than ever.

I don't want to leave Ivy with someone who thinks that. Who doesn't care if her mouth is throbbing and painful. Who doesn't even like to eat dinner with her.

The thought of her all alone in that dark, jumbled castle is awful—or even worse, the thought of her tormented and needled by Mrs. Cross.

But I can't take her with me. And I can't stay with Lorne.

It's an impossible situation with no real solution, just the hope that I can do something from a distance. A hope I don't really believe in at all.

Which makes my last day with Ivy incredibly painful. Though I'm trying not to let her see it.

Secretly, some desperate part of me is still hoping I'll learn something, figure something out, to truly help her.

Lorne comes into Ivy's suite without knocking. Ivy and I both stiffen when we hear the key in the lock, and Ivy shudders when she hears Mrs. Cross's high, staccato laugh. I frown because I did not think Mrs. Cross was coming along with us. I asked Lorne if it could just be the three of us. Maybe I would have been more likely to get what I wanted if I requested the opposite.

It's my turn to shudder when the pair steps inside. Lorne is dressed as Mr. Bones in a tight burgundy suit, top hat, and skull-painted face. Mrs. Cross has made her own Mary Poppins costume. This is both sacrilegious and highly disturbing because she much more resembles the Child Catcher in disguise.

"Who are you supposed to be?" Lorne's eyes crawl up and down my body. I don't like this face painting he's done—it makes it harder than ever to read his expression. "Aphrodite?" he guesses, smirking slightly. "Goddess of love?"

"Athena. Goddess of wisdom."

Lorne snorts in a way that's pretty insulting. "Okay."

My hatred burns and burns. Maybe I *was* fucking stupid when I laid eyes on Lorne—but I'm fixing that mistake tonight.

I can't wait to take his ring off my finger. Just a few hours left.

And most of all, I can't wait to be with Atlas. Not sneaking around, not hiding—safe in his arms, openly, gladly. By midnight tonight.

That's what I keep telling myself while forcing a smile for Lorne.

CHAPTER 33
ATLAS

This is the first Halloween in a long time that I've actually dressed up. And no less, in the costume I swore I'd never wear—our town's mascot and alter ego, Mr. Bones.

Dane can't believe his eyes. He, of course, has no choice about dressing up because he'll do anything for Remi, and Remi lives for Halloween. Which is why he is currently wearing one of his lab coats with a white fright wig and surprisingly realistic wrinkle makeup. Remi, the Marty to his Doc Brown, has on a puffy red vest and some pretty killer '80s sneakers. She's brought a skateboard, which, apparently, she actually knows how to ride.

She does a loop around us, leaning her entire body back in that gravity-defying way of skaters who seem glued to their boards by their feet.

"I thought you said Halloween was for overgrown kids?" Dane grins at me.

"I'm just wondering if you have to be some version of a doctor for every single one of your costumes. It's a little insecure."

"Oh yeah. It's much cooler to attend med school for no reason at all and then never put 'MD' on anything."

"It wasn't *no* reason—I got to avoid our parents for six years."

Dane smiles thinly. "That was my favorite part, too."

"Why didn't you tell us you were going to dress up?" Remi shouts at me, incensed, as she whips around another loop. "You could have gone as Biff!"

She jumps off her board, kicking it up neatly and catching it. Remi is petite, purple-haired, pierced and can work like a steam engine all day long. I've never seen anyone who can get more done in a day or who's cleverer at working with their hands.

But even for Remi, respected friend and potential sister-in-law, I will not be dressing up as Biff Tannen.

"He only dressed up to blend in," Dane observes wisely. "He's stalking that woman from the hotel."

"What woman?" Remi demands, instantly interested.

I give my brother a filthy glare. I only told him one or two very small pieces of information about Elena under strict instructions that he never mention them to anyone again, including me.

Dane just smiles and shrugs. "I tell her everything."

I shake my head in disgust. "What's happened to you?"

"I would have told her already, but we don't talk about you that much."

"*What woman?*" Remi is going to lose her mind if she's out of the secret for five more seconds.

"The one marrying the author," Dane says. "That's why he made us drive up to the castle that day—'cause he's jealous."

"*She's not marrying him,*" I say with way too much aggression.

Dane and Remi blink at me.

"Uh-oh," Remi says.

"Yeah." Dane grimaces. "That sounded pretty…"

"Murdery," Remi finishes.

"Don't finish each other's sentences, it's obnoxious. And I'm not going to do anything to him—as long as he doesn't do anything to her."

Dane and Remi exchange glances.

"Like…marry her?" Remi says tentatively.

"They're not getting married," I grit through my teeth.

Dane tilts his head, watching me. "She's leaving him?"

"Tonight."

"But you're worried."

"That's right."

Remi's expression grows serious, and she comes closer to me. "What are you worried he'll do?"

She's been tense since she saw my Mr. Bones costume in the first place. Remi had her own awful experience with a pack of Mr. Boneses at last year's Reaper's Revenge. She knows better than anyone how wild Halloween night can get in Grimstone.

I'm sure that's why she was riding her skateboard around in loops, trying to burn off her anxious energy. She's nervous as she peers up at me, picking at her vest.

"Hopefully nothing," I say. "But I'm going to make sure."

Dane comes and puts his arm around Remi. I'm almost jealous of how easily they slide into place against each other after a year of doing it every single day. It makes me want Elena next to me, today, tomorrow, every day for a year. And then for fifty more.

I never wanted to be part of a pair until I found my other half. Now I know how good it feels when we're connected...and how incomplete I am without her.

"He doesn't know she's leaving," I tell Dane and Remi. "And he won't be happy when he finds out. So I want to keep an eye on them...but not too close."

Remi says, "We can help."

It's not easy to follow unseen when you're a head taller than everyone else in the crowd and twice as broad as some. It wouldn't work at all without the Mr. Bones costume, the great equalizer at the Reaper's Revenge.

At least a third of the partygoers packing the streets are dressed as some version of Mr. Bones, including men, women, children, and pets. I see Day of the Dead Mr. Boneses, *Nightmare Before Christmas* Mr. Boneses, neon Mr. Boneses, and countless variations of the classic burgundy suit.

My suit is black and plain. My skull makeup is subtle. I want to draw as little attention as possible.

The noise and chaos stream around me like a river. Elena is the rock I focus on. I've never seen a crowd like this, Grimstone full to bursting with locals and strangers, indistinguishable for one single night. Which means that none of us have to live with what happens tonight—they can leave, and we can pretend we stayed home.

That's why this night becomes wilder and darker each year. Because when we wear masks, our shadow selves come out to play. Everything dark, repressed, and rejected, allowed to dance in public for one night of the year...

I see it with Lorne in his Mr. Bones suit. I see how he stands, how he walks differently, how he doesn't have to pretend to smile when a skeletal one is already painted on his face.

He barely speaks to Elena or Ivy. He lets them walk through the shops and sample the sweets and wait for their turn at the face-painting booth. It seems like he's letting them have their fun, but I see what he's really doing.

He's stalking Elena like a cat with a mouse. Letting her get ahead, get away, then coming up unexpectedly behind her. Slipping through shadows, waiting in doorways. Letting her pass. Following again. The way he walks, the way he moves, completely altered... because he's free to do it tonight when he thinks no one is watching.

My skin goes cold.

Lorne is good at stalking. A little too good.

I don't know where Mrs. Cross disappeared to. She was with her party at the start of the night, but she seems to have slipped away. Remi's keeping an eye out for her.

Elena and Ivy are staying in well-lit public spaces with plenty of people all around—or at least as well lit as you can get with the whole town done up like a haunted house.

But I'm not even close to comfortable.

The mood on Halloween night in Grimstone has always disturbed me. Last year wasn't the first time something terrible happened.

The feeling in the air can be shared. The more people who share it, the more powerful it becomes. That's the power of crowds, of mobs, of concerts.

Tonight, Grimstone is more packed than I've ever seen it. And the mood is the darkest I've ever known.

CHAPTER 34
ELENA

I worry I made a mistake bringing Ivy to the Reaper's Revenge. The crowds are worse than I expected, a line at every shop and booth and stand. Ivy claps her hands over her ears and keeps them there, which makes it difficult for her to enjoy the activities or even eat a caramel apple.

Then I remember that I brought my headphones, the noise-cancelling sort, which work very well because they used to belong to Mina, who prioritizes music over food or books.

Ivy gets the most adorable look of surprise on her face when I turn them on, like one of those babies trying a cochlear implant for the first time but in reverse. Ivy is thrilled to be plunged into blessed silence.

She calms down immediately when she doesn't have to hear all the shouts and whoops and chattering conversation—including mine. I'm relaxing a little myself because Lorne is leaving us alone and Mrs. Cross has disappeared entirely.

Lorne seems to be finding the street fair boring despite the explosions of color, sight, sound, and, most of all, smell emanating from every doorway. He's not engaging, hanging back, barely speaking.

That's exactly what I prefer. I'm here to spend time with Ivy. And if it's deeply tinged with guilt at the fact that I'm about to leave her high and dry, at least I can channel that into giving her the best damn Halloween night of her life.

She looks like a small brown snowman, wobbling along with her headphones, rounding her hood and her body padded with feathers. I wish I brought my camera along to take pictures of her, but I was afraid of it being jostled in the crowd. Ivy and I did, however, take a portrait before we left. I set the timer, and we posed together in front of the fireplace, pretending to be solemn like a formal portrait.

She has been somber, though. Like she knows I'm leaving. Maybe Lorne does, too. Maybe that's why he's barely speaking to me.

Once, I thought I saw Atlas—or at least, I saw a truly enormous Mr. Bones. It was far away and only for a moment, but it made me feel warm from my head to my toes. I hoped he would come to make sure that I'm safe.

It's that warmth, that feeling of invincibility, that tricks me moments later.

Lorne appears out of nowhere and grips my arm, steering me firmly toward the haunted house.

"Lorne! Don't you think that's a little scary for Ivy?"

"She wants to go in. It was her idea." Lorne jerks his chin toward Ivy, who's gazing up at the flat wooden facade, her feathered hood tipped back and her pale blond hair spilling down her back, her green eyes wide and almost dazed.

I don't know if that's actually true. The haunted house is painted in all kinds of bright neon colors and patterns, some spinning and moving. Ivy does seem…interested. But I'm worried she'll be terrified once we're inside.

Lorne is steering us in so forcefully that I'd have to physically resist to stop him. Ivy doesn't seem upset. And I just saw Atlas moments ago…

So I let him push me inside.

But inside is not at all what I expected.

———————

The interior space is as vast and winding as a labyrinth, with stairs and levels and elevators. I immediately start to get claustrophobic and want to leave, but we're shunted down the chute like cattle, more guests pouring in behind us.

Ivy is oddly calm, her hand in mine. Without the noise, she doesn't seem bothered by neon ghosts popping out at us or even killer clowns. She stays close against my side, so nobody actually touches her, but like with her *Firestarter* book, she does seem to crave a certain level of excitement.

Me, too. That's why I sometimes used to read ten hours a day if the bookshop was slow and Boyka wasn't around.

I'd read anything and everything that was beautiful, passionate, and exciting...all the things my life wasn't. But I wished it were.

And then I made that awful mistake, and my life became a nightmare, a clock ticking down to disaster...until Lorne showed up. And it seemed my mistake had become something miraculous.

But I should have known that miracles don't come from what I did...only consequences.

So in a strange way, I'm not surprised when Lorne suddenly grips my hair and yanks me through a side door, dragging Ivy after us. In the darkness and chaos, as he puts his arm around my throat and begins to choke, I can only think, *I guess this is what I deserved after all.*

CHAPTER 35
ATLAS

"WHAT DO YOU MEAN SHE'S NOT IN THE HOUSE?"

I'm bellowing at Marquis Henley, who has been Grimstone's sheriff for exactly one year.

Our last sheriff was murdered. This one is about to be murdered if he keeps telling me Elena is not in Lorne's house.

"I went inside personally. I looked."

"You searched every single room?"

"Yes."

"Then you didn't see her. If *he's* there, so is she."

Henley frowns. He is not a fucking idiot like Sheriff Shane, and he does not like that I'm talking to him like one.

"Look, Atlas, we went up there like you asked. Didn't have a warrant, don't have probable cause. He threw the door wide-open, invited us in. The fiancé's not there—only the daughter."

"Did you talk to Ivy?"

"You said the kid doesn't talk."

"She can still communicate!"

"Well, she didn't," Henley says flatly. "And I asked her. I said, *'You were at the fair with your daddy's girlfriend, right, honey? Do you know what happened to her? Do you know where she is?'* She wouldn't even look at me. Just stared at the wall."

"You have to go back."

"And do what, Atlas?"

"Arrest him!"

"For what? He had twenty, thirty minutes tops before we got up there. His kid was with him the whole time."

"*He took Elena!*"

I'm bellowing again. Henley places his hat back on his head to start the process of leaving. He's not going to take my nonsense, no matter how well we get along generally. "We're still searching the fair, the park, the beach…"

And you'll keep finding fuck all because I already know where she is.

But I don't bother saying that to Henley. It's obvious I'm going to have to handle this myself.

"You sure you got the straight story from this girl anyway, Atlas?" Henley stands with his feet apart, tucking his thumbs into his belt, creating a more impressive silhouette than when our old sheriff used to do it because while Sheriff Shane was turnip shaped, Henley resembles a mocha Mr. Clean. "Isn't she from some foreign country? Maybe she ran off."

Henley may not look like Sheriff Shane, but he's starting to sound like him.

I give him a cold look. "Shane used to say that, too, you know—when he didn't want to do his job."

Henley swells up and gives *me* a look like I just used up my one and only strike with him. "Watch yourself. I'm not him."

Remi waits until he's gone to come back into the lobby. "What'd you make him so mad for?"

This is rank hypocrisy since Remi was the number one person on our late sheriff's most-hated list. But I'll point that out to her another time.

"I've got to go."

"Well, hold on!" Remi chases after me. "I'm sorry for losing track of that old biddy. I was right there—"

"It's not your fault. I was right there, too."

Lorne swooped in like a bat and swept Elena inside the haunted house before I could move five feet through the crowd. By the time I got inside, they were lost in the warren of rooms. Dane circled around immediately to the exit, but as the groups streamed out, no Lorne, Elena, or Ivy emerged.

Precious minutes ticked past as I searched the rooms, shoving forward and backward through the crowd. Elena was gone, like she'd vanished.

The heat and noise were maddening, the howls of the dressed-up actors and the screaming crowd jerking me left and right, thinking one could be Elena.

When I finally found the side door and came out into night air that felt crackling cold, Remi ran up to tell me she'd seen a black delivery van speeding away, driven by someone in a Mary Poppins hat. Lorne's faithful servant, helping him abduct Elena, I'm sure of it.

But Sheriff Henley doesn't quite see it that way.

And where the fuck was Elena when he went up to the house? That's the part that's driving me insane. *He couldn't have hurt her already... He wouldn't... That's not what happened; that's not what's going to happen...*

Every minute the cops spent searching was torture, until sickening hours slipped past. And then it was all for *nothing*. I should have gone up there myself immediately; I should never have let her out of my sight. And now I'll never forgive myself if—

No, I can't even think that.

I have to believe; I have to *know* she's going to be okay.

Because I'm coming to get her.

I barrel through the front doors, striding for my car. Rain spatters down, but it doesn't deter the tourists choking Main Street, shouting and carousing with increasing levels of inebriation.

"Wait for us," Dane says sulkily, using his long legs to catch up with me. Remi has to sprint. He's sulky because he wanted to be alone with Remi long before now—the "other humans" portion of the evening was supposed to be limited.

"Your legs are literally two miles long," Remi pants as she jogs to keep up. She left her skateboard in my lobby, not that it would help her weave through the dense crowd. She jerks her head toward her rusty orange Bronco. "I'm parked over here."

I'd rather drive, but it's going to be a hell of a lot harder to get my car out from where it's parked.

Dane offers me shotgun for the first time in our lives, which concerns me. He must think something awful is happening.

"Drive, Remi," I say.

"I'm going, I'm going! I can't run over all these people…"

I wish she would.

Her Bronco inches painfully through the costumed jaywalkers until we can finally accelerate down the two-lane highway out of Grimstone, Remi's tools rattling in the trunk.

"New project?" I ask her, glancing back at the dusty pile of heavy implements.

"I bought the old Redbird place," she says. "Got a pretty good deal on it."

I don't doubt it. Redbird died fourteen years ago, and it's been empty since.

"How's the reno going?"

"I'll let you know when I get to the house." Remi sighs. "I'm still cutting my way through all the dead brush in the yard."

She's speeding, foot heavy on the gas, hands locked on the wheel. The roar of the engine becomes the sound of my agitation.

"You really think he kidnapped her?" says Dane quietly behind me.

I'm looking ahead, anticipating the appearance of the castle with its hunchbacked roof, its mismatching walls and chaotic corridors.

As the first twisted spires rise over the pine tops, I say, "I know he did."

CHAPTER 36
ELENA

I WAKE TRAPPED IN A TIGHT, TINY SPACE.

There's so little room that when I inhale, my ribs have to spread sideways.

It's completely dark, and I can't move. My arms and legs are so compressed that at first I think I've been encased in cement. And I start to scream.

A window slides open in front of my face.

The window is tiny, more of a slot just wide enough for me to peer through. It's positioned directly over my eyes. As if it were custom-made for me.

When it slides open, light blasts my face, or so it seems. Really, it's only a small amount of light, painful after the extreme darkness.

When my eyes adjust, they look directly into Lorne's. I keep screaming. He slides the window shut.

I shriek until my throat is raw and I'm sweating in the tight, humid, space. I lose my breath, and my head whirls.

When I falter, Lorne slides the window open once more. Air rushes in, cool and delicious.

"I wouldn't use up your air supply so soon," he says. "I had to soundproof these walls, so they're pretty airtight. You should conserve for when I have to close you off."

I shriek at him again, wild things, horrific things, the most rage-filled profanities I can muster in my native tongue. And then I'm crying and begging and pleading, and then sobbing with no voice at all, because no matter what Lorne threatens, I can't stop. I can't help myself; I've lost control. I can't bear to be trapped.

I'm stuck so tight I can't even beat my fists against the wall, can't squirm or fight.

All I can do is scream until my voice gives out.

And Lorne leaves the window open.

Because this time, he wants to hear me.

When I'm tired out, my throat so raw and swollen it can barely manage a husky squeak, Lorne steps in front of the window once more.

He was gone a long time. I don't know where he was. But I think I know where *I* am.

Without Lorne standing in the way, I could see all the way to the front door. I could see the oil paintings on the walls, the iron chandelier, the twin suits of armor standing at attention. I could look at the front entryway but from the back wall. I assume Lorne was standing just out of sight, enjoying my shrieks echoing off the walls. Until they turned to rasps and whimpers.

I remember this room, the first space we entered when Lorne brought me to his castle. He switched on the flashlight on his phone, and as the beam swung around, I saw a small tarp-wrapped niche, too small to be a closet. And I thought it must be somewhere to put a vase or a statue.

I think I'm inside that niche.

But it's not a niche anymore. It's completely closed in.

And I'm trapped inside with only a tiny window to look out. Like an iron maiden built right into the wall.

And when Lorne steps in front of that window again, I can't

move away. I'm stuck there, eye to eye with him, loathing him with every fiber of my being.

"Comfortable?" he says.

I would give anything to be able to spit in his face.

"Let me out," I rasp.

"So you can run back to Atlas?" Lorne smiles. The smile that I'm now one hundred percent certain is his only genuine smile—the one that's completely dead in the eyes. "I don't think so."

It's a good thing I can't spit on Lorne because I need my remaining saliva. My mouth is parched, and my temples throb.

"Where's Ivy?" I croak.

Lorne's eyes narrow. "What's the deal with you two? Why do you care about that little freak?"

Rage chills my chest. "Don't call her that."

"She's not even your kid." Lorne looks mystified. "I can't stand her. I almost got rid of her right after Linda, but I knew she could be useful. And she was, getting you to trust me."

Sweat slides down my body, tickling, irritating. I can't wipe it away, can't move an inch.

Lorne is right. I did find it disarming, all his talk about his daughter.

But it was also the first thing I noticed when the cracks started to show…that he didn't really give a shit about her. That he couldn't even pretend.

"Bad actors need props." My voice is almost too croaky to understand, but Lorne flushes.

"Fooled you easily enough."

"Well," I rasp. "I was pretty desperate."

"Not as desperate as you're going to be." Lorne slides the window shut.

He leaves me in the hot and airless wall.

And I realize I really should have asked for some water.

I doze in a kind of delirium. At one point, I think I hear muffled voices and see pinpricks of red and blue light. I try shouting again, but my throat is so hoarse, all that comes out is a mummified rasp.

The idea of mummies makes me go cold, even with sweat still drenching my clothes. A mummy might be exactly what I turn into if Lorne's plan is to leave me inside this wall. I'll die of thirst or starvation or suffocation, and a hot, dry hole is exactly the right condition for me to slowly wither and dry until I'm old leather and bones, wrapped in the shroud of my Halloween costume.

A horrible fate, trapped in Lorne's monstrous castle forever.

But maybe that isn't so bad.

I might *wish* that was the worst that happened to me....

Depending on what Lorne does when he takes me out of the wall.

I drift in and out in the dark. Wondering where Atlas is. Wondering if he's still at the Reaper's Revenge, looking for me.

If he's looking for me at all.

In the dark, crushed between the walls, barely breathing, head spinning, I begin to lose hope. I float back and forth between this night and one years before when I lay in a similar position, crushed and barely breathing...knowing that nobody was coming for me.

I wanted a family again. Not a borrowed one like Mina's, who let me sleep at their house and eat at their table but never treated me like a daughter.

I wanted a family of my own. A home of my own.

I thought that could be Lorne, Ivy, this castle...

And now I'll lie interred inside it forever. Sealed up alive inside its walls.

Maybe I deserve it.

I tried to escape my fate.

But too often when you flee your fate…you're only running toward it.

I think of the bookshop, the place that used to be my sanctuary and became my ticking time bomb.

I think of *that* night, too.

The night I never think about if I can help it.

The night Boyka stayed late.

The night I committed a terrible sin. *The* terrible sin, according to most religions.

I couldn't believe how easily it happened. You'd think it would be this long, drawn-out thing, but no…it was a matter of moments.

Boyka had always been a pest, you see. He was the manager of the shop when I first started working there, but very soon he turned the running of it over to me. I did all the work, every scrap of it, but he was manager in name and got more pay. For my side of the deal, he was supposed to let me run the shop how I liked, order my favorite books, not question my discounts, and mostly stay away.

But that night he didn't stay away. And he was being especially… pesky.

You know how men can be. Slapping, grabbing, touching. He pretended it was a joke, but this wasn't the first time he'd tried that sort of thing. It was just the first time he'd done it so aggressively, so late at night.

I thought he left, finally. And I went down to the basement where the book elevator was. I'd been waiting all night to bring up the stock. I didn't want to go down while Boyka was still there.

I didn't like going in the book elevator anyway; I'd been putting it off. I already didn't like small spaces.

And then, a hairy arm around my throat, his hot, sweating mass flattening me against the tight, metal walls…

I swung my arm back, hit him in the head. Only, I was holding the mallet I'd been using to unpack the crates.

It looked like a small cut, just above his right eyebrow. Until it started bleeding. He toppled over, blocking the door.

He lay there on the elevator floor, looking at me, long after he was dead.

And it took much longer than that to escape the little metal box.

But none of that was the worst part.

The worst part was the months that followed. Where I still ran the bookshop, never going down to the basement, sealing the door, stacking deliveries to the roof of the staff room, and never ever using the book elevator…that's what fucked me up.

Plus, the desperate need to get my broke ass out of Lviv before I was arrested for murder.

I already knew the bookshop had been sold. The clock was ticking down. And then…Lorne came along.

You can see why he feels like a punishment.

And why I might feel like I deserve it, on some level.

I think of Mina, wondering how many times she'll call my phone before she finally gives up forever—fifty? A hundred?

I wonder where Ivy is, if she even knows I'm here…god, I hope she's okay.

And most of all, I think of Atlas.

I don't know how long I've been in here. Time is losing meaning in the tiny, airless space inside the wall. Maybe it's been hours. Maybe it's been days. Maybe he never existed at all.

But I don't think so.

No. I think…I did a bad thing. And maybe Lorne *was* my punishment.

But Atlas was my heaven. And I was there for a while, tasting it…what it felt to be safe and happy and cherished.

That heaven felt just as real as Lorne's hell.

When the air gets low, when my head spins, when my mind

wants to break apart, when it would be easiest to drift away, that's what I cling to:

He'll come for me.

The window slides open, startling me awake. Lorne's bloodshot blue eyes stare in at me.

"Your boyfriend's here."

I try screaming again, hoping that Atlas will hear me, but all that comes out is a croak.

Lorne just laughs. "He's not inside, idiot. He's outside the gate. Want to see?"

Lorne touches the security monitor next to the door. A black-and-white image of Atlas appears on its screen, distorted somewhat by the heavy rain. Even so, I can tell he's standing right outside the gates.

"Atlas! Atlas! Atlas!"

It's like a nightmare—no matter how hard I try to scream, barely any sound comes out of my swollen throat. Lorne barely glances back at me.

"Looking for something, Atlas?" he says into the intercom.

Atlas's head jerks up. He's not looking toward the intercom—he's gazing toward the house.

In a low, calm voice, he says, "Open the gate, Lorne. I just want to talk."

"I don't think so. I already spoke to the police you sent up here." Lorne laughs nastily. "You make it too easy, Atlas. I loved showing them the new place."

"This doesn't have to turn ugly," Atlas says. "We can keep it civilized."

"Oh, I'm not worried about that." Lorne smiles serenely, safe behind his iron gates and his stone walls. "There's not going to be any ugliness. In fact, this will be remarkably clean." He leans forward, hissing into the microphone, "You'll never find her. No one will."

Atlas stands there in the rain, a dark figure looking steadily toward the house as if he knows that if he could only x-ray the walls, he'd find me inside. But after a moment, without saying another word to Lorne, he turns and walks away.

I stare at the video screen, unbelieving.

Is he actually leaving?

The screen remains blank. No movement but the wind and rain, no figure by the gate.

Lorne snorts, turning his back on the video monitor, returning to the wall so he can sneer right into my face. "I told you, Elena. He just wanted to fuck you."

"He loves me," I whisper in my ruined voice. "He'll come for me."

"It doesn't matter if he does." Lorne's demented smile stretches wider. "I have twenty hiding places in this castle deeper and darker than this. Pits in the ground, cupboards in the walls, torture chambers in the attic…I've spent years planning, Elena, and months building. I can't wait to show you what I've prepared for you. Racks to stretch those lovely limbs, tools to mark your skin, irons to brand you, sensory deprivation chambers to blind and silence you until you won't even remember the sight of sun or the smell of grass, only my voice in your ears and my hands on your body…"

He lists my future tortures in a calm, almost beatific tone. As if he's describing a religious experience.

"The cops were already here earlier tonight, and they walked past you five times. You can scream yourself raw right in the same room, and all they'll hear is the wind in the chimney. I can hide you places in this house that Atlas wouldn't find you for a thousand years, no matter how long he search—"

An enormous crash echoes from the upper floor. It sounds like something very large and metallic was pushed over, maybe a suit of armor like the ones by the door.

"What is she—" Lorne's head snaps up, listening. He smirks at me. "Stay right here."

As he turns, the smirk falls away, leaving a cold and fixed intention that makes me extremely afraid for Ivy.

"*Run, Ivy!*" I shriek, but it's even more useless than before.

Lorne sweeps out of view in the direction of the stairs.

"*Ivy! He's coming, Ivy!*" I thrash and fight inside the wall, barely able to move, scraping my skin raw against the wood and stone. There's a tug on my ring finger, and then sudden lightness as Lorne's ring pulls free and tumbles down the gap in the wall.

And suddenly, there she is, Ivy, right in front of me, wide-eyed, filthy faced, frantic. She's scrabbling at the wall, trying to do something, something I can't see. *O Bozhe*, she's trying to free me.

"Never mind that, Ivy! Get out of the house; run down to the road!" I'm praying that Atlas hasn't actually left, that somehow she could find him. I'm terrified of what Lorne might do to her now that he no longer needs her as bait.

But Ivy won't leave the wall, won't leave me.

"You've got to get out of here; he's coming back!"

Too late—Lorne thunders down the stairs. Ivy sprints off like a white rabbit.

And then, on the security monitor, I see something that makes my heart soar:

Atlas scaled the wall and is striding toward the house, carrying an enormous axe.

CHAPTER 37
ATLAS

CASTLES ARE FORTRESSES, AND LORNE'S IS NO DIFFERENT. HE'S built it with iron gates, high windows, stone walls…

But he forgot about one thing.

His door is made of wood.

I stride back to the Bronco, wrenching open the trunk.

"Shouldn't we call the cops again?" Remi asks nervously.

"You two can head back if you want." I shove aside Remi's rake and hedge clippers, wrapping my hand around the handle of an axe. "I'm not leaving Elena here overnight."

Remi looks at Dane. "The little girl's in there, too?"

He nods.

"Then I'm going in."

"You stay right next to me," he tells her firmly.

I'm already scaling the wall.

CHAPTER 38
ELENA

THE BOOMING ON THE DOOR IS LIKE A BATTERING RAM. THE IMPACT hits again and again, deafening, relentless. I don't know where Lorne is, or Ivy—all I can see is the patch of room directly in front of me, mostly the front door. So I see the moment the axe bites through, glinting steel breaking through just above the latch.

I'm screaming for Atlas though it's less than a whisper. I keep screaming as he hacks through the door, the axe taking enormous bites of the wood and wrenching them away.

He makes a hole, and the wind and rain come pouring through. He hacks and cuts and smashes until his whole Goliath frame bursts through, scratched by splinters, drenched with rain, bloodied, furious, and fucking gorgeous.

He's barely through the door before Lorne leaps out at him, and I see a slash of silver as he whips a knife down Atlas's side. Atlas howls, a long gash opening up on his shirt, showing a strip of blood-ied flank. He clouts Lorne backhand across the face and follows with a swing of the axe that might have taken Lorne's head off if Lorne didn't slip on the wet slate and tumble all the way backward.

The axe embeds in the door directly over Lorne's head. He stares up at my furious and bloodied lover attempting to wrench the axe out of the door and apparently loses the last of his courage. He dives through the Atlas-sized hole in the door.

Faintly, in the rain-drenched yard, someone shouts.

The rain thunders in, mud pouring under the door. Atlas is dripping wet as he yanks the axe free of the wood and crosses the flagstones, hand clasped to his side, the blood running down his fingers black as pitch in the crack of lightning.

I'm pounding the wall with all the momentum I can muster in the fraction of space I have to move.

It makes no sound, but it doesn't matter—Lorne left the sliding window open, and Atlas can see my eyes peeking out at him.

He strides across the room, shoulders hunched, thick arm pressed against his wound. The axe glints wickedly in his red-drenched hand. "Elena! How do I get you out?"

"I don't know," I say in the faintest raspy whisper. *"I don't know how I got in…"*

"Are you standing upright?"

I nod.

"Are your hands at your sides?"

"Pretty much…"

"Then close your eyes."

Atlas lifts the axe.

———————

He lifts me out of the wall and carries me in his arms, like a bride over the threshold. Only, we're exiting the castle and going home to the Monarch Hotel.

I know this like I know my own name, as I nestle my head against Atlas's chest, my arms around his neck.

I'm already home.

CHAPTER 39
ATLAS

I CARRY MY BRIDE HOME IN MY ARMS AND TAKE HER DIRECTLY TO our room. I tell her ten more times that Ivy is safe with my brother's girlfriend, happily making pancakes. She still won't lie down until I threaten her with an actual hospital if she won't at least let me take a look at her.

My hands are shaking while I check her over. They calm when I finally see the worst of it is scrapes and bruises. On the outside, at least.

Then I can only hold her.

She insists on seeing Ivy before she goes to sleep, and I take her to Ivy's new room, which used to be my mother's.

Ivy is watching a movie with Remi, but she jumps off the bed and runs to Elena the moment she sees her, throwing her arms around her waist and hugging her for a long time.

When she finally lets go, it's only to push her notebook into Elena's hands. Elena looks at the page, at the word written there in uneven, scraggly letters. *Sorry.*

I recognize the writing. I can see Elena does, too. Her eyes fill with tears. She touches Ivy's shoulder, looking into her face. "Oh, honey. You were telling me to get out? To get away from your dad?"

Ivy nods her head miserably.

Elena wraps her arms around her. "Don't worry, *solnyshko moi.* I'm not going anywhere. Not anymore."

I thought it must have been Ivy who trashed the room when I saw that Elena's camera wasn't damaged. And of course, I'm the one who showed Ivy the dumbwaiter. I knew that would come back to bite me in the ass—or in this case, cost me two rolls of wallpaper and three new locks.

How the hell I'm going to keep her out of the dumbwaiters in the future is the bigger problem...they go all throughout the hotel. And Ivy is going to have a lot more freedom in the future, for better and for worse.

Problems for another day.

I care about one thing and one thing only tonight.

"Put her to bed," I say to Elena. "I need you."

CHAPTER 40
ELENA

I LIE ON ATLAS'S BED, WHICH IS TWICE THE SIZE OF A NORMAL BED and covered in furry blankets that look like bear pelts. This is necessary because his room is as cold as a cave. In most ways that matter, it *is* a cave, with a glass wall on one side.

I was reading his character sketches in the bath, and now I want to talk to him about them, but he is finding this highly embarrassing. Also, his tongue is busy between my legs.

"They were beautiful. I'm telling you, Atlas, you should at least send one to a magazine or—"

He lifts his head. "I will gag you."

I laugh and push his head back down where it's been for the better part of an hour. "Fine, stay down there. I'll only say sexy th—oh, *bozhe chortove, tse nespravedlyvo...*"

After that, I can't talk at all. I can only cry, and beg, and whimper.

He pulls me on top of him, rolling me onto his chest, which is warm and broad, and raises and lowers me several inches with each of his breaths. Lying with my cheek over my heart sends a thud like a tide through my body. I have never been more relaxed.

He massages my back, all down my spine, creating raindrops with his fingertips. He slowly and systematically unknits every painful knot, every place I'm tense and strained. When he reaches my lower back, I groan, on the very edge of pleasure and deep, painful release.

"This is the first part of you I fell in love with…" Atlas's fingers patter up and down along the base of my spine.

I look down at him, my hair falling down all around his face, then bend my head to kiss him softly on the mouth. "I loved your hands first. But now…it might be your tongue."

He kisses me so deeply, I taste what I tasted the night he told me he loved me—that pure, essential, longing part of him. I drift, euphoric, until he pulls back a little and says, "No, I lied. It was when I looked into your eyes."

He looks at me now in this glass box in the cliff, full of light reflected off the ocean. I see the bits of green that glimmer brightest in his eyes when he's happy. When he's looking at me just like this.

I say, "I saw you, and you saw me. And we both knew it. We knew what happened. We knew what we felt."

I drop my lips down onto his. Atlas grips my waist and pulls my hips down, pressing me against him. Letting me feel his cock harden with every touch of our tongues.

I press against him, letting the head of his cock slide into position, letting it push against my entrance.

I'm dreading and longing for that feeling again, that tight and almost tearing friction, the very edge of what could possibly feel good. That's how it starts. But then the wetness grows, the sliding and the heat of Atlas's hands on my waist and his body beneath me, his cock inside me like a throbbing brand, and what's warm and pleasurable builds and builds, and pain becomes nothing more than accelerant to everything that's good.

Everything about him arouses me: his strength, his size, the texture of his skin, the scent that rises from his body as he fucks me.

But nothing matches how he touches me. There's skill, consideration, sensitivity…When he finally rolls on top of me, he positions his weight on his own arm, his body lying almost alongside mine, my knee hooked over his hip. He fits his cock inside me, our bodies slotting tightly together.

He scoops his elbow under my knee, lifting my leg a little higher, pulling me closer. The pressure is intense, but he's careful, smooth. Slowly, he begins to slide me back and forth, almost in a rocking motion. Back and forth, back and forth…

There are many kinds of climaxes, I'm learning. Some in waves, some in pulses.

Atlas's weight presses down on me, but for once, the sensation doesn't make me panic. It only spikes my adrenaline and the intense pleasure radiating outward from every point our bodies touch.

It's the weight of Atlas that is his strength, his solidity.

Atlas is my fortress; he is my castle. I'm safe right here with him.

I wrap my legs around his waist and my arms around his neck, lifting my mouth to kiss him. He drives into me deeper, arms like pillars on either side of my face, dark eyes gazing down at me.

That feeling builds, builds, builds, with every pound of the hammer. This is the other thing I'm learning: the longer it builds, the bigger the blast. As Atlas drives inside me, I'm almost frightened of what must be coming.

But I hold on to his neck and look into his eyes. And when he finally groans and gives one last heave and drives in all the way, crushing me in his arms and kissing me, the shudders of his body flow into mine, and the twitches and pulses inside me set off a chain reaction.

The explosion erupts inside me, surging down my veins like molten lava. We come together, wrapped up tightly in each other's arms atop the pile of furs, the air seeming to shimmer like the heat from a furnace.

But when we sit up, flushed and sweating, snow falls outside the window. White flakes drift down from the sky, melting into the slate-gray ocean. And the frost on the glass blooms like roses.

———————

Late into the night, I whisper my secrets to Atlas, and he whispers his to me. We tell each other our dreams, our desires, our fears, and our fantasies.

Atlas tells me what happened to Lorne after he dove through the hole in the door, how he ran out into the woods in the storm, Dane chasing after him.

Construction slowed when the workers wouldn't work in the rain. But as it turned out, they were right—Lorne got barely a hundred feet from his castle before he was swept down the mountain in a river of mud.

Dane narrowly escaped the same fate.

Atlas says, "Dane came staggering back to the house covered in mud, white as chalk underneath, saying, *'He's dead; there's no way he survived that.'*" Something confirmed the next day when Lorne's broken body was found at the base of the mountain.

I tell Atlas everything that happened with Boyka, the whole awful truth.

"My love," he murmurs, "that's not even a mistake; that was an accident."

And maybe he's right. Because the next morning, a genuine miracle occurs.

Mina calls me. That's not the miracle—the miracle is what she says.

"Sprout...I've got horrible news."

Mina has been my best friend all my life, not just a cousin. Which is why I don't leap to conclusions when she says she has "horrible news"—that could mean a rise in movie theater prices or the breakup of her favorite celebrity couple. Mina is a little dramatic.

This morning, however, she sounds unusually subdued. And Mina is never subdued. Something really bad must have happened.

"What is it?" I ask hesitantly.

Mina can hardly get it out. "Well...you see...ah..." She lets it out in a rush. "I'm sorry, Sprout, but they demoed your bookstore!"

I'm silent for a moment as this slowly sinks in.

"You mean…they took down the whole thing?"

"Yes!" Mina sobs. "They boarded up the whole block, destroyed it all! They're putting in condos instead."

"It's…gone? The whole bookstore? Everything inside of it?"

"Everything. Oh, Elena, don't cry, I'm sorry… Are you so sad for all your beautiful books?"

"Yes," I sob out, half laughing as well. "I'm crying for the books."

Really, I'm crying with relief because, deserving of it or not, I'm finally free.

Free to settle down to a new life.

EPILOGUE
ELENA

MOVING INTO THE MONARCH IS EASY BECAUSE I ALREADY LIVE there. A fleet of bellhops carries my belongings down six flights of stairs and then down to the hotel-beneath-the-hotel where our little family resides.

Ivy is thrilled with her new room. Atlas's mother had a flair for the dramatic, decorating what's now Ivy's room in sumptuous scarlet silk and glowing lanterns. Ivy has been smuggling in little treasures from all over the hotel, turning it into a proper pirate's cave.

Making it Ivy's permanent home takes a lot more work.

Step one is a quickie marriage between Atlas and me. Turns out, immigration is a bit of an "ask for forgiveness afterward" situation when it comes to weddings. Once Atlas and I are married, I'll be allowed to stay in the country and apply for a new visa even though I'm technically breaking the rules by getting hitched without one.

We marry in the rose garden at the Monarch Hotel, with Ivy as our flower girl and Dane and Remi as our witnesses. The snow falls thickly down, blanketing the bushes, catching in our hair.

Atlas has never looked handsomer, tall, dark, and glowering in the snow.

I'm too excited to be cold, and anyway, I've got a long white cape on over my dress. The dress, however, isn't white—it's the teal silk from Vivian's shop. The skirt looks blue as sea glass against the snow flowing like liquid across the grass.

My bouquet is white roses with several large lilies mixed in.

"I thought you didn't like that scent anymore?" Atlas says.

I lift the bouquet to my nose and inhale the peppery-sweet smell of Atlas's garden and the sad, nostalgic scent of lilies.

"I'm so happy today…I want to love it again."

I take another deep breath and then kiss Atlas, the smell of fresh blooms lingering in my nose and on my lips.

All through that day and into the night, I carry the bouquet with me and breathe in that scent, welding it slowly and forever to the start of something new.

———

Lorne is gone, but his castle is not. The police comb through it over the next several weeks, uncovering more details of the *surprises* Lorne had in store for me. Besides hidden dungeons and torture chambers, Sheriff Henley located over thirty different "cabinets" where Lorne could have stashed me, including some under the floorboards and others high in the rafters. But the ones that made me shudder most were the ones that were Ivy-sized.

Dubbed the "Murder Castle" by the press, Lorne's house has since been sold to an investor who turned it into an extremely popular Airbnb. You can stay in any number of the rooms where Lorne planned to torture me, for just four hundred and ninety-nine dollars a night. Twelve hundred a night during the week of the Reaper's Revenge.

"This town is getting so fucked up," Atlas says.

"*Getting* fucked up?" Dane raises an eyebrow at his brother. "It's just getting more obvious."

———

The adoption of Ivy takes six more months, several lawyers, and a lot of money. That part doesn't matter too much because Atlas has a lot of money, and eventually, so does Ivy.

As it turns out, Ivy's mother Linda was *very* wealthy, as Lorne knew. He inherited everything at first. But with Lorne dead…there's a new heiress in town.

That's what makes the adoption complicated—several of Ivy's relatives come forward when it's clear an inheritance is at stake. Luckily, the judge takes Ivy's wishes into account. She's been progressing enough in her typing therapy that she's able to write him a very clear note on her brand-new keyboard.

I wish I could tell you that something terrible happened to Mrs. Cross. Ivy wrote a statement about how she was treated by her father and caretaker. It was not considered sufficient evidence, not even when I supplied photographs I'd snapped of Ivy that showed the blue shadows of bruises.

Though Mrs. Cross still lives in her smoky little witch's cabin outside of Grimstone, Atlas solemnly promised Ivy that if she ever stepped foot on the property of the Monarch Hotel again, he'd toss her off the sea cliffs.

Atlas looked quite terrifying as he said it, huge as a mountain bending over Ivy, eyes dark as the grave, shoulders blocking out the lamplight.

Yet Ivy smiled up at him with trust and adoration. She's only my shadow half the time now, often choosing to trail after Atlas as he sees to the business of the hotel. And—break my heart, little traitor—drawing in her notebook the design for her own velvet suit.

But hearts don't break or even burst. They only shrink or swell. And sometimes you can bruise them. There is no bruise seeing Ivy safe and happy, following along after Atlas.

We take a portrait on the stairs of the hotel to celebrate when the paperwork is complete and we're officially a family.

We hang the printed photograph in the same spot above the

stairs, joining the generations of Covetts inside those frames who lived and loved and laughed inside the Monarch.

That's not the only photograph I have to take. I promised one of a very particular sort to Atlas in exchange for reading his writing.

And I'm a woman of my word.

I take the pictures in our bedroom on a rainy day when droplets streak down the glass. I lay the bearskin blankets out and pose nude in front of the window.

The last photograph is the one Atlas likes the best, the one where I stand in front of the foggy glass, hair hanging down over my breasts, the blankets bunched beneath my feet. He says he had a fantasy about me like that once, rising out of the ocean like Venus.

I print him a smaller copy he can keep in the breast pocket of his suit, like the icon of a patron saint. I've seen him take it out and kiss it when he doesn't know I'm watching.

I feel the same about my ring.

It's been my lucky talisman ever since Atlas gave it to me—I don't think I've had a truly dark day since. And I've never slept better than when I'm wrapped in his arms, his ring upon my finger.

Because the picture and the ring mean the same thing.

They mean, *I'm with you. I love you. I'll protect you, I'll take care of you. Carry me with you always and keep me in your heart. Because you are there in mine.*

ACKNOWLEDGMENTS

Monarch is my first frontlist release with Bloom, so first and foremost I need to thank Dom, Christa, Pam, Madison, and the rest of the Bloom team. It has been such a pleasure working with you. I feel extremely lucky to be teamed up with such a brilliant and inspiring group of women.

Thank you to Nicole, who designed this beautiful, spooky cover, and much thanks as always to my artist Line, who illustrates all of my books.

Thank you to Letty for your observant and insightful editing, and to Grace for sensitivity reading. Thank you, Katie, for your copy and continuity edits and trigger warnings.

Thank you to the rest of the Sophie team, Maya and Brittany, who handle the nuts and bolts of the business, and Kerry, who helps take care of the littlest Lark.

Thank you to my boys, Weston and Rhett, for growing into such good men.

And most of all, thank you Ry for being my Atlas. You're my mountain and my home, my safe refuge in the darkest night.

About the Author

Sophie Lark is the *USA Today* bestselling author of *Brutal Prince* and the Sinners Duet. She lives in Southern California with her husband and three children. Her favorite authors are Emily Henry and Freida McFadden, and she looks forward to Halloween every year.

The Love Lark Letter: geni.us/lark-letter
The Love Lark Reader Group: geni.us/love-larks
Website: sophielark.com
Instagram: @Sophie_Lark_Author
TikTok: @sophielarkauthor
Exclusive Content: patreon.com/sophielark
Complete Works: geni.us/lark-amazon
Book Playlists: geni.us/lark-spotify